As always, for Susan.

Abaddon Resurrection

An Adam Dekker Novel

Lawrence Clayton Miller

Also by Lawrence Miller

Abaddon Consortium

Abaddon Rising

Abaddon Resurrection
By Lawrence Clayton Miller

Sunset Media Group
5105 Sevilla Ave. NW
Albuquerque, NM 87120

Cover design by Jason Miller, fluiddesigns@yahoo.com

ISBN-10: 0983943591
ISBN: 9780983943594

Printed in the United States

CHAPTER ONE

THE LATE AFTERNOON WAS DREARY; the dark clouds, thick with moisture, threatened to release a downpour that was sure to be uncomfortable. The man searching through the impenetrable tangle of bushes and trees in the Black Forest looked up, certain he would be caught in the terrible weather. His two assistants trudged behind him, carrying large sacks across their backs and trusting in the elder's leadership.

The trio stepped into a clearing and the man looked up again, certain he had only minutes before the deluge, and then looked around—he recognized this place. It was no longer groomed as he remembered, but it was the same. A large, flat stone roughly fifteen feet square occupied the center of the alder grove clearing—like an altar. Grass and scrub brush grew around the stones that defined an area that had once been holy.

"The Alder Grove," he whispered. "I have found it. I have found Krugerschloss."

The man had to search for the path leading to Abaddon's ancient dwelling, hidden deep in the mountain— but he found it. The track was overgrown and all but indistinguishable from the rest of the forest. He ordered the younger men to follow and it led them to the base of a granite cliff. Looking left and right across the wall of rock, the older man located the disguised entry he knew was there.

He opened one of the sacks carried by the younger men and extracted a torch, one of several he had prepared. He reached into a pocket, took out a handful of wooden matches, and ignited the oil-soaked pine hemp tied to the torch. The strict tenants of the Brotherhood forbade all mechanical contrivances. Lighting two more torches, he handed one to each of his assistants, and then took his first step inside. There was a bright crack of lightning, followed almost immediately by a great boom of thunder.

The passageway was narrow and dark but high enough to ward off feelings of claustrophobia. Despite the torches it was only through his previous knowledge of Krugerschloss that they could move through the cavern with assurance. The torchlight flickered and danced on the walls of the passageway as the men moved, creating an ever-changing pattern of shadows.

They arrived at a closed door, and the man knew once he opened it, forces would be set into motion that could not be stopped. Hesitating, he placed a hand on the thick oak door, wondering again if he was certain he wished to go through with this. "I have waited many years," he said more to himself than to his companions, "endured much hardship, and watched the dissolution of my ancient Egyptian heritage. Desert tribes have overrun us and they have no respect for the Ancient Ways and Old Truths, and I will correct this wrong." With that pronouncement, Kamenwati pushed open the door.

Torchlight could not illuminate the entire hall, but from his position Kamenwati saw a glowing blue platform. It was otherworldly—shimmering with a cold, blue life. This was the place Abaddon had reached out to control the world.

Abaddon built a criminal organization he called a Consortium along with the religious Brotherhood—a two-pronged approach driven not so much by ideology as greed.

He'd achieved a systematic takeover of the Brotherhood, a small remnant of believers in an ancient religion who were scattered in small groups around the world. The Brotherhood was easy to seduce because Abaddon knew the Old Truths, could use the Flows, and was able to control thought and action half a world away. He was formidable and frightening to the Brotherhood, and one by one, the Brotherhood groups came under Abaddon's sway until he controlled them all.

The stepped-in pyramid carved into the back wall of the cave gave the agate altar an illusion of great depth and almost infinite reach. But today there was no band of adepts circling the altar and no crowd of acolytes filling the hall. Kamenwati imagined the power represented here: the power to control men, and the power to influence worldwide events.

It had all been lost five years ago when Abaddon was defeated and imprisoned. Now, only his blue altar remained, and there was no one left to worship before it. *That will change,* he thought, *as soon as I can accomplish the resurrection.* It was a dangerous gamble to bring Abaddon back from his stasis prison. Abaddon would still be a powerful practitioner of Magick, the ancient mode of rationality that looks to invisible forces to influence events, effect change in material conditions, and present the illusion of change.

Kamenwati was himself a powerful practitioner who studied his entire life and was, in his estimation, more widely accomplished than Abaddon. Abaddon had long ago chosen to pervert his powers and focus his energy on those aspects of Magick allowing him to dominate and kill men. This was not the Ancient Way, the true way, and it troubled Kamenwati deeply for years. But now he was confident he could control the unpredictable Abaddon, because he had the threat of returning him to the stasis prison; it would be unspoken but understood—if Kamenwati could get him out, he could put him back in. Abaddon was sure to be suspicious of Kamenwati's motivation and he must deflect it from the beginning. A subservient, submissive posture would get him through the first moments, but he would quickly have to demonstrate that Abaddon must respect him. His plan was simple and clever: He knew much of Abaddon's history and his vulnerabilities. He would remind Abaddon of this from the very first, punctuated with the additional threat of the small box he carried.

Kamenwati ordered his two assistants to put down their packs and extract the alabaster jars they carried. He directed the young men to place the jars evenly around the perimeter of the altar. When the task was complete the two young men took up positions at the rear of the altar, flanking the pyramidal wall structure.

The effect of placing the two assistants in the rear with their torches was dramatic. The pyramid structure glowed with silver and gold, crafted in such a way that the filigree patterns intertwined and seemed to float in front of the wall. The agate platform itself glowed with cool blue light from the torches now positioned at the rear, revealing an intricate network of channels, looking very much like veins, feeding life-giving blood into the heart of the great stone.

Kamenwati adjusted the placement of a few alabaster jars and removed a black, hooded cloak from his pack. When he pulled the cloak over his head and put the cowl up, he presented an imposing and frightful image. He stepped to the center of the altar and began the process of entering into a trance. He turned slowly with his eyes closed and arms extended symbolically over the jars around him.

A low moan became a more audible chant. The younger men did not understand what Kamenwati said, not surprising because the chant was in ancient Egyptian, a lost language. Kamenwati's spinning stopped and his chanting grew in volume and intensity of delivery. He took a step to the side and then to the front, issuing orders to no one in particular. Then the mystic lifted his arms straight up, clapped his hands, and moved back to the pyramidal structure. Once in the pyramid, a bright flash of light shot up from the center of the agate platform. The light struck a point on the ceiling high above and split into twelve new beams focusing on each of the alabaster jars. As the jars were struck with the light, they glowed a fierce red.

The two assistants looked with amazement at the sight, not knowing what to expect next. There seemed to be an exchange of energy in the beams, from the jars to the point above, as the light beams pulsed back and forth. A small cloud formed in the cavern ceiling, its translucent gasses swirling with many colors. The cloud grew and the swirling colors intensified, and the young men began to perceive a rectangular form within the cloud. The cloud grew deeper and wider, covering the cavern ceiling over the platform, and then began to descend. The inside the rectangular object they distinguished a body.

Clapping his hands again, Kamenwati issued a shout. The light beams flowing from the jars up to the central point in the ceiling switched focus in the blink of an eye, now pulsing at the large cube in the center of the platform. The intensity of the light grew unbearable until a loud *crack* was heard, leaving the platform in darkness.

It took a moment for the young men's vision to return and they gasped, seeing a swirling residue of smoke and a crouching, naked man.

Kamenwati moved quickly to the man on the platform, carrying another cloak from his bag. Going to one knee and holding the folded cloak forward, he addressed the apparition. "Lord Abaddon, you have returned. Accept this cloak as a temporary covering until proper attire may be arranged."

The crouched figure snatched the offered robe and, in one smooth move, stood and swung the garment out and around him. He looked carefully at the man before him, and with growing recognition spoke. "I know you. You are Kamenwati. How did you accomplish this?" Abaddon arose, closing the cloak around his frame and pulling the full cowl up over his head to prevent the young men, who were staring in awe, from seeing his face.

"I harnessed the power of the twelve great mystics, represented here in these jars filled with their ashes. Together we broke the stasis holding you, and now, together, we will complete what you began—the transformation of mankind to a preindustrial place of dependence on Magick and those who wield its power."

Abaddon looked at the mystic with suspicion. "I do not take partners. I am The Abaddon; my will and purposes prevail over all."

"Nevertheless, you will have me, and you will temper your legendary pride. Our goals align, and you will be supportive."

"Or else?"

"Or else I return you to stasis—one you can never escape." Kamenwati leaned in close to Abaddon, only he could hear. "You see, I have the ashes of the Succubus that conceived you." Kamenwati showed him the little box and saw the hesitation in Abaddon's eyes. "Yes, I see you understand its importance. You came from the unholy union of that Succubus and your mother, the Baroness Kruger. What you did not know is that your father, the Baron, shocked and humiliated to his core, hunted down the Succubus and burned him at the stake in the alder grove as punishment for defiling his wife. The fire completely consumed the evil creature, leaving only gray ashes. The Baron collected the ashes and stored them in a small box as a protection from further encroachment by evil forces. Even you did not know of the box, and when you killed your father to assume his titles and property, you did not know the makings of your undoing were in a simple, wooden box."

Abaddon jerked his head back. He wanted to punish the Egyptian for his insolence but thought better of it and held his tongue. *I will have plenty of opportunity to deal with this man.* He switched gears and focused on a new topic. "How long was I captive?"

"Five years, my lord."

"Five years! How could so much time go by?" Abaddon's eyes narrowed and he balled his fists. "And those who confined me? What of them?"

"The female Adept died during the struggle," Kamenwati said as he ticked off the participants. "Galdur, the Icelander, has retreated to his frozen hole, and Dekker returned to America."

"Dekker." Abaddon almost spat out the name. "He was at the heart of all my troubles. I want him. I want to crush him." Kamenwati took a conciliatory tone, seeking to calm the dangerous man.

"My lord, there are some matters we need to address before chasing a single man." He placed a hand on Abaddon's shoulder, steering him to the rear of the altar. "I suggest we go into your chambers to relax and plan."

"I'll never relax while that man still breathes. I want him. I want him dead."

"And so it shall be, but we must first assess the overall state of affairs and attempt to reassemble your followers. Then we can deal with Dekker."

ABADDON SPENT THE time following his return evaluating the state of his network and was surprised how completely his organization had been dismantled. He started broadcasting a daily summons through the Flows, calling his followers, and Kamenwati was surprised at the response. After all, Abaddon's Consortium and his Brotherhood were the most hunted people on Earth, and even a hint that someone was associated with Abaddon was enough to warrant a long jail term. Even so, he found a number of Adepts and acolytes, once scattered by fear, willing to return to Krugerschloss.

Kamenwati proved himself a proficient manager, setting the growing population of Krugerschloss to the many tasks of cleaning, repair, and restoration. They began with the Great Hall—the heart of the refuge. They restored one of the residence caverns, Triberg Hall, where all could easily occupy residence apartments. Kamenwati chose Triberg because it was the source of water within Krugerschloss thanks to an underground stream diverted for everyday use. The systems of control were primitive by the modern world's standards, being largely wood and ceramic tubes and channels, requiring regular repair and replacement. Kamenwati considered it fortunate that five years of neglect in this closed environment had resulted in little damage to the overall system, and repairs were rapidly made.

"DEKKER. I KNOW it is Dekker behind this!" Abaddon shouted one day, clearly angry at a report in his hand. Kamenwati wondered if he could ever keep him on track and focused on the task of restoring Krugerschloss and rebuilding his Brotherhood.

"Another enterprise lost, and all the revenue with it." Abaddon swung his arm angrily, sweeping papers and small items off his desk and scattering them on the floor. He shouted at Kamenwati. "You fool! Why can't you control these situations? Where are my Adepts? Send in my Adepts!"

Kamenwati did not have to go looking for the Adepts. The shouting seemed to have brought them out of the woodwork, and two young men appeared at the door. "We hear and we obey, Master!" The appearance of the two Adepts quieted Abaddon. He sat at his desk.

"Good, good." Abaddon looked around the room as if Dekker were going to spring from the walls and attack. "Now, listen to me carefully. You two will find Dekker and kill him."

Kamenwati stepped forward, sensing the fragile balance of Abaddon's mind and sanity. "Master, you are overreacting. You are only just now discovering losses that took place months and even years ago."

"Don't try to sooth me with your talk, Kamenwati. I will not rest while I know this man lives."

"We share your passion, Master. But have you considered that Dekker need not be killed?"

"What are you saying? Of course he needs to be killed! As long as he lives, he will torment me."

"Why not drive him here to Krugerschloss where you can deal with him personally?"

The thought seemed to hit a mark in Abaddon's warped psyche, but then, just as quickly, was rejected. "No! I want him dead. I want his family dead. I want everyone and everything associated with him dead!" He turned to the

Adepts standing before him. "And I want you two to find him in America and carry out my orders."

The Adepts looked at one another with fear in their eyes. "As you wish, Master Abaddon. We will seek him out and kill him." The pair spun around and left the room, happy to be out but concerned about their assignment.

Kamenwati could only shake his head in resignation.

CHAPTER TWO

ADAM DEKKER PULLED BACK ON Blackjack's reins, bringing the tall, black Arabian horse to a stop as he came in sight of Vallecito Ranch—his home. The house was a rugged yet comforting sight, a Territorial-style main house set on a tree-studded mesa, with the Jemez Mountains forming a backdrop.

He stopped to take it in. His dark hair peeked from under the wide brim of his Stetson hat, and his weathered face, tanned from years spent outdoors, made his six foot two-inch frame look rugged and mysterious, something women found irresistible. Blackjack interrupted his thoughts by pawing a hoof, indicating he was eager to get to his stable. Sasha, his Black Russian Terrier, had already abandoned his master, dashing into the house.

Dekker smiled and thought what a blissful existence this was, without trouble or conflict to disturb the peace of the mountain valley. He came around the front of the house and saw his four-wheel-drive truck parked at a casual angle in front of the wide porch. Kelly sat in one of the porch rockers, and seeing her husband, jumped up waving. She walked out to him, her left hand grabbing one of the supple leather straps attached to the horse's bridle.

"Welcome home, cowboy," she said, looking up to him, admiring his good looks and strong body. "I've got a special night planned for you. I think you'll like what I got in Santa Fe."

Dekker dismounted and grabbed the bridle from the other side. The couple walked the horse to his stable in an adjacent building. After brushing down the horse, putting away the tack, and making sure there was plenty of hay and water, they walked back to the house. "I'm afraid I smell a little horsey, so I'm going to shower," said Dekker.

"An excellent idea. I'll have cocktails waiting on the patio."

He remembered again how he and Kelly met and fell in love. Her grandfather, Horace Rimmer, a scientist at the Los Alamos Laboratories, developed an astounding theory that was nothing short of revolutionary. It was based on World War II experiments to mask warships from radar, code named Project Rainbow, but better known as the Philadelphia Experiment. What was developed in those days frightened even the War Office, and the Philadelphia Experiment was quickly shut down and forgotten, until decades later when Rimmer uncovered the original plans and formulas, envisioning an entirely new field of study in gravity resonance. He worked on the theory for many years, convincing the Labs' management his theories could be the answer to interstellar travel.

A spy group, led by an Estonian woman named Rina Kask, discovered Rimmer's work and set about stealing it— and the Labs top secret particle beam project. Her first move was kidnapping Rimmer, but he was uncooperative, so Rina found new leverage: His granddaughter, Kelly. Rimmer was cowed when he learned Kelly had been kidnapped and imprisoned. Kelly escaped and set off a tangled web of espionage and deceit that ultimately swept in Dekker. Their adventure led through many harrowing situations, but during that time they came to love one another. And that is what Dekker chose to remember.

Dekker came out to the patio with a light breeze moving through new buds on the oaks surrounding the house, the Ponderosa pines framing the view whistled and hummed with a music all their own. He bent down and kissed Kelly, a little longer than was necessary, and she responded with a small giggle. "Long time on the trail?"

Dekker played along. "Little lady, I'm so parched I could lick the sweat off a mule!"

"Oh, ick! Don't go that far—how about a single malt scotch?" She grabbed one of the glasses sitting on the small table and the bottle, offering him a drink.

"I thought you'd never ask." Kelly poured a glass of Sauvignon Blanc for herself. They chatted about the ranch, neighbors, and acquaintances. Kelly talked about **funny or annoying people at the Smithsonian Institution where she worked, and Adam tossed in anecdotes with typical, self-effacing humor.**

The sun was setting on the mountains, spreading a pink glow over the countryside. "This is the most beautiful time of day, don't you think?" Kelly commented, leaning her head on her husband's shoulder as she enjoyed the sunset colors.

"Do you want me to start the fire?" Dekker asked as he arose to get the pit prepared. Kelly lifted his glass, offering to refresh his drink. He declined. "One is plenty at this altitude. You don't want me to be a blubbering drunk, do you?" Kelly laughed and went inside to prepare herself for the evening. Dekker went happily about the work of setting a fire and cooking the fine-looking strip steaks Kelly brought home from Santa Fe.

As he placed the meat on the grill, Kelly walked out in a dress he hadn't seen before. "New?" It was pretty and filmy.

"Found it today and just had to have it. Do you like it?" The color showed off her auburn hair, and the plunging neckline accentuated her pearl-colored skin. The cut of the dress made her look every bit the woman she was.

"Oh, yes. I like it."

Adam grilled the steaks and the couple ate, devouring each other with their eyes as much as the food on their plates. "I love it when your hair is down like this; you look absolutely beautiful, and I love you so very much."

Kelly got up to remove their plates from the table, bending over more than necessary to be sure her husband could take in her nakedness beneath the dress. Dekker's attention and imagination were riveted. "Um, what's for dessert?"

Kelly put the dishes on the kitchen counter and walked slowly toward the hallway leading to their bedroom. She looked over her shoulder and cooed, "It's in here, darling." As she walked down the hall she dropped the dress to the floor, revealing her perfect, opalescent skin and petite figure.

Dekker needed no more coaxing and followed her into the bedroom.

THEIR LOVEMAKING WAS passionate and intimate, each knowing the other's preferences and most erogenous places. Fully spent, with arms and legs entwined, they fell into a blissful sleep. Dekker slept soundly, the troubled dreams and visions that haunted him for the last year driven away.

Until his sleep was disturbed by a scraping sound.

Dekker knew every sound in his wilderness home, coyotes sniffing around for an easy meal, raccoons and owls, even the occasional mountain lion down from the high country. But the sound that brought him awake was none of those. This was a man-made sound.

Where was Sasha? He never let anything get near the house, and he was strangely quiet.

He untangled himself from Kelly, taking care not to wake her. He stood and pulled on a pair of jeans and boots, listening for the sound again. He went to the antique Spanish armoire, opened the doors, hoping the slight creaking would not disturb Kelly. If she heard it, she only shifted around beneath the sheet, rolling over and clutching his pillow.

He found his SIG Sauer 220 Compact in the top drawer, checked to be sure the clip was full, and closed the armoire doors. The SIG is a small but powerful handgun, and with a nine-round clip of .45ACP ammunition, it packed a punch in close quarters.

Dekker held the pistol with practiced assurance and opened the bedroom door. He listened for the noise to repeat, but there was only quiet in the house. He began a careful inspection, beginning with the living room and kitchen area. The dishes were as Kelly left them, and everything else seemed normal. A cool glow of moonlight flooded through the French doors leading to the patio, allowing Dekker to inspect the entire space without turning on a light.

He saw that one of the patio doors was slightly ajar, and he wracked his mind to remember if they had closed the doors when they came inside with the steaks. He couldn't recall, closed the door, and continued with his survey of the room. No furniture was out of place, and no items on the bookshelves had been moved; he couldn't imagine what had made the sound that awoke him.

Dekker finished inspecting the living area and began thinking the sound was imaginary, another of his dreams. He stepped outside the front door onto the porch, circled the house, and went along the edge of the corral to the barn. He had no light with him, but the bright moon gave him all the light he needed; he realized if someone was prowling, the moonlight would make him an easy target.

He began focusing on his proximity sense, the "danger radar" that served him so well over the years, and was now pinging off the scale. He crouched down to reduce his visible profile, giving him time to determine the source of danger. Moving into the barn he saw a dark shape on the ground. Coming closer, he realized it was Sasha lying on the dirt floor like an old, discarded garment. He knelt down next to the great dog, stroking his head and seeking any sign of life. There was none. How could someone kill this big dog without a sound of struggle, and without an apparent wound? He was shocked by the implications: only one force he knew could accomplish this terrible act, and he had seen it firsthand five years ago. *This is a Brotherhood strike, and they are attacking my house.*

He heard a scream. Kelly! He jumped up to run to the house but found he couldn't move. It was like a pair of great arms held him, restricting his movement. "No!" he shouted, realizing a Word of Power held him. "Kelly! You have to resist!"

Dekker feared the worst. He knew the only way to break a Word was to combat it with another. He forced himself to focus and calm his mind, and soon came to a state where he could wield a Word of Denial, taught to him by Galdur, the Icelandic mystic. The mental struggle was fierce; whoever held him was a seasoned practitioner of Magick. Dekker did not have the deep training, but as Galdur told him, it wasn't about how much one studied on the topic, it was a matter of the will.

Dekker felt the hold breaking as he concentrated his efforts on denying the force holding him in its grip. And then, with an almost audible *crack*, he was loose. Dekker wasted no time and ran to the house.

CHAPTER THREE

DEKKER THREW OPEN THE FRONT door, shouting for Kelly. The house was quiet and there was no reply. An icy fear gripped Dekker's heart as he moved down the hall toward their bedroom. His Ranger training demanded he check each of the rooms before the master bedroom at the end, an instinct he did not want to follow, but one he couldn't ignore.

He looked into the guest room where nothing was out of place, and moved on to check his office. Stepping inside, there was nothing immediately noticeable. His gun safe was locked and untouched, and the mess of books and papers on the desk were exactly as he had left them.

He turned around and realized instantly the Abaddon mask and robe were gone. He had taken these as a remembrance of the struggle with Abaddon. Had it not been for Galdur, and especially Kara, who'd died in the fight below Abaddon's lair in Germany, he would not have survived. Since that time Dekker displayed them on the wall with other souvenirs of previous missions. Nothing else was touched, only the Abaddon artifacts.

He went to the door of his bedroom, his hand frozen on the handle, his mind not willing to accept what might be beyond. He pushed open the door with a final effort of will and saw Kelly, sprawled naked across the bed, her eyes frozen wide in fear, her mouth open in a silent scream.

Dekker dropped to his knees beside the bed and grabbed her hand. He let out a deep and anguished cry, the grief in his heart so great he thought he would die. He couldn't think, he could only cry beside the bed.

He had no recollection of the passage of time, only the swirling memories of the bright, wonderful, and brave woman he now held in his arms. He rocked her back and forth, squeezing her lifeless body, muttering her name, hoping beyond hope she would awake. She had become the bedrock of his life, an anchor keeping him steady in all situations. Now she was gone, and he refused to accept it.

Dekker grieved for several hours, disbelieving, accusing himself, and spiraling into a pit of despair. He knew that wasn't good or healthy, but he didn't care. Kelly had been taken, and he couldn't accept it. As the sun came up he knew he would have to contact someone. He couldn't leave his wife like this, naked and terror-stricken in death. He dressed Kelly in a pretty nightie and carefully arranged her on the bed, taking care to smooth the sheets and blankets. He also closed her eyes, kissing each. She looked much more peaceful, almost like she were sleeping. This set off a new round of anguish in him and he screamed out a single word: "Abaddon!"

MIDDAY AND EVERYTHING was a blur. An emergency medical team was first to arrive, followed by Deputy Sheriff Ortega, and someone from the medical examiner's office in Santa Fe. Dekker knew they were investigating as if this were a homicide, and it was, but not due to forces they would understand. Dekker couldn't even begin to explain what happened in a rational, understandable way, and so remained mute throughout the preliminary investigation.

He was hardly aware that all the officials had gone when Horace Rimmer, Kelly's grandfather and his friend, showed up. Horace looked as terrible in his shock and grief as Dekker. "How could this happen?" A sob caught in his throat as he came to Dekker's side.

Dekker could only remember the bright, vibrant woman who became such a central part of his life, helping lift him from a very dark and lonely place in his psyche, giving him hope and a reason to go on. Now she was gone. What could he say? How to answer the old man's heartfelt question? Dekker had no good explanation, but he did have an idea. "Abaddon—that's the only explanation."

Rimmer stayed with Dekker through the afternoon and seeing no real change in his grief, invited him to come to his home in Los Alamos. Dekker looked at his friend with sad, grateful eyes, but declined.

"You shouldn't be alone, Adam," Rimmer advised him. Dekker could only nod his head, seeing another meaning in the statement. "You're right, Horace. I shouldn't be alone, but a madman has cut me off at the knees, leaving me here—alone. No, I want to stay."

Rimmer left Dekker alone in the house.

At first Dekker simply sat but then realized despite all grief, he was hungry. How long since he last ate? He couldn't remember; he supposed it was dinner with Kelly the night before, and that brought on a new wave of sorrow. He kept recalling her face, her voice, and her smell. He sat with his eyes closed, fighting back tears, telling himself a Ranger does not cry. That thought only created more conflict in him and he became angry. He was angry with everyone and everything, but most especially, he was angry with himself for failing to protect her.

THE NEXT MORNING he received two telephone calls, one from Jim Lynch, his boss at the National Counterterrorism Center, offering shocked condolences and telling Dekker he would help out any way he, or the NCTC, could. To Dekker, that sounded like the bugle call of the cavalry, someone who shared his history with Abaddon. *Perhaps he can explain Kelly's death to the authorities*, he thought.

He looked around his house, a place he loved dearly but now felt empty, and he grieved for the loss of the heart of the house, his Kelly.

The next telephone call was from Deputy Ortega, who wanted Dekker to come into Santa Fe to "answer a few questions." That sounded an awful lot like he was a suspect, and he didn't like it. Dekker responded that he could come by in a day or two, but the deputy sheriff became a little firmer. "No, Mr. Dekker, we need to see you today, as soon as possible, in fact." There was a long silence. "There are some troubling facts in your wife's death we need to clear up. How about I come up there and we can talk?"

"No. I'll be down there in a day or two." Dekker's mind was finally firing on all cylinders, realizing the "talk" was the first step toward labeling him a suspect in the case. He simply could not be detained for any period of time; he had to find Abaddon, and he would not be stopped by local law enforcement.

THE NEXT DAYS passed in a blur for Dekker. The ME's office ruled Kelly died from asphyxiation, specifically strangulation, although there were no signs or ligature marks on her neck. They could only surmise that a pillow or some other means was used to cut off her air supply and she simply stopped breathing. Dekker was the only other person in the house, except his purported invaders, so it became reasonable to believe he killed his wife for reasons unknown, and blamed it on intruders. "It's happened before," commented Ortega. "And strange things happen out here in the wilderness."

The ME and Sheriff's Department wanted to do more investigating into Dekker's life and relationships, but because he had powerful friends in Washington, they would proceed with caution.

Kelly's body was released to a funeral home and Dekker applied for, and received, approval to bury her at Vallecito Ranch. He prepared a plot near a stand of oak trees, shaded and beautiful, with a view of the expansive mesa and the mountain peaks beyond.

Horace Rimmer knew Kelly's heart and her love for the land and was confident this was how she would like to be buried. Dekker fenced off a plot for two because he intended to be buried beside her when his time came. Horace asked Dekker to make it big enough for three, that he, too, would like to be buried next to the granddaughter he raised as his own child. For Dekker, there was no question and he expanded the site to accommodate three graves, along with another for Sasha.

DEPUTY ORTEGA CAUGHT up with Dekker before the funeral. He could see the deputy was uneasy and wondered what he had to say. Ortega stuck his thumbs in his utility belt, looking like he was working up the courage to speak. "Mr. Dekker, you know we still have questions about your wife's death, and I'd like you to keep yourself available."

"You mean, 'don't leave town,' don't you?"

"I mean the investigation is not closed, and we will want you available." Dekker nodded, but his eyes said otherwise as he watched the Deputy Sheriff walk to his vehicle.

Jim Lynch, who'd come from Washington, DC for the funeral, spotted Dekker talking with the local sheriff and moved to his side as soon as the deputy drove away. Lynch noticed how tightly Dekker held his body and the faraway look in his eyes. Both he and Dekker knew who was behind the murder of his wife, and Lynch was certain his friend would not let Abaddon get away with it, even if he had to hunt for a hundred years.

"Adam, I want you to take time off—as much as you need before reporting back to work. And I also want you to know that the NCTC will help you any way we can." Lynch watched the departing deputy's car. "And don't worry, Adam, we'll cover you with the cops."

Dekker looked at his boss and friend, the hard look softened, and he nodded. He and Lynch went back many years, to a time when Dekker was a Special Ops officer in the Army and Lynch a CIA field operative. They'd worked together on several operations, and Dekker saved Lynch's life more than once, so when Lynch was recruited into NCTC in the aftermath of the 9/11 World Trade Center attack, he naturally turned to Dekker as a resource. Having left the

Army, Dekker did not want to be a government staffer, which suited Lynch just fine. Dekker was offered a consulting contract, and from that time forward his relationship with the NCTC was equitable and profitable.

Dekker was thankful for his friend's support, but he knew the help he needed would not come from the agency's extensive computer and terrorist interdiction technology. Instead, he would have to go to the heart of the conflict and meet the monster on his own turf; "analoging" was how he thought of it.

Dekker surveyed the few mourners surrounding the grave. There was Jim Lynch, of course, but also Horace Rimmer, deeply saddened by her death. Miguel, his ranch hand, caretaker, and friend, stood off to one side. Two representatives of the San Jacinto Pueblo were also there to mourn Kelly's passing: Eagle Claw Hurtado and his eldest son, Frank. It was Eagle Claw who'd helped Dekker through the anger, hurt, and confusion when he'd first come to New Mexico. Back then he arrived knowing no one and bought this ranch, Vallecito, for its remote location and its separation from civilization. It was a place he went to hide—from himself, from his thoughts, and from his memories.

He spent days hiking the canyons and mesas above Valles Caldera in the Jemez Mountains, coming to love the environment for its inspirational mountains, soothing forests, and cleansing mesas. He became interested in the history of the land and its peoples and was intrigued by the many legends of Indian warriors, bandits, and lost treasure.

Exploring gave Dekker something to do and a way to occupy his attention so he wouldn't have to think about his prior life, particularly his last mission to rescue an American student who mysteriously vanished from her hotel on Cozumel. It turned out she had been abducted by Yang Wei, a Chinese slave trader and a Consortium operative, who worked in South America funneling young female abductees to his rich clients in the Gulf region. Dekker tracked down the girl but was unable to save her. He had her, but she was so traumatized she didn't know what to do or who to trust. In the end she ran away from him and straight to Yang Wei. He watched a broken and forlorn young woman fly off to her doom, a situation that caused him to doubt everything he had done and every thought he believed in. Because of that incident, he'd retired from the private security firm and retreated to the mountains of New Mexico, to forget and do penance.

No one knew Dekker, the man, like Eagle Claw. He first met the tribal elder when he sought out a local expert on some Indian relics he discovered on one of his hikes. Eagle Claw was impressed this Anglo would even care to know the history of the relics, much less seek him out to give him an evaluation. Eagle Claw's respect for Dekker grew as he continued visiting the tiny San Jacinto Pueblo and began making friends. But Eagle Claw sensed Dekker was deeply wounded, not the type of wound that could be bound, but a deep wound of the spirit. One day Dekker came to him seeking help, and he was glad. The old man had seen into his very soul and helped him put aside his demons, emerging from an ancient kiva ceremony a new man. It was shortly thereafter he became entangled in a sinister spy operation centered on the Los Alamos National Laboratory and Dr. Horace Rimmer's gravity resonance experiments.

AFTER THE MOURNERS were gone Dekker sat under the oaks in remorseful remembrance, seeing Kelly in her dusty clothes, fresh from one of her archeological digs in the mountains; he saw her in her curator's office at the Smithsonian Institution, surrounded by artifacts, books, and samples; and he saw her in the soft blue dress she wore for their last meal, her lovely shape revealed by the clinging fabric and the light of the setting sun. These and many more memories crowded his mind and fed the ache in his heart.

His grief came in paralyzing waves. He sat by Kelly's grave for hours, sitting on a tree stump, letting the loss wash over and through him. Funerals were supposed to provide closure, but he was nowhere near that. The more he thought, the more certain he was he had to find Abaddon. He made up his mind to leave at sunup—and he would not tell Deputy Ortega. He had to pursue this on his own terms, in his own way, and he did not need entanglements.

The next day Dekker arose early, spoke with Miguel, his caretaker about watching the ranch and his horse while he was gone, and walked out of his home. He didn't look back.

CHAPTER FOUR

LORD GEOFFREY STAPLETON, ENGLISH nobleman and member of Parliament, was astounded when he heard the call through the Flows, learning of Abaddon's return. He responded quickly when the Master's call went out for the faithful to return to Krugerschloss.

Lord Geoffrey, a privileged and proper English gentleman, sent several of his local followers in response to the call, hoping to curry favor with the newly returned leader. He got a twinge, a tightening in his bowels, as he recalled the collapse of Abaddon's empire. Abaddon groomed him, raising him to a high position in his organization, ultimately directing Consortium operations in Great Britain, North, and South America.

In the unsettled period after Abaddon's defeat, Lord Geoffrey felt like he was in a small boat being tossed about on an angry sea. Much of his Consortium operations in arms trading and drugs had been confiscated, seized, or shut down by government zealots. Miraculously, Lord Geoffrey himself remained undetected and untouched during the witch-hunt carried on for the first year after Abaddon's defeat, a fact for which he was most grateful. Nevertheless, he kept a low profile for years, quietly rebuilding his operation and focusing his attention on managing the few remaining money-making schemes—including human trafficking and drug smuggling.

Now, with Abaddon back in Krugerschloss, he was certain business conditions would improve, since fear of Abaddon and his abilities drove all loyalty within his operation. Lord Geoffrey was confidant by using fear, it was only a matter of time before the Consortium got back into full operation. The summons for his personal appearance before Abaddon seemed an ideal opportunity to gain favor with the Master, and he eagerly collected background information for a report on Consortium operations during the last five years.

He set out for Germany, ready to show his Master he could resume full business operations.

CHAPTER FIVE

KAMENWATI SAT BEHIND A SIMPLE desk in a large inner office in the administrative center of Krugerschloss. The facility had none of the bustling activity it enjoyed during the long years leading up to the collapse five years ago, but the population was once again growing. Residents had increased to about one hundred, giving Kamenwati the range of skills necessary to finish the renovations, including building a fine, handcrafted desk for Abaddon. The desk pleased the master greatly and put him in a pleasant mood for several days.

Triberg Hall, deep in the heart of the mountain, was almost full and new arrivals were assigned to Germania Hall. The three residence halls were themed in their décor, and ultimately, their interests. The residence apartments of each were built into the granite walls in three levels, all connected by wide staircases and porches. Each residence had a distinctive façade made from intricately carved beams and pillars, decorated and carved with brightly colored nature themes, like flowers, leafy trees, running streams, and rugged mountains. The effect was like a fairy tale village.

All Halls included open structures on the main floor that housed tables and chairs, similar to an Oktoberfest biergarten. Smaller structures scattered around the main floor offered spaces for smaller groups to gather.

Germania Hall, the most recently reoccupied, was themed differently. It had the feel of a deep forest with huge trees soaring upward to the cavern ceiling, and grand staircases circling and climbing the great trunks. At several points large platforms protruded, offering more places to gather. At two points up the trees there were wide bridges leading to the dwellings in the cavern walls.

Kruger Hall, the final and still unoccupied residence in the mountain, had the look and feel of a Medieval Castle, with great tapestries hanging on the granite walls, heraldic symbols relating to the Kruger clan, and all manner of axes, bows, swords, and shields, all artfully displayed. Unlike the other residence halls, the public area was entirely open, with lines of great wooden tables and benches. The residences were defined by façades as in the other Halls, but not so finely carved, nor were they painted or decorated. The feel was a decidedly more utilitarian in Kruger Hall, not uncomfortable, just simpler.

Kamenwati received word that the two Adepts dispatched to America to eliminate the man so distracting the Master were on their way home, and carrying news. When they arrived, the Adepts were immediately escorted into Kamenwati's presence, even before dressing in the gray cloaks signifying their rank.

Kamenwati stood as the pair entered and looked with expectation at the bundle under the arm of one. "Report."

One of the Adepts said, "We bring presents for the Master." The man holding a bundle stepped forward and put the package on the desk. Kamenwati untied it, and seeing the bright copper mask atop the folded black cloak, let out a breath.

"You have done well. Tell me, Klaus, about the man and how you dealt with him."

Klaus began the story. "First, finding Dekker's home was difficult. It is located far into the western mountains of America. We feared we could not find it, but a chance meeting with a local criminal enterprise associated with the Consortium gave us the break we needed. Their leader was very familiar with the area and agreed, for a price, to lead us to Vallecito Ranch, Dekker's home. As you know, Dekker has certain skills and we considered him very dangerous. We were taken as far as the dirt road leading to the ranch and we snuck up in the dark, so Dekker wouldn't know we were there. Our first problem was a large black dog that was in the barn. We used our powers through the Flows to constrict the dog and to strangle the life from it without making a sound; our plan was to kill Dekker the same way. But Dekker somehow knew we were there and surprised us when he came into the barn and attacked. Brother Bernard here stayed behind while I ran out and around to the house."

"I tried to constrict and strangle Dekker," Bernard said, "but couldn't. Dekker knew what I was doing and used his own Word of Power to stop me."

"I made it inside the house," interrupted Klaus, "to carry out the plan to kill the woman, if we couldn't kill Dekker. It was easy; she was sleeping, but unfortunately she was able to get out one loud scream, which I stopped as fast as I could. After she was dead I went on a quick search and discovered the Master's artifacts in another room—the mask and cloak hanging on the wall like trophies. I took them and got out of the house. I knew Dekker was alive, but with his wife dead, I was sure he would find his way to Krugerschloss for the Master to deal with."

Kamenwati rewrapped the mask and cloak, placing a hand on top. "You have done well. Now go, refresh yourselves and retrieve your Brotherhood garments. I will take this to the Master." The Adepts left Kamenwati pleased their work had been acknowledged and commended. He watched them walk out of his office and sat down, placing his forehead on the bundle. Had someone been watching him, that person would have said he was praying. In a way, he was: In his heart he said, *This should be mine, and one day I will wear these and wield the power of Abaddon.*

Caressing the bright, gleaming mask, Kamenwati pondered yet again the reasons he embarked on this dangerous path. He could simply have established himself, much as Abaddon had many decades ago, taking over one Brotherhood cell after another, becoming connected to the civil power base, and subverting authority. He simply could not wait fifty years to gain the kingdom, and he couldn't continually look over his shoulder, wondering if Abaddon managed to escape and was coming to reclaim what was rightfully his. No, he must make a clean coup of it, killing the man Kambrian, who was Abaddon, and assume his place as the recognized leader and ruler. It was dangerous, but something he felt could be accomplished. And seeing how Abaddon's mind deteriorated almost daily, he was certain when he made his play, Abaddon would put up little resistance.

He stayed for a long time with his head down and arms outstretched in a meditative state until interrupted by an acolyte. "The Master is asking for you, sir." Kamenwati looked up, his reverie broken, and waved off the intruder. He stood up with a small sigh; he left the office with the bundle held close to his chest, carrying it to the Master's chambers.

ABADDON NOTED THE Egyptian's manner was slightly less deferential than usual and wondered for a moment what caused this change. He supposed it was the news of success he brought, knowing it was a welcome difference from the typical report. Just as quickly Abaddon remembered Kamenwati's threat from the moment of his resurrection, the ashes of the Succubus, and he was once again on guard.

"Good news from the team sent to America, my lord," Kamenwati began as he set the package in front of Abaddon. "And here is a prize you will appreciate." Abaddon took the package, holding it underneath with one hand and stroking the top with the other hand.

"And what of Dekker?"

"Our men were unable to contain him, but they did kill his wife and his guard dog. I'm sure he will be seeking us out soon, Lord." Kamenwati began to show discomfort under Abaddon's darkening countenance. "After all, it is what you predicted."

"Our people failed!" The explosive anger set Kamenwati back a small step. "How can that be?"

"The Adepts did their best."

"And they were found lacking. I will not tolerate incompetence and failure! You will bring them to the assembly chamber at sunset for punishment."

Kamenwati knew what this meant, and he was sorry for the young men. "Lord, if you will allow your anger to cool, you will see this is not a setback, only a foreseen development in your wider plan." Abaddon was clearly not disposed to listen to the Egyptian, no matter the logic of his argument.

"Leave me. I will meet you in the assembly hall tonight when all have gathered." He watched closely as the Egyptian retreated from the room. What he didn't see was the anger on Kamenwati's face. Abaddon's unchecked arrogance rankled Kamenwati, which fed the growing plan in his heart.

With the Egyptian gone, Abaddon opened the bundle before him, carefully holding up the bright copper mask, the candlelight in the room making it sparkle and dance with a life of its own. He placed the mask over his head and looked out the familiar eyeholes. It felt comfortable and reassuring, a feeling compounded when he placed the cloak around his shoulders. Now he felt complete, and once again, invincible.

CHAPTER SIX

LORD GEOFFREY ARRIVED AT KRUGERSCHLOSS in the evening, tired from the trip but excited to deliver good news to the Master. He entered the administrative building and was immediately concerned when he found no one there. He realized the mountain castle was still regrouping and repopulating, but this absence in a place that should be humming with activity caused him concern.

Geoffrey walked to the various offices and found no clue to the reason for a vacant facility. He went to a rear door, the one leading to the residence halls far up the tunnels, and peered inside. It was dark, not surprising as the dictates of the orthodox Brotherhood belief system prohibited modern technologies and instrumentation such as electric lights.

He recalled his own induction in this very place. His father, a believer and practitioner with their Brotherhood cell based at Stonehenge, had pledged his only son to Abaddon's service. The Master was pleased to receive the young Englishman and took a personal interest in his training and development. Geoffrey always feared meetings with the Master; frightened by his power and by the golden mask he always wore when outside his chambers. The mask made Abaddon look unholy and unreadable, and that scared young Geoffrey.

In time, he became used to both Krugerschloss and Abaddon, and on the day he learned his father had died, he was secretly pleased. He was ordered to return to his ancestral home and take charge of the Brotherhood group based there and manage Consortium activities in Great Britain and the Americas. Released from Abaddon's pre-industrial utopia in Krugerschloss, Geoffrey headed home to assume his role in the Brotherhood and take his father's place as a Peer of the Realm in the House of Lords.

He shook his head at the futility of Abaddon's orthodox restrictions and wondered what the Brotherhood thought the "restored" world would look like when Abaddon's vision of mankind under his complete control was fulfilled. He wondered himself, but knew it would never be the pre-industrial paradise Abaddon's rhetoric promised. Geoffrey selected a hurricane-style lamp from among several on a table next to the door, lit it, and headed left along the back passage; a route he knew led to the Great Hall.

Geoffrey began to hear distant noises as he walked—one noise, actually: The low sound of many voices talking at once. When he reached the door to the Great Hall he recognized the sound as a crowd of Brothers, and opening the door and stepping inside he saw them milling about, waiting for something. He estimated there were almost one hundred men and women in the hall, most in the white robes of acolytes, but several in the front dressed in the Adepts' gray.

The Great Hall was ablaze with light from the many torches held in mounts fixed to the walls and the numerous lamps, like the one he carried. The agate platform at the front of the Hall glowed with the same eerie blue color Geoffrey remembered, the tint cast up on the walls, shimmering with the movement of people and air in the room. Geoffrey knew he'd walked in on an important assembly and turned to leave when someone called out his name.

"Geoffrey! Lord Geoffrey Stapleton—please join us."

Geoffrey turned and saw a man in a black robe beckoning him to come forward. At first he didn't recognize the man and then he remembered—it was the Egyptian mystic, Kamenwati, a man he had not seen for many years.

"Please, Geoffrey, my brother, you are welcome here. You have arrived at just the right moment,"

Geoffrey moved up to the Egyptian. He noted two young men on the front edge of the platform standing at stiff attention. He could see only their backs. "What have they done?" Geoffrey asked.

"You will see in a moment," responded Kamenwati.

Four red-robed men emerged from doors to the left and right of the platform, two from each side. The red-robed men moved to the sides of the platform, and then turned toward the back wall with the stepped-in pyramidal carvings.

The central pyramid carving soundlessly slid open; dark smoke issued into the room. The haze quickly covered the platform and spilled over the edge. Abaddon stepped out of it, in full robes and wearing the brightly burnished copper mask. Geoffrey had to admit it made an impressive and terrifying sight.

The faithful standing behind Geoffrey and the Egyptian looked on in rapt attention, their sense of expectation palpable. Low at first, and then building, they began the familiar chant.

> *Great is Abaddon.*
> *Great is his power.*
> *He is the bringer of death and he is the giver of life.*
> *Great is Abaddon*

Abaddon moved to the center of the agate platform and gestured for the red-robed attendants to move in. They did so, standing around the two subjects awaiting judgment. One of the subjects began blurting out excuses and supplications.

"Enough!" Abaddon commanded. "You are both Adepts and therefore know my laws. You were given the task to capture and kill the American named Dekker."

The other young Adept spoke up. "Master, it was my companion," he gestured with his head to the Adept on his left, "who remained in the barn to corner and kill the man, while I went into the house. There I used the tools of Magick to choke the life from the woman as you ordered, and then retrieved your property."

Abaddon focused his inscrutable golden stare at the young man. The Adept gathered confidence and continued. "I ran outside to find my brother, only to see the man, Dekker, running into the house. I confess that I panicked for a moment and ran, but soon I mastered my emotions and stopped. My partner here"—again with a gesture of his head to the left—"I found cowering in the underbrush. I grabbed him and we made our escape. While it was not a perfect mission, we accomplished most of the objectives."

Abaddon clasped his hands behind his back, thinking. "No, as you say, not perfect. But where in my instructions were you given the option to disobey and fail me?" The Adept who had been speaking began again but Abaddon lifted his left hand toward him, stopping the reply with a gurgling cough. "This was a simple enough assignment: Kill him and kill all others with him."

The second Adept dropped to his knees, groveling. Abaddon moved his golden gaze back and forth between the two young men, and then, lifting the other hand, he seemed to grab the Adept by his shoulders. Although separated from the young men by a distance of eight feet, he levitated both Adepts into the air. When both were hovering over the platform, Abaddon unleashed his wrath. He lifted his arms high and the two Adepts flew up to the stone ceiling of the cavern; Abaddon held his position for a long moment, and then dropped his arms. The two doomed men crashed to the platform, bodies broken and twisted, as a gasp came from those watching, including Lord Geoffrey.

Abaddon looked out over his assembly, fixing them with a stare. He turned and re-entered the pyramid at the rear of the platform.

When Abaddon was gone there was a collective relaxation, as if all in the room had been holding their breath, and let it out as their Master departed. *So, Geoffrey noted, none of the Master's intimidation skills have diminished. If anything, he has grown stronger while in captivity.*

Soon after Abaddon's departure one of the red-robed attendants came back, asking for Lord Geoffrey. Geoffrey looked to Kamenwati for some interpretation or guidance, but the Egyptian could only shrug his shoulders. The attendant stood before Geoffrey and issued an order to follow him, adding, "The Master is waiting."

Geoffrey couldn't imagine what his transgression might be, so he began assembling a mental list of excuses and retorts.

ABADDON RECEIVED LORD Geoffrey in his offices behind the altar. He always stood during formal audiences, elevated on a six-inch platform to enhance his diminutive five-foot, seven-inch height, and increasing the visitor's feeling of insignificance. This occasion was no exception. Geoffrey was a little surprised since he had seen him many times without the mask, but he supposed the Master needed the prop to bolster his ego. Geoffrey stood at mute attention, waiting for whatever the Master had for him.

"Lord Geoffrey, I understand you have been able to keep the greater part of our Western Consortium intact."

Geoffrey nodded and began fishing for the documents he brought. "Yes, I have, and I've brought information that will bring you up to date with the remaining operations, as well as my new plans."

Abaddon waved off his offer. "Not now. My immediate concern is this man Adam Dekker. He must be found and eliminated. Nothing else happens until I am rid of him." This last statement was delivered with a hiss and it was clear to Geoffrey that the Adepts' failed mission would now become his. "You, Geoffrey, will mobilize your organization to locate Dekker and either capture him or drive him here to me. The Adepts were right—I must be the one to deal with him. Do you understand?"

"Completely, Master," said Geoffrey, choking back a string of questions, not the least of which was Dekker's location.

"You may go, but do not forget the price for failure." Abaddon turned around with the dismissal, his back not receiving any questions. Geoffrey knew this was a terrible position to be in, and was certain the task would be difficult.

"No, Master, I will not forget."

CHAPTER SEVEN

DEKKER'S MIND CHURNED QUESTIONS AS he drove, chief among them Abaddon's status. He struggled to recall what Galdur told him about the stasis holding Abaddon, and all he could remember was it was supposed to last a very long time. Could he really have broken out in only five years? Did someone intervene, effectively resurrecting the monster? The Brotherhood's assassination strike at his ranch came out of the blue; there was no warning. This had its own set of unanswerable questions of who and why, equally confounding without more information.

Dekker drove aimlessly, chewing on the questions troubling him.

He'd left Vallecito Ranch with no clear notion of a destination, unconsciously driving east and stopping when he realized he was entering Nashville, Tennessee. He had only a dim recollection of the trip and stops for fuel. He was grateful he had not been involved in a traffic accident or pulled over for reckless driving. But he had to ask himself, where was he headed? His brain and body were on autopilot, so he knew his subconscious had a destination.

After sitting in a diner, drinking coffee, and chewing on a surprisingly tasty sandwich, the revelation came: He was headed to Northern Virginia, to his condo near the National Counterterrorism Center. It was a place almost nobody knew about, a place he called his "safe house," and somewhere he could take cover with little probability of discovery.

The thousand plus miles he had driven caught up to him and he rented a room in a motel next to the diner. Dekker dropped onto the bed, fully clothed, and immediately fell into a deep sleep. Eighteen hours later Dekker awoke.

At first the surroundings of the motel room confused him, but then the memory of the diner, and his understanding of where his subconscious was taking him, came back. He grappled with a flood of renewed grief for several moments before rubbing his stiff muscles and realized he needed a shower.

After the shower Dekker checked out of the motel and went back to the diner for a late breakfast of eggs, grits, toast, and coffee. The food was like a tonic for his body, reviving and refreshing. He filled the pickup truck with gas and continued east on Highway 40, headed for Washington, DC.

CHAPTER EIGHT

LORD GEOFFREY BUSIED HIMSELF AFTER leaving Krugerschloss with the task of locating Dekker, something easier said than done. He could have asked for Kamenwati's help, but he was somehow suspicious of the Egyptian. Abaddon's sweeping directive may have been possible to achieve five years ago, but today with a reduced Brotherhood population and a severely restricted Consortium, the order seemed impossible, even foolish.

Geoffrey first had to identify the places Dekker was likely to be found. New Mexico was certainly one place to look, but more research into his career revealed a dozen more possibilities. Geoffrey hadn't the resources to cover so many places; even in New Mexico he had only the Mestizos motorcycle gang, a tenuous connection through the Consortium's cartel partner in Mexico.

It was a similar story in the other cities, states, and countries Dekker was associated with, but he had to make an effort or face the consequences. Abaddon was demanding regular reports and the strain of devising something new each day grew into a true burden on Geoffrey. After all, he did have responsibilities in the House of Lords and to Parliament that could not be ignored. None of that mattered to Abaddon and he became more insistent Dekker be found.

Geoffrey had a discussion with one of the few Consortium groups still intact and operating in America, the group led by a man named Origen. The group was based in suburban Maryland outside the nation's capitol and had served Geoffrey well over the years. At first Origen was not happy to hear from his titular Brotherhood "superior," a man he had never met face-to-face.

Origen had heard Abaddon's calls in the Flows, of course, but was reserving his support until he knew more. Now came this insistence by Lord Geoffrey to begin searching for a man that may or may not be in the DC area. "Adam Dekker works for the National Counterterrorism Center and it is likely he will be there, or somewhere in the area," Lord Geoffrey told him.

Origen, a man accustomed to leadership and the respect of others, took the information with frustrated anger. "Great; this guy Dekker is a spook. Just the kind of person we need to be avoiding, not finding."

Origen's operation consisted of warlords, gangsters, corrupt generals, and venal, self-serving politicians. Each needed the influence and power Abaddon wielded, and so had joined in his strange alliance. The Consortium was an enterprise in criminal and illegal activity, not a religious-fanatic cell as the Brotherhood. The Consortium held no religious beliefs, only the belief in amassing money and power.

Origen was a long-time "information broker," selling military and intelligence secrets to the highest bidder. The Consortium recruited him long ago, promising funding and resources to continue building his operation. He would keep fifty percent of all proceeds for his local organization, and the remainder going to offshore Consortium accounts. The prospect of regular funding and support had been appealing, but giving up half his revenue—that was a bit much, even if the volume rose as they'd promised.

Origen had no desire to enlist in Abaddon's activities, and declined that first offer. Shortly thereafter a man clad in a gray cloak appeared at his door, reiterating the Consortium's offer. Origen had had no time for ridiculous offers and slammed the door in the man's face. At least he'd tried to. He was stunned to find his mind working but his body unresponsive. In fact, it felt like someone wrapped him up with strong ropes, completely immobilizing his arms. He'd tried to shout for help but could not. His throat would not work, and it felt like he was being choked. Fear flooded in and Origen panicked. *Is this the way I'm to die?* He'd struggled to get loose, but the more effort he'd put into it, the tighter the binding became. Just as he was about to black out, the strangling sensation around his neck ceased.

Taking great gulps of air, he'd choked out, "Who are you?"

"I am an Adept, sent by Abaddon to persuade you to come into his fold."

"What if I don't want to join this Abaddon?"

"Then you will die where you stand." It required only a moment for Origen to reconsider his options.

"I accept your offer. Please let me go."

IN RETROSPECT IT had been a good trade for Origen. His reach and business grew beyond his wildest dreams. He purchased an estate home at the end of Patuxent River Road in rural Maryland and he developed moles in every important government organization, including defense, intelligence, and law enforcement. These assets provided a steady flow of plans, deployments, payments, virtually any element of intelligence that might interest his now worldwide circle of clients.

Origen learned quickly that Abaddon's power wasn't limited by distance. When one of his people totally fouled up an Abaddon assignment, the man spontaneously combusted, burst into flames like some protesting Buddhist monk, in the presence of his entire staff. The lesson sunk in immediately and dramatically: No one ignored or failed to carry out orders from Abaddon, or anyone in the Consortium, again.

So, after Lord Geoffrey's call, Origen assembled a team of men to explain their task. "First things first: We have to find out where Dekker lives, and what he does off the clock."

NCTC is located in suburban Virginia, in the upscale bedroom community of McLean. Since his particular Consortium cell was not especially orthodox in their Brotherhood beliefs, they had no problem using the Internet and Google Earth to help them locate the agency. They brought in a color print of Google's satellite imagery and explained it to Origen.

"It isn't exactly hidden," said Mitchell, a senior member of his staff began. "They just don't make it easy to find. I'll bet most of the people living in the area aren't even aware the agency is there. NCTC is surrounded by a thick band of forest right at the intersection of the Beltway, the Dulles access road, and Dolly Madison Boulevard. Lots of traffic going all around it, but nobody's really paying attention."

Another member of the team, Reggie, a young man who was sometimes overenthusiastic, stepped into the conversation. "The agency was established after 9/11. It's a central clearing house for intelligence on terrorists and their various plots. It was also meant to bridge the institutional silos of CIA, FBI, and the NSA. It's worked fairly well, and other than homegrown attacks, the militant Islamic groups have been kept at bay."

"And what about Dekker?" Origen asked. "What does he do there?"

"He's a special agent, like James Bond, sir," Mitchell said. Referring to notes, he continued. "He began in the Army, as a Ranger. His specialty was search and recovery, and he saw action in every hotspot in the world, which caught the CIA's attention. They began borrowing him to lead extraction teams in Bosnia, Iraq, Somalia, and even in South America."

"A man of action," Origen said.

"Oh, he is. And when the NCTC was created, they immediately brought Dekker on as a special operative. But then there is a total blank in his history, like he disappeared from the face of the earth."

"Do you know where he lives?"

"That information is hard to find, but it seems he lives—at least part time—in New Mexico."

"Where does he live when he's here in town? Surely there must be real estate records."

"So far, nothing, sir." Reggie looked to his colleague for support, but found none. "I'll keep digging."

Origen was done with the meeting and gave orders to the team "Use the photo from Google Earth and start a surveillance schedule on the facility. Begin searching the neighborhoods and developments around the headquarters. Chances are he has a place close by."

The pair left Origen, staring at the photo of Dekker. "Who are you, and what is your connection to Abaddon?"

CHAPTER NINE

DEKKER OPENED THE DOOR TO his condo in the Colonies at McLean. The air inside was a little musty since the windows were closed and the air conditioning turned off, but it caused him to choke up with emotion. He could smell Kelly in the condo, and all the heartbreak held back by his anger broke through. He could hardly move and it was a struggle just to close the door behind him as he collapsed on the living room couch. The coffee table still had small bits of dirt from the artifact she'd been so excited about the last time they were here. She'd brought the piece in from a dig in Arizona and would log it into the Smithsonian collection in the morning, but she hadn't been able to wait to tell him all about the trip and the artifact.

Dekker remembered opening a bottle of chardonnay and pouring two glasses, listening politely while Kelly poured out her story. She was never more beautiful than when she recounted her archeological adventures, her eyes bright with excitement. She showed off her prize, holding it carefully but showing Dekker every angle of the piece. He loved her passion, and now, remembering this last time in the condo, it hurt his heart deeply.

"Damn you, Abaddon. You will pay for what you have stolen!"

Dekker went to the refrigerator in the kitchen, opening it to see what might be there. He found a bottle of chardonnay, grabbed it, and went back to the living room with a glass and an opener.

"Here's to you, Kelly, my love."

DEKKER AWOKE WITH a headache. *My god, I drank the whole bottle of wine*, he thought, slightly annoyed at himself. He went to the bathroom and found a bottle of ibuprofen, took out three tablets, and washed them down.

Forty-five minutes, a shower, and two cups of coffee later, he felt ready to face the world. He began with a call to Dennis Allende, the brilliant young computer expert at NCTC who had been part of Dekker's ragtag team that took on Abaddon five years before. Dennis was now chief of the Forensic Information Investigation Unit (FIU), his skills and insight moving him steadily up in the organization. Dennis was a key man in Dekker's various operations in these intervening years, and was a trusted confidant. Dennis was also one of the few who knew what Dekker would be facing, and it was Dekker's hope Dennis' computers could answer some of his basic questions.

"Dekker! Glad to hear from you, man!"

"Glad to talk to you, too. Listen, Dennis, I'm going to need your help. I assume you heard about what happened on my ranch in New Mexico?"

"Yes, and I can't tell you how sorry I was to learn about Kelly. I've been trying to figure out why someone would want her dead, but I get nowhere."

"It was Abaddon," Dekker said with a choke in his voice. "He sent a team of Adepts to my home. I was the intended target but they couldn't get me, so they killed Kelly and Sasha, instead."

"The dog, too? I loved Sasha."

"I did, too, almost as much as Kelly. I am going to avenge my loss, and the loss of everyone else who's had the misfortune to cross paths with that sociopath."

"I agree. How can I help?"

"We need to find out if Abaddon is really back, which is the only way this makes sense. And we need to know who his accomplices are."

"It's hard to believe anyone would help him, or why."

"Personally, I believe the only way that monster could escape the stasis is with outside help, and that's why I need you to get me a list of known Adepts and deep practitioners who might be his accomplice, or accomplices."

"No problem. Do you want to come in to the office?"

"I want to keep a low profile, Dennis. I sort of left New Mexico before the police were done with me. Is your social life still about your computers, or can you get away?"

"You know me—highly focused and no relationships outside the office, so getting away is no problem."

"Why don't you come to my condo? You remember where it is, right?"

"Sure. I'll come over right after work, say about five-thirty?"

"Perfect. I'll be looking for you."

Dekker hung up and realized he had several hours to kill, but he was energized. He would use the time to begin his own investigation, and it would start with Paul Prentiss, the disgraced—and imprisoned—former Federal Reserve Chairman.

Prentiss was the lynchpin in Abaddon's scheme to seize control of the world's major currencies. It was Abaddon's careful planning that placed him in control of the US currency by grabbing him early smoothing his way as a young man.

Dekker was been present at Eilean Donan Castle in Scotland when an energy ball hurled Benjamin Wilton, the previous Fed Chairman, out a window to his death on the courtyard below. It was a low point in Dekker's career and his first exposure to the Brotherhood and the powers of Magick. It was after the tragic death that Dekker met Ulrig who, it turned out, was an elder in the Brotherhood, but one of the few who did not blindly follow Abaddon. It was Ulrig who'd opened his eyes to the wider world of Magick and spiritual powers, setting Dekker on a course that would intersect Galdur, Kara Triberg, and ultimately, Abaddon.

Because of the nature of Prentiss' crime he was being held as a terrorist in the Anacostia Naval Station brig in the District of Columbia. Dekker knew this because it was very important to keep Prentiss isolated and unable to communicate with anyone outside. Who knew what mischief he could still cause? Dekker would need a special high-level clearance to visit the man. He needed Jim Lynch to make the call.

"Jim, I need to take you up on your offer to help me," said Dekker when he called.

"Adam, where are you? You aren't here in DC, I hope."

"Never mind that, Jim. I just need your help."

"Of course, what is it you need?"

"I need clearance to visit Prentiss."

"Why in the world do you want to talk to him?"

"I think he may have some insight into my current situation." Lynch knew Dekker was hurting, and did not want to set him back.

"Adam, I think you're fishing a dry hole."

"It may be, but it's a place to start."

"It's going to be difficult to get clearance to see Prentiss. He is very much isolated — and for good reason."

"No one knows the reasons better than me, Jim." Lynch looked out his office window, holding the telephone receiver, taking time to weigh the consequences of what Dekker was asking. Dropping his chin to his chest, he acquiesced.

"Ok, you'll get it."

Dekker let out a sigh of relief, and said quietly, "Thank you, Jim," and hung up the telephone.

DEKKER PULLED UP to the front gate of the Anacostia Naval Station and was directed to the brig. It had been two days since his talk with Jim Lynch, but he finally got word he could interview Paul Prentiss, but only briefly. Driving into the brig area was like entering a world away from the rest of the base. Set well off from military operations, a high fence topped with razor wire surrounded the brig compound. Dekker was glad he was not an inmate in this dismal place.

Armed Marines patrolled the perimeter as well as manning the security station where he checked in. After several minutes of processing, and the guard looking through databases, Dekker was handed a visitor's badge. "Keep this on and in plain sight at all times, sir," instructed the corporal checking him in.

Dekker nodded and an electronically locked door clicked open. Another Marine escorted Dekker to a low, red brick building with no windows.

"Cheery place," Dekker commented lightly. The Marine did not see the humor. They entered the building through another manned security door where Dekker was handed off to a new set of guards. He was given verbal instructions on how he was to act with the prisoner, and he was informed the meeting would be recorded. He inquired about the inmate's privacy rights and was told in stern terms, "Prisoners in this section have no rights."

Dekker stepped inside the prison blockhouse and the guard reminded him of the last provision of his visit. "You will have thirty minutes, and there will be no note taking." Dekker knew half an hour wasn't enough time to establish a rapport or get any sort of meaningful information, so he had to come up with another angle of attack, one sympathetic to Prentiss.

He was shown into a stark cinderblock room with only a door. Flush light fixtures in the ceiling were covered with heavy wire mesh and a microphone hung from a wire directly over a small table bolted to the floor. There were two institutional wooden chairs, and like the table, one was firmly bolted in place. He assumed the unsecured chair was for him, so he pulled it out and sat down to wait for Prentiss.

A few minutes later Marine guards escorted Prentiss into the room. They marched him to the bolted chair, sat him down, and stepped back to the corners of the room. Their eyes never left their charge and they looked like tough hombres.

Prentiss was singularly nondescript. He was neither tall nor short, skinny or fat. In fact, he was the very image of a forgettable government functionary. Dekker supposed a tailored suit and a briefcase would alter the impression, but Prentiss was a cowed enemy—totally defeated and accepting of his fate. The heights he had imagined for himself, the kingdom he planned for his estate in Little Washington in the Virginia countryside, were not to be, could never be—thanks in no small part to the man standing before him.

"Mr. Prentiss, my name is Adam Dekker." He reached out to offer his hand but the guards took a step forward and one said, "No physical contact with the prisoner." Dekker quickly withdrew his hand and went into his pitch. "Mr. Prentiss, I don't know if you know who I am—my name is

Dekker, and I was involved in dismantling Abaddon's mad plan five years ago."

"I know who you are. Why are you here, to gloat? I've already told them everything I know."

"Yes, I'm sure you have. But I want to talk with you about something else. I was attacked a couple of weeks ago—a Brotherhood attack." That bit of information caused Prentiss to look up sharply. "They used their powers to restrain me and kill my wife."

"Why didn't they kill you, too?"

"They tried and failed. Unfortunately, they succeeded with my wife and got away before I could catch them. When I found Kelly," Dekker's eyes almost burst into flames at the memory, "I vowed to catch the man who ordered it."

"Odd they would choose to attack you after so much time…what do you want from me?"

"I am hoping we have a similar motivation to, ah, seek retaliation."

Prentiss eyed Dekker closely, and then leaned on the table between them. "What are you suggesting? Surely you can see that my mobility and resources are limited."

Dekker looked at Prentiss with stern, cold eyes. "I believe someone has released Abaddon from his stasis, and I want you to tell me who might have helped him—who could help him."

"Who could resurrect Abaddon? You're crazy. It's my understanding only Abaddon has the power to create and dismantle a stasis chamber."

"Yes, but if someone else, or some special group, had the power, who would that be?"

Prentiss sat back in his chair with a curious look. "What's in it for me?"

"Can you help me? If you can, I'll work on something for you," said Dekker.

"I need more specifics," answered Prentiss. "Can you get my sentence commuted?"

"No, Mr. Prentiss, I can't do that. But I'm sure there are privileges that can make your life in here a little easier."

"Why should I want to help you, Mr. Dekker? You were the architect of my destruction."

"Because Abaddon has destroyed both our lives. Wouldn't you like to be instrumental in recapturing him and get rid of him forever?"

"Assuming he has been released, and assuming you can catch him, I doubt you could ever kill him."

Dekker stared at Prentiss with a stony resolve and an almost palpable anger. "I can do it. I just need a place to start."

He remembered the showdown in the ancient monolithic stone temple in the field below Krugerschloss. There he, Galdur, and Kara faced Abaddon, enduring the wrath he rained down on them, and most importantly, keeping him off guard. They formed a stasis cube above the unsuspecting Abaddon, his attention focused on his renegade Adept, Kara. Before he could react, they lowered the stasis down and around him, trapping the evil.

Dekker's resolve transfixed Prentiss and, it seemed, swayed him. "Let me think about it, Mr. Dekker." He stood up, flanked immediately by the Marine guards, and left the room. Dekker put his head down on the table, took several deep breaths, and lifted it back up.

Another guard came into the room to escort Dekker out.

CHAPTER TEN

SAMMY PUCKETT, ONE OF ORIGEN'S men, parked his car for the third day in the cul-de-sac at the end of Old Maple Square Street. This was a quiet and affluent neighborhood, and a perfect place to leave his car. He used the paved walk to Windy Hill Road, which crossed Great Falls Road, and provided an unobstructed view into the NCTC facility. From a grassy play area he watched everyone coming and going into the agency, but his particular mission was to look for any of Adam Dekker's known associates, or Dekker himself.

Sammy was beginning to tire of the monotonous routine. This day he brought a folding camp chair and a small collapsible cooler with drinks and a couple of sandwiches, and by eight o'clock was settled in for another day of observation. Sammy was grateful the residents were only sporadic visitors to their park area since it wouldn't do to have nosy neighbors asking questions.

The morning dragged on, cars coming and going; Sammy carefully observed each with binoculars. A young woman pushing a baby stroller went by, but Sammy displayed his props of bird-watching books, a sketchpad, and a camera, which seemed to answer her unspoken question of identity and purpose. He was harmless, not casing homes in the neighborhood, and was forgotten as soon as the baby fussed and needed attention.

The day was ending and he was about to pack it in when an old Volvo caught his attention. The car itself was out of place, a brand and a lifestyle statement that was out of sync with everyone else at the agency. Sammy inspected the driver with his binoculars and looked at the photos he had placed in the pages of his sketchpad. It was a hit! The driver was Dennis Allende, some sort of technology geek and known to have been in Germany with Dekker for Abaddon's defeat.

Sammy made sure he had the license plate number and quickly packed up his chair and birding paraphernalia, heading as quickly as he could to his car. Sammy was lucky.

The rush-hour traffic had Great Falls Road backed up and he saw Allende turn the Volvo onto Chain Bridge Road.

After crossing under the Dulles Toll Road Sammy followed the Volvo onto Old Meadows Road, into a condominium complex. It was perfect, Sammy observed. He could park without attracting attention. He drove around a bit, as if looking for a particular building, until he found Allende's Volvo parked in front of an end building. Sammy took a parking place well away but still in a position to see what Allende was up.

He watched Allende approach one of the units and ring the doorbell. It looked like nobody was home and Dennis turned to leave just as a car pulled up. Sammy saw the primary objective, Dekker, get out and call out to Allende. This was great luck for Sammy and he called in the find. Origen was very pleased and sent another team of observers to take over for the hero of the moment.

"We will soon have our man," Origen gloated.

"DENNIS!" DEKKER CAME up to Allende, wrapping him in a bear hug. "I'm sorry to be late, but the traffic from Anacostia held me up and being on the run, I can't afford to have a cell phone someone can track."

"What were you doing over there?"

"Meeting an old friend. Come inside and I'll fill you in."

Once comfortably settled, the NCTC technology expert sat down. His buzz-cut hair stuck up in a million tiny spears, very much in style for younger men. He wore an open casual shirt, untucked and unbuttoned, over a t-shirt with a huge tongue sticking out—a tribute to the Rolling Stones. He was the classic geek, and he idolized Dekker.

"It is really good to see you, Dennis."

"Yes, and it's good to see you as well. What's up?"

"I think I'm going to be away from the agency a while longer."

"Given Kelly's death and all you've been through, no one will think less of you." Dennis shifted around in his seat.

"But why are you *here*? This town with all its intrigues, deceits, and double-crosses, is the last place you need to be." Dekker grew very serious and had a look on his face Allende had never before seen. He realized it was anger—no, more than anger—hatred. It scared Dennis, and he didn't know what to say.

"This is the right place for me to be, because here is where it all began five years ago."

Dennis realized Dekker was talking about the Abaddon adventure, an experience he would not soon forget: Racing through the halls and tunnels of Krugerschloss, pursued by Brothers intent on their death; breaking into Abaddon's private chambers behind the altar in the Great Hall and finding the most amazing technology setup; sparring with— and defeating—the computer system in the process of taking over the US economy; and the final meltdown of Abaddon's systems when he introduced an unsolvable equation that totally consumed the computer system. It was all very exciting, and also very scary.

Dennis was confused; Abaddon was confined and out of the picture. He waited for Dekker to calm down and continue.

"I think Abaddon has escaped. The attack on my ranch was the work of the Brotherhood and a clear sign Abaddon wants to make good on his promise to kill me and everyone I care about."

"Mr. Lynch mentioned your suspicions about Abaddon when I met with him today, but I told him I couldn't imagine how that could be. I clearly recall Galdur's explanation of the stasis and that it was, for all intents and purposes, eternal."

"What can be made, can be unmade, and I need to know who 'unmade' the stasis—and what Abaddon plans to do."

"I want to help," said Dennis with a firm conviction.

Adam told Dennis about his meeting with Prentiss and what he hoped would come of it. "He knew what Abaddon's plan was, and more importantly, who the major players were. I need to know who in the Brotherhood circle has the power to undo the stasis, and then, who still supports the mad scheme."

"Why not come into NCTC and use our resources?"

"Because of the fugitive thing. I can't tell the police what it really is, or they'd for sure think I was nuts and jail me just for that."

The pain in his voice was unmistakable, an expression of his deep sorrow and anger; first at Abaddon and his people, next at the authorities for thinking he could ever hurt his wife.

"As someone whose world is defined by data and logic, I can appreciate their skepticism," Dennis said. "It's very hard to accept the powers that Abaddon and his followers have, and even harder to explain to someone who hasn't experienced them."

"I believed they were going to arrest me as a suspect, that's why I left."

"Now I understand," said Dennis. "And I also get why you wanted to start with Prentiss. But I think there is a different route we can follow, if you're willing."

DENNIS LEFT THE condo an hour later under the careful watch of Origen's men. They had orders to ignore all others and capture or kill Dekker. Four men had been sent to relieve Sammy at the condo, and now they moved out to complete their mission. These men were not Adepts or knowledgeable in the traditions of Magick. They knew about it from Origen, whom they considered to be very strange—they were simply hired muscle used to collect and enforce.

Inside the condo, Dekker was calmer than he had been in days. Dennis had been a good call, someone who could analyze and come to conclusions he might miss. Dekker sat on the couch in the darkened room, considering the new options Dennis presented.

His mind drifted and felt his consciousness reach into the Flows, a pleasant experience and oddly refreshing, when his danger radar brought him up short. He re-focused his attention to the threat and felt a group of men approaching outside. They were intent on his death. Dekker looked around, glad he had the lights out, but concerned he was trapped in the condo. He had to get outside, and quickly, if he hoped to gain any sort of advantage over the attackers.

CHAPTER ELEVEN

DENNIS WENT STRAIGHT BACK TO the NCTC to work on details of the plan he suggested to Dekker. He would also put in for immediate vacation and comp time, which he had coming, giving him the freedom to help his friend. He, too, was angry about the attack and Kelly's murder. She was a smart, accomplished, beautiful woman, and the thought that Abaddon had her executed caused a righteous anger to well up.

The NCTC, like most government agencies, tended to clear out at 4:00 in the afternoon. But there were a number of people whose jobs were not regular and so were in the facility at all hours. His department, the FID, operated around the clock and several technicians were onsite. He was greeted with surprise since his position rarely required his presence at night. Dennis simply waved them off and went to his office.

Dennis emerged in the middle of the next day, a sleek laptop in one hand and a canvas bag full of documents in the other. He was ready to go hunting and he believed he had the information Dekker could use to drive a stake through the heart of evil, stopping it once and for all.

DEKKER MOVED CAREFULLY from window to window, looking and listening. He held the SIG Sauer Compact he brought with him from New Mexico, and scanned for movement. He had to get out of the condo, but the front door was definitely out. He went to the bedroom and opened the window overlooking the woods behind the complex. It was about twenty feet down, due to the slope of the ground, but he had long ago prepared this escape route. He opened the bedside end table where he kept a burner cell phone for just such a situation, picking it up, he inspected the device to assure it was charged. As he placed the cell phone in his pocket thanked the heavens he had prepared to this level.

Retrieving a rope he had stashed under the bed, he fed one end through a D-ring installed on the side of the building. He paid the line out until it reached the ground and dropped the remainder to double the line. He tucked the SIG into his waistband and grabbed both sides of the rope. Stepping out carefully and holding himself at an angle away from the building wall, he closed the bedroom window. His plan was to make it look like nobody was home, and he thought it unlikely they would find his escape route.

Dekker descended to the ground, pulling one end of the rope back up and through the D-ring, dropping the rope in a heap at his feet. He gathered up the rope, wrapped it in a mountain climber's bundle, slung it across his shoulders, and headed for the cover of the trees. His biggest concern at the moment was the chance the intruders might have night-vision gear. If so, even the trees would not provide cover. He simply had to trust to luck and get back around his building. He went into autopilot mode, trusting training and instinct to guide him through the next minutes.

Once around his building, Dekker dashed across the parking area to another building where he could stop and observe his front door. Two men stood on either side of it, each holding a compact machine pistol. As he waited he saw two more men moving stealthily toward each side of his building, obviously to cut off any rear retreat. Dekker was thankful he acted quickly and got out, because now there would be no way to escape unseen.

The men at the door were frustrated by their inability to pick the door lock; clearly they were unaware that Dekker had installed the **Schlage M492P High Security Electromagnetic Lock** that was virtually impossible to pick. The team at the door went into a huddle, with occasional exclamations heard and squelched. The men seemed to have decided on another means to open the door and one of them left his position and trotted down the parking lot to a panel van, curiously marked "Bottner Center." A few moments later the man emerged and returned to his colleague at Dekker's door.

Dekker had no idea what the attackers planned, but short of blowing down the door, nothing would disengage the electromagnetic lock system. He was interested in the dark green van the attackers used and moved to it, letting the vehicle hide him from view. Entering the van was no problem since his attackers left the doors unlocked. Dekker reasoned it was to facilitate a quick getaway, but it also made breaking in much easier. He searched for clues to the identity of the attackers, not only who they were, but who sent them.

The Colonies condo community was a quiet place, all professionals, working primarily for the government in one capacity or another. So the explosion was jarring and Dekker knew what the attackers had done—they'd blown the door. Definitely not subtle, but it gave them the entry they desired. The only problem was, Dekker wasn't there.

Dekker found a spare set of keys and an envelope in the glove compartment, which also held a registration certificate identifying the owner, as the Maryland Agricultural and Wildlife Management Agency. He was not surprised to find a photocopy of his own picture with a reference to someone named Origen. "That's an odd name."

There was nothing more to be gained from the van and Dekker slipped out. He noted the license plate was Maryland, a little unusual given they were in Northern Virginia, but the registration gave him a clue to a location. Dekker left the van and watched his condo until the two men reemerged and headed toward the van. There was a short conference as the confused men decided what to do. As they walked back to their van Dekker heard some of their conversation.

"That damn Sammy, he sent us on a wild goose chase!"

"Yeah, he probably followed a girl back here and imagined himself the super-spy."

"Just wait until we get back."

"Just wait until Origen hears this operation was a bust." Sirens wailing in the distance sent the four quickly to the van.

Dekker headed for his own car as well, pulling out just as two police cruisers drove into the parking area. The sirens and flashing lights brought several residents from the surrounding buildings to see what was happening, and it didn't take long for the police to assess the blown-in door and determine there had been some sort of assault and break in. The only problem was, they found neither victims nor assailants to aid, or arrest, and a quick check of owners within the complex revealed only the condo was the owned by the government.

CHAPTER TWELVE

WHILE DEKKER FOLLOWED THE VAN he used the burner cell to call Dennis and asked him to get background on Origen, and his connection to this whole affair. "What kind of name is origin?" Dennis asked. "Is it foreign, or some kind of alias he uses?"

"Don't know, buddy, but my guess is it's some kind of criminal handle he uses."

Dekker trailed the assailants' van across the Beltway into Maryland until it became US Route 95 heading south. He followed the green van off the Interstate onto Route 50 and then to Davidsonville Road. A short ride brought the van to Bottner Road, clarifying the sign on the side of the van. The road came to an end at an Agricultural and Wildlife Station, a larger facility than Dekker expected. Set in the middle of a forested area, the institutional buildings were nondescript, in a government architectural way.

Dekker held back following because they were alone and there were no real residential communities in the area. With headlights off, he proceeded slowly along the road, pulling into a front parking lot while the van circled around toward the rear. He was curious to know why such an agency should be trying to kill him, and walking around the buildings where the van went, discovered a motor pool marshaling area. His assailants parked the van neatly into a row of three other identical vehicles and were now walking across the wide field, headed away from the facility.

They stole the van. Smart. He wasn't going to lose his quarry now, and thanks to the wide-open field bordered by thick woods, he was able to see exactly where they went. He watched until they disappeared into the woods and then sprinted a quarter mile to the place he last saw them. Dekker found a trail leading into the woods, but it was disguised in a way that even an experienced woodsman might miss. It was only because he watched where the men entered the trees that he was able to find it, realizing the camouflage was to disguise their rear access to the wildlife facility. Dekker was even more impressed with this Origen, and he decided to take more care following the four men.

The trail snaked through the forest, ending at the rear of a large estate house. The men were inside, but Dekker didn't need to see them to know this was home base. He saw a man, a guard, walking the perimeter of the house; he carried the same armament as the would-be attackers, plus he had night-vision goggles hanging around his neck.

Dekker had to get inside the mansion but the guard was an obstacle, and he had no idea what additional security measures were in place. It didn't really matter because he knew enough for the moment and headed back through the woods to his car.

Dekker could not return to his condo. The police and their questions, and the curious neighbors, would put him right back into the bind he escaped in New Mexico. He was much better off checking into a hotel. A nice La Quinta Inn off Route 50 provided the hideaway he needed, while still remaining close to Origen's estate. He got some food from a nearby Denny's, returned to his room, and slept.

CHAPTER THIRTEEN

DEKKER AWOKE LATE IN THE morning, deep in thought about Kelly, Abaddon, and the entire tangled mess. He wandered down to the registration area where a complimentary breakfast was still available. The coffee was weak but welcome, and the yogurt with trail mix and fruit made a decent breakfast. He sat at a small table in the corner, well away from the television set mounted on the wall, allowing him to make a phone call without undo noise. It took three tries to get Dennis to answer his cell phone, and when he did, he told him about the discovery the night before.

"Wonderful," Dennis answered with enthusiasm, surprising for someone who had been up and working all night. "I've got some very interesting stuff for you, too. Since we're on this Origen thing, let me begin there. I started by searching the name, or word, 'origin,' that's with the letter *I*.

There were lots of references to the origin of life, of the universe, in science, mathematics, medicine, biology, and myths. None of it seemed to fit a person, much less someone who is involved with our friend Abaddon.

"Then I found a reference to a third century theologian named 'Origen,' spelled with an *e*. I won't bore you with the details, although it turns out this cleric is very interesting. He espoused a philosophy that all souls are pre-existing, and that in the beginning all intelligent beings were united to God. He wrote and taught that all souls would eventually be reconciled and return to God—even Satan. You can imagine this set off the church establishment and he was declared a heretic and posthumously excommunicated. Well, this all seemed to fit the weird spiritual world of Abaddon, so I ran with it. It wasn't until nine o'clock this morning that I finally found a contemporary reference, right here in the DC area."

Dennis said there was a story in the *Washington Post* fifteen years prior, and promised he would text it to Dekker. It only took a minute for the text to arrive and Dekker read the article. It followed a series of FBI raids and arrests in an influence-peddling scheme involving someone named Dmitri Kosygin.

"It says this Dmitri used the alias 'Origen' to denote his 'heavenly' authority," Dekker commented. "I'd say he was a Russian spy."

"Not Russian—Romanian. It seems he is an ethnic Romani, that's a Gypsy to you and me, and needless to say, the FBI didn't buy the 'mission from God' story and put him in jail. Scan a few paragraphs down and you'll see that Dmitri/Origen was released for lack of witnesses. Everyone involved with him died under mysterious circumstances, so the feds had no case. There's no record of his name, either one, after that time."

Dekker closed the text document. "Our boy went off the grid."

"That's right, but not completely," Dennis said with satisfaction. "Nobody escapes 'Allende's Net' when it's cast."

Dekker chuckled at Dennis' joke and realized it was the first time in many days that he'd found anything amusing. He immediately admonished himself, determined to keep the pain of Kelly's death at the forefront of his mind.

"What I mean is, with this much information I was able to expand my search to include financial transactions, bank accounts, real estate purchases and sales, even church memberships. Do you know what I found?"

"No, but I'm certain you'll tell me."

"Dmitri/Origen has no job or income; he does not own a car; he has no known means of financial support, yet ten years ago he was named on a deed for an estate on Patuxent River Road in a very tony area of Maryland."

"Yes, I've been there."

"Are you kidding? How could you do that? It took me hours with the most sophisticated computer technology in the country to come up with that, and you casually say you've already been there." Dennis was always a little thin-skinned when it came to others beating him to the punch in research.

"Take it easy, Dennis, I simply followed a group of bad guys who came looking for me, and they led me to a house not far from here."

Dennis was not pleased to be scooped, but he did settle down.

CHAPTER FOURTEEN

AN ACOLYTE KNOCKED ON KAMENWATI'S office door, waiting sheepishly. "Enter," came a voice from inside. The young man stepped into the office with eyes downturned and hands clasped together before him. Without looking up from his desk Kamenwati asked what the acolyte wanted—he was busy.

"Sir, the master is acting strangely. What I mean is, he seems to be thrashing around more than usual, and criticizes us when no wrong has been done."

"I see. And what do you want from me?" asked Kamenwati, looking up at the acolyte.

"Sir, we were hoping you might speak with him and find out what the problem may be. We are here to serve, but we are afraid."

Kamenwati dismissed the acolyte with vague assurances, and when he was gone, sat back with a grin on his face. "It seems to be working."

He had been careful to implement his plan to topple Abaddon and assume his position. It was bold and relied heavily on the Master's deteriorating mental state, but his original assessment seemed to be holding true: The man was a sociopath with a grandiose sense of self, and absolutely no sense of remorse or guilt, exhibiting no emotion, and lacking empathy. And now these escalating outbursts of rage—it was perfect and he was clearly headed in the direction Kamenwati wished.

"Just keep up the pressure, feed his obsession to dominate mankind, and let him self-destruct."

Kamenwati knew it was a long-term plan and he was well experienced in waiting, but he wondered if he'd have the strength and the tools to bring down the man who'd been the Master for so long. He needed an ally, someone he could use to push Abaddon faster and harder. Hw sat considering the possibilities, wondering who could be trusted, who could be taken into his confidence, and who would be willing—and motivated—to attack Abaddon. In the end he could think of only one name, the man singularly responsible for the previous fall of the master and dismantling his enterprises.

"Dekker."

The name had become a catchphrase in Krugerschloss, a name used as a pejorative among the acolytes and Adepts. Yes, he must recruit Dekker to his cause and convince him the only way to achieve vengeance for Abaddon's crimes was to join forces. The more Kamenwati thought about it, the more he liked the idea, although locating Dekker seemed to be a problem. He would start by circling back around to Lord Geoffrey.

LORD GEOFFREY'S BUTLER moved through Dungannon Manor like a ghost, seeming to float through rooms, making no sound and leaving no evidence of his passing. While Benton's employer was the titled and hereditary peer, the reality was he was the practical lord of the manor. There were no secrets he did not know, no skeletons in closets he could not reveal. Benton was secure in his position and fiefdom of Dungannon Manor.

This morning Benton was somewhat concerned. Lord Geoffrey had been locked away in his office for several hours and there were periods of shouting, pleading, and demanding. This was not normal. The Consortium business supporting the estate, while greatly reduced in scope and income, was nonetheless operating at a steady pace. Benton was confident that equilibrium would be restored in a few short years. But this present shouting and upset could only be about the ridiculous search for the American.

Lord Geoffrey burst out of his office and seeing Benton, began issuing orders. "Benton, we have some planning and logistics that must be done now!"

"As you wish, sir. What is it I may do for you?"

"I have spoken with Origen, our man in America, and he tells me his people found Dekker."

"They have captured him?"

"Not exactly, and that's what we need to straighten out. Now, have Jane get my plane ready for travel to America."

"Any place special in America, sir?"

"Yes, you fool! Baltimore."

"Very good, sir."

"And call Westminster and notify the Lord Chancellor that I will be taking a leave of absence."

"What reason shall I give?"

"I don't know. Tell him I've been diagnosed with early stage lymphoma and that I will be undergoing treatment that prohibits work during its term."

"Very good, sir. It will be done right away." Geoffrey went back into his office while Benton headed for his own smaller office on the opposite side of the house, shaking his head. "What foolishness," Benton said to no one, and began making calls.

Lord Geoffrey was somewhat appeased but still needed to vent, so he called Origen. It took quite some time for the assistant answering the telephone to locate Origen, and the longer it took the more annoyed Lord Geoffrey became. Finally there was a new voice on the other end of the line.

"Lord Geoffrey, what a pleasure to hear from you so soon," Origen said smoothly. "I have no new reports for you, but we hope to have the American by tomorrow, or the following day."

"That's wonderful. But that is not why I called." Geoffrey waited a breath, and then continued. "I am coming over there." Origin paused with this news. It was not good. The last thing he needed was someone looking over his shoulder and second-guessing decisions.

"How wonderful, Lord Geoffrey. May I have one of my people pick you up?"

"Yes. I'll be arriving at the private aviation terminal at BWI. And please have the guest suite readied. I plan to stay with you until this matter is resolved."

Origen could only roll his eyes at this news, but accepted it as inevitable. "Fax me your itinerary and we'll handle everything else."

"Thank you, Origen. I knew I could count on you."

KAMENWATI RETURNED TO his office after a difficult interview with Abaddon. The man was obsessed with the American and he would discuss no other topic. He demanded the Egyptian contact Lord Geoffrey and push harder for results. He told his master these things simply took time, but Abaddon would hear nothing of it. His perception was everyone was lying down on the job, that they lacked commitment and motivation. He vowed to motivate them all with some well-placed executions. It was only after Kamenwati argued such action would have the opposite effect that Abaddon relented, saying, "Nevertheless I wanted results—and quickly."

After calling Lord Geoffrey with Abaddon's ultimatum, Kamenwati felt a little better. Geoffrey reported that Origen, one of his lieutenants in America, had actually located Dekker and was moving to capture him. That was certainly positive news and played well into Kamenwati's plans.

"When you have the man in custody, be sure you tell me first."

CHAPTER FIFTEEN

ORIGEN WAS NOT PLEASED ABOUT the prospect of Lord Geoffrey coming into his territory. He realized the man was his organizational superior and he had to accommodate his wishes, but now he was sorry he ever took the Consortium's money. He would have been better off just freelancing as he had done early in his career. He even thought about an escape plan should this whole thing blow up. It had been many years, but he knew he could go to Europe and hide in the Romani community there. He could live anonymously among his kin in France, Poland, Germany, even Romania, although the last did not hold much appeal for him.

He would have to give this idea more consideration. But now, he needed to find Dekker. The original order had been to capture or kill the man, but now it had become capture only—they wanted him for some other purpose.

Origen did not care, so long as they found, captured, and got rid of this enormous nuisance.

Origen called in his men and sent them out in groups of two to find Dekker. "You were idiots for leaving that condo complex last night. You should have searched for him there."

"Yes, sir, but the explosive we were forced to use to get into the condo alerted neighbors, and they called the cops," Richards, one of the four assailants, explained. "The police were swarming the place when we left."

Origen rubbed his hand across his face in frustration. "Okay, I understand. The question now is: Where would he go?" Sammy, who'd missed all the excitement after turning over surveillance to the team of four, had a theory. "I'd say he would head for the NCTC." The others groaned at his statement.

"It's obvious he was trying to stay away from the agency," Richards said. "As a matter of fact, I just found out this morning that the police in New Mexico are looking for him in connection with the death of his wife. Our FBI informant, Stawicki, says the local search has expanded and an Agent Donald Strickland from the NCTC Field Investigation Unit who's been assigned to look into possible links here."

Origen considered this information and had an idea. "I want two of you to find that agent and follow him; perhaps with new intelligence we can nail this guy down."

"Yes, sir," Richards said. "I'll get on it with Johnson." He indicated the man standing next to him with a nod of his head.

"Good. Now get going." Origin looked at the remaining men. "You other two fan out. It's possible he followed you back here." Then, turning to Sammy, "I want you to go back to the condo and see what can be found there, then resume your surveillance at the NCTC." Sammy looked disappointed to be on the crud detail again, but accepted it.

NCTC FIELD AGENT Don "Rusty" Strickland sat at a table outside Camille's Sidewalk Café, across from the Verizon Center on F Street. He brushed back his mop of dark red hair—the source of his nickname—while seeming to read *The*

Washington Post. In reality, he was watching a vacant building across the street. The Kevlar vest under his shirt was making him hot and he prayed they wouldn't have to wait too long.

Strickland was among the new generation of employees Director Lynch was recruiting to meet the growing demands of the agency. They were no longer an agency passively collecting, sifting, and interpreting information; rather, NCTC now engaged directly in certain interdiction and apprehension cases. It was a change necessitated by the nature of terrorism itself. The extremist and revolutionary groups exploded across the world, and moved very fast. That kind of challenge meant the United States and its allies had to develop a more nimble operating model, and Jim Lynch believed he had an answer using Adam Dekker's methods. He set out to find smart, capable young men and women who could work on a team but think for themselves. He found his new recruits in surprising places, from universities, to law enforcement, and even museums. Rusty Strickland, a former US Army bomb squad officer with experience in both Iraq and Afghanistan, was perhaps the best of the dozen new officers in the Investigations Unit.

Rusty was on the trail of Michael Muhammad, an American citizen who had been radicalized in college, converted to Islam, and was now a known terrorist with an acknowledged gift for bomb making. As a homegrown terrorist, Muhammad worked his way up the underground hierarchy and was connected to several high-profile plots, the most sinister of which was a planned strike at Disney World in Florida.

NCTC received a tip about the Disney threat through an NSA surveillance program and immediately swung into action. Rusty was the lead on a team sent to stop the plot and arrest those involved. The terrorists had no idea the government was on to them and were supremely confident their planned attack using the horse-drawn carriage ride along Main Street would not only kill many infidels, but would make every family in the park flee in terror. They were actually surprised when Rusty's team appeared, seemingly from nowhere, to arrest them as they were booby-trapping carriage. The park guests didn't know what was happening, and the NCTC team, with support from the FBI and local police, had it under control in moments.

Unfortunately for Rusty, Muhammad was not among those captured. The Disney World operation was seen in the intelligence community as a victory, yet the success had a bitter taste. The threat was very real and it had come too close to success for comfort, but the greater threat had not been contained.

In the aftermath of the Disney incident, Rusty's team was assigned the job to track Muhammad and capture him. They thought they had him in Atlanta, but once again he slipped their grasp. Based on intelligence he received from Dennis Allende, the chief of the NCTC Forensic Information Investigation Unit, Rusty's unit was led to this warehouse on F Street. The team of two men and one woman were watching all sides of the building, waiting for Muhammad to show up.

As Rusty turned the page of his newspaper he spotted a man walking past the warehouse and looking at it a little too closely. The man made a quick look around and Rusty identified him as Muhammad. He spoke into the sub-vocal microphone attached to the base of his throat. "We have something here...Muhammad's in a dark suit. Hold on, he's going around the east side of the building."

Rusty abandoned his newspaper and the table as soon as his target was out of sight. He rushed across the street to follow, peeking around the corner of the building just as Mohammad opened a side door and entered.

"Our man just entered the building. Did you see him, Judy?"

"I did," the hidden agent said.

"You follow him into that entrance, I'm going in on the F Street side. Everyone else proceed inside with caution." Rusty received a short affirmation of his order from the other agents and moved back to the front of the building where he slipped into a small door adjacent to the main entrance. *It seems everyone has keys to this building*, he thought.

Inside the building was dark, and dust kicked up in small clouds with each step. It was quiet, and if he had not seen Muhammad enter and given the order for his three agents to enter as well, he would have thought himself alone. Moving with practiced stealth, Rusty hugged one wall and moved into the building, alert for Muhammad's presence.

After moving through the entrance area into a hallway, he couldn't help but wonder where Muhammad was.

"Anyone see him?" He received negative responses from all members of his team.

Where the hell has he gone? Rusty wondered.

There was a large room at the center of the building and all four NCTC agents met there. They spoke in soft voices, but the tension was obvious. Where the hell had Muhammad gone? "Judy, you followed him in that alley door, did you spot him at all?"

"No. By the time I got in, he was gone. Sorry."

"I suppose you guys didn't see or hear anything either?" he asked Dave and Bill, the other agents. They both shook their heads and looked as perplexed as Rusty.

"The only answer is he went up," Rusty said, pointing toward the ceiling.

"Or down," added Bill.

"Yes, or down," Rusty acknowledged. "We're going to have to separate and expand this search. He's here somewhere." Rusty gave directions to the team and the three went toward stairs leading to upper floors. Rusty went in search of a basement level and hoped Muhammad hadn't slipped their grasp again.

He made his way to the exterior wall and followed it to a set of double doors. Opposite those doors was a stair leading down. *Eureka,* he thought in triumph. Going down into a dark and unknown space made him uneasy, like chasing al-Qaeda into their mountain caves. He knew the defender had the advantage, and he must proceed with caution.

Rusty reached the bottom of the broad stairway without incident. He stood at another double door, the obvious entry into the basement area. Looking around he saw there were no alternatives, and carefully pushed one of the doors open. He moved into the basement, staying low. He was surprised to learn the basement wasn't a large open space, but a series of rooms. He paused to fill in his team.

"Team, I am in the basement. Nothing to report so far — anything on the upper floors?" There were three floors above and they had divided, taking one floor each, and all three reported negative on Muhammad.

Rusty continued into a maze of rooms and looking around a corner, saw something promising. It was a faint glow coming from under a closed door. Had it not been so dark, he doubted he would have seen it. As he approached the door he heard voices. Rusty stopped to call his team on their tactical communication system.

"Judy? Dave? Bill? I've got voices down here. It seems our friend Muhammad is meeting accomplices, but for the life of me, I can't understand how they got in the building without us knowing."

"You want us to come down, Rusty?" Judy asked.

"Yes. There's a stairway across from a double door on the outside wall. Come down and I'll meet you at the bottom."

The NCTC agents met as Rusty suggested and moved down the hall to a point where they could observe the door. Just as Rusty described, there was a faint light seeping from the bottom of the doorway. The light seemed to vary from time to time.

"Someone's walking back and forth," Dave said. Rusty and the others nodded.

Rusty used hand signals to disburse his team in preparation for a rush on the room. But before they could get into position the door was flung open and an animated group of men spilled into the hallway. They all appeared to be of Middle Eastern descent except for the man at the rear, who was clearly Anglo. It was Michael Muhammad and he was unhappy about something. Muhammad's anger kept the group of militants from noticing the NCTC team crouching in the dark hall.

Still unseen, Rusty motioned for his team to stay low and still. To everyone's surprise the terrorists did not turn to move up the hall to the stairway, which would have immediately revealed the NCTC team huddled in the dark. Instead, they went the opposite direction, deeper into the basement maze. Rusty looked to his team and saw the same look of relief that must have been on his own face, and signaled Judy and Dave to search the now empty room while he and Bill followed the group.

After two minutes, Rusty received a call from Judy. "Rusty, you won't believe what we've found in this room. I know you can't talk, but let me give you a summary: The room is a bomber's paradise. It has stacks of boxes filled with explosives—C4, I think. We need to get this stuff out of here before something bad happens."

Rusty was caught in a dilemma: Should he and Bill turn around and take care of the stash of explosives, or continue trailing Muhammad's people? The departing terrorists made the decision for him. They came to a wall and waited for their leader to catch up. Muhammad looked around nervously, as if he knew they were being followed, and then deciding nothing was amiss, he stood before the blank wall.

Rusty was well back and out of sight, peeking around a corner every few moments to keep up with what his target was doing. He was startled when he saw Muhammad push a section of the wall in, revealing a passageway beyond. *Now, where did that come from?* Rusty watched as the men moved into the passage and the section of wall swung closed. Because the wall was brick, the seams were hidden, making it completely invisible. *Must have been a secret escape from the Prohibition era,* Rusty reasoned.

With the closing of the wall door, silence was no longer necessary. Rusty and Bill hurried to the spot they watched open, looking for a lever or switch. "Damn! Where is it?" Rusty was impatient.

"Hold on, I think I may have it," Bill said. They heard a soft *click* and saw a small crack appear on the right side.

"You did it, Bill! Good work."

The pair moved carefully down the dark hallway, mindful of the terrorists ahead. They arrived at a door, looked at one another, and opened it. Light flooded in, hurting their eyes that were accustomed to the dark environment of the basement. Pushing the door wider they found themselves in the storeroom of what had to be a restaurant.

"Smells like a Persian restaurant," said Rusty.

"Persian?" Bill asked. "How can you tell that?"

"By the smell; there's no other quite like it."

They moved out of the storeroom and into a kitchen. Rusty held up a badge, which seemed to quiet the cooks. He looked into the dining room.

"Not here," he said. He called Judy to deliver the bad news. "Judy, we've lost them. Are you still with the explosives?"

"I am, but I sent Dave up top to get an FBI bomb team here to move this stuff out."

"Good work."

"Sorry we missed Muhammad again, Rusty. We'll get him next time."

He received a text from Deputy Director Jim Lynch asking him to check in as soon as possible. As he stood on the sidewalk in front of Camille's Café watching the FBI team move the boxes of C4 into a secure truck, he called the office, connecting with Lynch's assistant, Marilyn Stamm. "Hi, Marilyn, it's Rusty. I got a text from the boss."

"Good afternoon, Rusty. Yes, he seems eager to speak with you. I'll connect you."

A soft click and a moment of music was replaced with the voice of Jim Lynch. "Rusty, where are you?"

"Downtown, sir, chasing the terrorist, Muhammad."

"Well, I need you to chase down someone else." Lynch paused for effect. "Adam Dekker." Rusty's surprise was complete. Dekker was his mentor and his friend.

"What are you talking about?"

"You know about the attack in New Mexico, right?"

"Sure, we all know. Still can't believe someone killed his wife."

"And his dog," Lynch added.

"So what's the problem? You know he didn't do it."

"I know it, but local law enforcement doesn't. They asked him to stay around and available, sort of a house arrest. Well, Dekker declined their invitation and has gone AWOL."

"Making him look guilty," Rusty said. "Do you know where he'd go?"

"Yes. Right here."

"Here? Why? It seems the last place he'd want to be."

"This all circles back around to Abaddon."

"Abaddon," Rusty whispered the name. "I've only heard rumors and pieces of the story. It all happened before you recruited me into the NCTC. But I thought that was done years ago."

"So did I, but apparently not." Lynch went on to tell Rusty what he knew of the attack on Dekker's ranch and Kelly's death, a killing that was not so mysterious when you knew about Abaddon and his methods. Rusty listened carefully, and began to understand what Lynch was telling him.

"Dekker told the authorities about the peculiar powers Abaddon wields, and I even backed him up on it. But it all sounds so outrageous, it's hard to believe. Very few people know the whole story of the Abaddon incident. We have no idea if Abaddon is back on the loose, but the circumstances of the attack on Kelly, and the dog's death, are consistent with what we saw five years ago. Dekker believes that somehow

Abaddon has been released from the confinement stasis, and he's determined to find out who did it, and why. Add to that his anger over his wife's murder, and you have a man moving with a single purpose—to strike back."

"So he's gone rogue?" Rusty sounded concerned.

"Not exactly, but we need to catch up with him."

The conversation ended and Lynch called his executive assistant, Marilyn Stamm, asking her to have Dennis Allende come up to his office.

"I'm sorry, Mr. Lynch, but Dennis is out."

"In that case, call his cell phone. I need to see him."

CHAPTER SIXTEEN

THE NORMALLY HEAVY GUARD AROUND Origen's manor house was minimal because all the staff was out looking for Dekker. The lone security person, a young man new to the organization, was the only watchman, and he had to rely on a few perimeter cameras. The young guard was not especially worried since it was full daylight and his cameras gave him a good view of all four sides of the manor house. He heard his boss' superior, Lord somebody-or-other, was on his way and should arrive shortly, with one of the teams escorting the Consortium chief to the house.

DEKKER MOVED DOWN the trail behind the agricultural station, following the route from the night before. He assumed there would be video surveillance and had prepared for it.

Once at the edge of the woods surrounding the house, he took the small field glasses from the equipment bag he always kept in his truck and surveyed the upper edges of the house. He spotted a security camera and stopped to consider his options. The sun was up, just over the roof of the manor house, making him squint slightly. That gave him an idea to blind the camera long enough to get across the open space. The sunlight was creating reflections from pieces of silica shale scattered on the ground, and Dekker thought if he could find a large enough piece, it might just work.

He had had to backtrack to the field behind the Bottner facility and soon found an even better solution. Small research huts were placed around the open space, each growing different plants. Several of them had large sheets of silver Mylar to insulate and heat the interiors. Making mental apologies to the facility, Dekker "borrowed" a large section of Mylar, cutting it with the multi-tool he carried in his pocket.

Moving back to the edge of the woods surrounding the house, Dekker set to the task of making a mirror. In a few minutes he created a frame, stretched the silver fabric over it, and looked for a good, sunny spot to set his device.   In   the security office, the young guard saw a monitor flare white. He knew it was reflected sunlight but was unsure what he should do since his entire chain of command was out looking for Dekker. He decided to go outside and investigate.

While the security office guard was wondering what to do, Dekker made his way across the twenty yards of open space to the rear of the house under the cover of his improvised camera blind. He stood beside a short stairway leading up to a small deck and a door. There were windows on the back wall, but not many, and they were all situated several feet up, due to the elevation of the structure over a basement. As Dekker considered his next move, the back door opened and a young uniformed guard stepped out. The guard looked in the direction of Dekker's mirror, squinting to see the cause. The guard spotted a slight reflection and descended the stairs, leaving the back door open.

Dekker slipped up the four steps without making a sound and stepped into the house. He knew the young man would be returning soon, so he had to find a hiding place and make his plans.

The guard found Dekker's makeshift mirror, but still didn't understand its significance. "I better show this to the boss," he muttered, carrying the stick-framed Mylar structure back to the house. He went first to his security office, checking all cameras. There was no activity. He gathered up his courage and called Origen's office to reported the incident.

"How convenient," Origen muttered at the news, and then issued an order to the young guard. "Get everyone back here right away. We're being attacked." The young guard couldn't imagine who would be attacking them or how the boss knew, but he began making telephone calls with Origen's order to return.

At that same time one of the manor cars pulled up to the front entrance. A well-dressed man stepped out of the rear seat, straightened his coat, looked around, and ordered one of the attendants to show him in. The guard made another call to his boss to report the arrival.

"Just perfect," was Origen's dry reply.

DEKKER STOOD BY a parlor window, watching the arriving limousine. His proximity sense told him he was all but alone in the large house, but he wasn't taking any chances. He watched a well-dressed man get out of a car, walk to the front entrance, and then pass out of sight, and he realized he knew the man: Lord Geoffrey Stapleton.

It seemed to be coming together, because he knew Geoffrey was a direct link to Abaddon. Dekker had to know the Englishman's purpose here; he strongly suspected it included him.

"Lord Geoffrey," came the overly friendly greeting from the figure moving quickly down the hall to intercept the new guest. "I am honored by your visit." Geoffrey took the offered hand and with a slightly superior look, returned the greeting, albeit with less enthusiasm. Origen began an incessant babble, directing Lord Geoffrey to the very parlor hiding Dekker.

I'm not going to be trapped in here like a rat in a trap, Dekker thought, and searched around for a place to hide.

There was only the other door. It was the one he'd used when he found this room, situated opposite the door to the hall—the door Origen and Lord Geoffrey were about to enter. He was able to slip out just as the main door opened. He was safe for the moment.

He stood in a service hall, one that led all the way to the back of the house, and it was thankfully empty. For the moment Dekker was alone, and he stayed at the door, ear pressed to its smooth, white surface, listening to the men inside. It was all mundane and formula chitchat that filled time until they got to the true topic at hand.

CHAPTER SEVENTEEN

LORD GEOFFREY DECIDED TO END the pleasantries and get to the subject most on his mind. "And what of Dekker? Do you have him?" Origin answered somewhat uncomfortably.

"Not exactly. He's a slippery one and difficult to capture." An indistinguishable muttering signaled Lord Geoffrey's displeasure. "But we're on to him, and should have him for you today," he announced with a surety he did not feel.

Dekker pressed in to capture every word and every nuance, ignoring his other senses, particularly his proximity, or early warning sense, which meant he didn't know the young guard was watching him on the video surveillance system.

AT FIRST THE young guard couldn't believe what he saw: A man stealing out of the parlor, and then stand at the door, listening. Once again he didn't know what to do and was in a fair tizzy waiting for the rest of his security team to return.

The two men from the limo were unloading luggage and taking it up to the guest suite on the second floor. The guard watching his monitors saw the men mount the stairs and disappear into the guest suite. He flicked his eyes back to the intruder in the service hall and was startled to find the man gone. At the same time two cars rolled up to the side portico, the staff entrance, and let out several of the men. The young guard heaved a sigh of relief.

Dekker's anger deepened again when he learned that Abaddon sent Lord Geoffrey to personally oversee his capture, confirmation that Abaddon was truly back, and that he had a vendetta for Dekker. He pulled away from the parlor door, fists shaking and ready to strike at Abaddon and everything that was his. But somewhere in his mind a calming voice cautioned him to wait. Dekker was unsure if it was his own conscience talking or something else. Concentrating on this question calmed his anger and he could once again reason. He knew it was time to get out of this house; there was only danger here, and a high probability of entrapment. He spun and moved quickly back up the hallway, heading for the rear door, his proximity sense back on, warning him that danger was near. He stopped and stepped into a storeroom to get a fix on where the danger was.

He leaned against a wall and calmed himself, letting his mind take over. When he had a good mental picture of what was happening in the house he began making an escape plan, with the briefest of nods to his own wonder as to why he hadn't done that before he went in the house.

THE SECURITY ROOM guard ran to the portico entrance and intercepted the returning men. "Hey, guys, we've got an intruder!"

"What are you talking about?" admonished one of the returning men. "We've never had an intruder."

"Well, we've got one now. I've seen him on the security monitors. We need to find him, and quickly."

"Is this intruder alone?" asked another security man.

All of the security team was angry that someone infiltrated the manor house. "I suppose our mistake was leaving this kid alone here," said one security man.

"How did he get through the defenses?" asked the older guard of the group. "I've been here ten years and I've never seen anyone get through. Never seen anyone find the place, for that matter. Never mind, everyone take a COM and let's get at it."

"All I know is the intruder is here and prowling through the house. Let me show you."

The young guard went to a keyboard and called up archive footage from the hallway and discovered his intruder leaving in a hurry, then, following on other cameras, he saw the man stop as if he heard something, and then go into a storage room.

"Attention everyone," the guard said into his radio. "I've spotted the intruder entering a north storage room on the service corridor. I have no visual coverage inside the room, but it looks like he's still there."

Origen's men gave one another a congratulatory punch on their shoulders and headed toward the service hall.

DEKKER SENSED AT least six men, perhaps more, converging on his hiding place. He looked around for another exit, knowing the door he entered led to the hallway with no escape except the rear door of the house. He would never make it, and simply had to find another alternative. He couldn't believe he was in such a position. Never in all his years in the Special Forces had he failed to have an escape plan. He was slipping, and he knew it, and he knew it stemmed from the attack on his ranch.

Looking around he found no other exit from the room and pulled the SIG from his waistband, taking some comfort from the solid feel of the powerful pistol. He had to breathe deeply to center himself, and then coolly considered the situation. He searched the walls for a concealed hatch or something similar. Nothing. And then, behind a stack of boxes containing tomato sauce, he saw what he was looking for—a dumbwaiter. Older houses such as this had these small service lifts in the kitchen, laundry room, and in storeroom areas, to facilitate moving things between floors. This one seemed idle or infrequently used, due no doubt to changing the function of certain rooms above.

Dekker considered the conveyance, telling himself it was something, but too small. Try as he might, he simply could not fit into the tiny opening. He needed another plan.

He left the dumbwaiter and squatted at the wall by the door, making himself as small as possible.

Origen's men pushed open the door in a SWAT-style entry. A man on either side of the door peered in from a low crouching stance, and then signaled the others to enter. They filed in, weapons at the ready, alert to danger. They scanned the room and saw nobody, but one man noticed the disturbed boxes of tomato sauce. He motioned for the others to cover him and moved carefully to see if their intruder was hiding there. The dumbwaiter lift was discovered, its hatch slightly ajar as Dekker left it.

"Here he is, boys," said the lead man. "Looks like he's in the service shaft." He peeked in carefully, not wanting to attract a bullet. "Not here. He went up or down, but my money is on down."

Dekker watched the entire scene with some amusement. His little trick of misdirection seemed to work, and he was amazed he had not been discovered. Dekker thought he might just be able to make a break for it and slowly moved around the open door, ready to dash down the hallway and out the back. Unfortunately, one of the men happened to turn as he sought a better position to observe what was going on at the dumbwaiter, and glimpsed Dekker at the wall. He immediately trained his weapon on the crouching intruder and shouted the alarm.

"Got him! He's over there here, cowering like a scared rabbit." The others turned in unison, each raising a weapon in Dekker's direction. Dekker knew he had been caught, and facing such odds and firepower, resistance was futile. He carefully placed his pistol on the floor, pushing it out of reach.

"Now there's a man who knows how to be captured," said the leader of the group. "No need for bloodshed, right?" He walked over to Dekker, picking up his SIG along the way. "Nice piece," he said and pocketed the pistol.

He turned to the other men, ordering them to take him, and once they had him securely tied the leader came up to Dekker, looking him over closely. "I do believe we have the man Origen is looking for, boys. You're Dekker, aren't you?" Dekker said nothing. "All right, then, we'll let you talk to the boss. He'll know what to do with you."

Dekker was roughly handled and shoved out into the hallway, but instead of going to the back door, they headed back the way he had come just minutes before. When they reached the rear salon door the leader knocked and then entered, dragging his prize with him.

Lord Geoffrey's expression matched the surprise on Origen's face. "We've got your man, sir," announced the guard holding Dekker.

The looks of surprise changed to smug satisfaction.

CHAPTER EIGHTEEN

KAMENWATI READ THE COMMUNICATION FROM Lord Geoffrey with a sense of relief. He leaned back in his chair, whispering, "That's it. Now I can put my plan into action." He drafted up a reply to the Englishman telling him to bring the American to Strasbourg, France, where he could be interviewed prior to presentation to Abaddon. Kamenwati was careful to restate that no word was to be sent to anyone about the American until he had the opportunity to question him.

He called in one of his growing staff of acolytes and instructed him to contact the Brotherhood house near Strasbourg and have them to prepare for his arrival.

Kamenwati felt victory on the horizon, and after all these years it felt good. He cautioned himself to keep his thoughts under control so Abaddon would get no hint. Discovery now would mean death, undoubtedly in a horrible and painful manner.

Geoffrey received Kamenwati's reply with a scowl. Something was up, but he couldn't figure what it might be. He'd intended to take Dekker directly to the Master and get him off his hands. This diversion to Strasbourg seemed suspicious and he wondered what Kamenwati's game was. Despite his misgivings, Lord Geoffrey informed Origen he would be leaving in the morning with the prisoner.

Origen was all too happy to have the Englishman go, and for Lord Geoffrey to take the prisoner with him. He felt as long as the two of them were in his territory and under his roof, there would be nothing but danger.

RUSTY STRICKLAND DROVE past the Mall on his return to the NCTC and was stopped by a police cordon near the World War II memorial. As he leaned over the steering wheel to observe the action he noticed a dark sedan with tinted windows. He couldn't explain why, but he sensed it was following him. "Muhammad, perhaps?"

The roadblock turned out to be a standoff between the police and an old veteran, apparently upset by denial of benefits he believed the government owed him. As the police escorted the old man away Rusty looked around for the suspicious car, but it was nowhere to be seen. *Now how did he find a way out of this gridlock?* The entire way back to his office, Rusty couldn't help but wonder about the tail, who it was, and what purpose it served.

ALMOST AS SOON as the Origen soldier reached the Mall, he received a text message instructing him to return to the manor house. It was a little odd, but his was not to reason why, simply to obey.

He arrived a little later than the other teams and was disappointed he'd missed all the action. It turned out the young kid in the security office was the hero of the day, something that rankled the rest of the staff. They had cornered an intruder, the man Dekker for whom Origen so fervently searched. Even now he was being questioned; the man decided this was a good thing, and life could get back to a normal routine.

AS HE PACKED up for the day, Rusty thought of something he wanted to try in the Dekker case. He searched around for a cell phone number, and finding it, called.

"Hello, Dennis?" Rusty asked when the call was answered.

"It is. Who is this?"

"It's Rusty Strickland. Do you remember—we met on the Monument suicide case?"

Dennis recalled the strange case when an NCTC employee had somehow climbed out an observation window at the top of the Washington Monument and taken a swan dive to the pavement below. Dennis consulted on the investigation to identify the man, and he met Rusty Strickland in the process.

"I want to talk with you about a colleague of ours, Adam Dekker."

There was silence for a long moment. "Yes, I know Dekker. What is it you want to know?"

"I need to meet you to talk about it. The phone is too impersonal, too easy to hack. Can we meet?"

There was another period of silence from Allende. "That would be fine, Rusty. What did you have in mind?" Strickland suggested breakfast the next morning at a restaurant near Tysons Corner, thinking it would be a convenient off-site place for Allende.

"I'm actually on leave right now. How about something in Fairfax?" Rusty agreed and the meeting was set.

THE NEXT MORNING Rusty pulled into the Potbelly Sandwich Shop on Chain Bridge Road near Main Street in Fairfax. He had never heard of this place, but Dennis seemed to like it, and it didn't really matter to Rusty. He was there to get information for the Dekker case.

Dennis walked in a few minutes after Rusty and found him sitting in a booth toward the rear of the restaurant. "Thanks for meeting with me, Dennis," Rusty began. "Do you want to order?" Dennis shook the agent's hand and led the way. "I always order the egg and sausage on sourdough."

"Sounds pretty good. I've never been here before."

"It is good, and they top it with tomatoes and green chili. A little spicy, but very tasty."

"I guess I'll order the same thing." They returned to their table with the order while a waitress came around with coffee.

After a couple of bites, Rusty commented, "This is really good. Thanks for the recommendation." More bites and then Rusty continued. "Lynch just put me on the search for Adam Dekker. It seems he left New Mexico before the local authorities were done with him. Do you have any ideas? Can you tell me where he is? I can't help thinking Dekker needs some help."

Dennis put his breakfast sandwich down to think about his response. There were aspects of the Abaddon case that were highly classified, and he was unsure how much he could—or should—say to Agent Strickland. *He is an NCTC agent, after all,* Dennis thought. *He is, by definition, cleared for secret information.* Dennis looked around to see if other patrons were close. He liked Strickland from the start; he was open and honest, much like Dekker, and Dennis thought a little help would go a long way to assisting Dekker. He decided to give Rusty more background than most people had about the Abaddon case.

"This all began five years ago when Dekker received a videotape from a friend in the broadcast news business. That reporter, Nick Strong, uncovered what looked like a worldwide conspiracy to murder the heads of finance of their respective countries. The deaths went largely unnoticed because they seemed accidental, but an inspection of available video footage showed something quite different. They were all pushed, shoved, or choked to death in public, and no assailant was seen or detained. Nick Strong put the pieces of this puzzle together and was going to expose not only the conspiracy, but also the man behind it all: Abaddon.

"The night Nick was going to reveal what he found, he died—in the studio. The circumstances were odd, but there was no evidence of foul play, and it was called a heart attack. Then Dekker got involved. Knowing heads of finance were being targeted, he was very concerned for the safety of then Federal Reserve Chairman Benjamin Wilton. Jim Lynch got him assigned to the security detail while Chairman Wilton attended a secret meeting of finance ministers in Scotland. All seemed to be going well when Dekker witnessed a glowing ball fly through the air, striking the chairman, and throwing him through a window to his death on the courtyard below. Dekker became deeply involved right then and discovered Abaddon and his secret Brotherhood were behind it all."

"Why? What could they hope to accomplish?"

"This Brotherhood has a belief system quite different from any other group in the world. They believe mechanization and reliance on knowledge have upended the natural order. They hold that Magick—that's capped and spelled with a k—and what they call 'the old truths' are the way man is supposed to live and interact with the world. In short, they were working to achieve a collapse of the world's financial systems as a means to plunge mankind into a new Dark Age. Of course, Abaddon's goals were slightly more selfish—he, along with his hand-picked government replacements, and his Adepts would rule."

"Abaddon wanted to rule the world? Like in a James Bond movie?" Strickland couldn't believe such a plan.

"Yes, and he came very close to achieving it. It's been kept Top Secret, but Dekker, Galdur, Kara Triberg, and myself stopped his plan as it was being executed."

"Wait, Dennis. That's a lot to take in. First, who is this Kara person? And how about Galdur?"

"Kara was an Adept, devoted and sworn to Abaddon. She was sent to kill Dekker when he started to make trouble for the plan. She chased him across Europe and to America where, with the help of an Icelandic mystic named Galdur, Kara was turned to our side. She was fundamentally uncomfortable with Abaddon's plan, but because she was so programmed, like a cult, she had no way out. Dekker and Galdur gave her a way out and she joined our little force headed to a place called Krugerschloss in Germany's Black Forest. Our objective was to stop the plan from working.

"When we finally got into the mountain fortress, we discovered Abaddon had a technology setup second-to-none. For the man who decried technology, it was a serious anachronism. For him, it seemed, the anti-technology, anti-mechanism line was just a tool to control the Brotherhood cells around the world, and it was the very technology he condemned that he intended to use to collapse the financial systems worldwide.

"It almost worked. Dekker and the others lured Abaddon down to an ancient temple site in a field below Krugerschloss where they used the same mystical powers Abaddon wielded to bind him in a supernatural stasis. It was mostly Kara who did the binding but Abaddon was so blind with rage at the defector Adept that he didn't notice Galdur and Dekker, both helping sustain what Kara created. In the end, Abaddon was contained in a stasis cube, but Kara was killed by a collapsing stone pillar."

"And what about all the computer setup you said Abaddon had?"

"I was left to disable the computer system. It wasn't easy, and in the end I employed a trick to draw more computer resources to solving a problem that is unsolvable. Eventually the system's logic circuits were fried, effectively ending the financial takeover."

Strickland sat back, his breakfast sandwich forgotten. "That is hands-down the most amazing story I ever heard. And it's true? Why wasn't this publicized? You and Dekker and I suppose Galdur, too, were all heroes. You guys literally saved the world."

"Certain people decided that nobody would believe several aspects of the saga, particularly the elements of Magick and the use of the Flows. Besides, the threat was averted and the evil megalomaniac contained, supposedly forever. So we all moved on, except Dekker. He was most deeply affected by the whole affair, and it was Dekker that Abaddon cursed as he disappeared into limbo, promising to kill him and everyone close to him."

"And now an attack on his home," Rusty commented.

"Yeah. Kelly, his wife, was killed—just like the various finance ministers years before. Dekker knew the MO, knew who was behind the hit, and he went ballistic."

"I guess I can understand now. How did Abaddon escape this 'stasis' you described?"

"We haven't been able to confirm that Abaddon is back, but indications are it's true. If it is, Dekker will find Abaddon. That's why he ran from New Mexico; he couldn't afford the time it would take for a drawn-out inquiry. He needed to move on Abaddon before his power was again consolidated. As to how Abaddon escaped, I don't know. It involves a lot of mysticism I don't understand; I can appreciate it, having witnessed the power first hand, but I don't understand it. All I can do is venture a theory that a powerful member of the Brotherhood came forward and reversed the process that bound Abaddon."

"I thought you said the Brotherhood was crushed and disbanded."

"Yes, for the most part that's true. But something like the Brotherhood can't be totally eradicated. It's like crabgrass in your yard: You can pull it, dig it, beat it to hell, but it will inevitably return. And some practitioners, the deeply skilled ones, have the ability to hide themselves from scrutiny. They could ride out the storm and regroup at a later time."

Strickland pondered Dennis' story and then arose, dropping some tip money on the table. Dennis followed suit and the pair left the restaurant. Outside, Strickland had a final question for Dennis. "Do you know where Dekker is?"

"Yesterday I would have answered yes. But today, I don't know."

"Something spooked him?"

"More like someone attacked him—apparently agents for someone named 'Origen.' Dekker asked me to research the name and yesterday I gave him a report on the phone. It began with the spelling of the name. Once I figured out the odd spelling I was able to understand the reference. Origen was a historical figure, a prolific third century writer, weighing in on many branches of theology and philosophy. He lived in Alexandria, Egypt, giving me a clue to the Abaddon connection."

"That name is unusual. Where can I find this guy?"

"He has a large property in Maryland. Let me get you the address."

"Thanks, Dennis. I appreciate the help."

CHAPTER NINETEEN

DEKKER WAS STILL DRUGGED WHEN Origin's men guided him out of the salon. Origen was quite clear about taking precautions with this prisoner, telling the guards he was a dangerous man—and they heeded the advice. They injected him with a mixture of scopolamine and Ambien, an old trick to keep a prisoner docile yet mobile. There was some discussion about where to keep Dekker until it was time to leave, and they agreed a closet in the hallway was the best answer. "Besides, he won't care where he is," one of the men said.

In Colombia where the plant originates, scopolamine is dried and ground into what is known as "zombie" powder. It is a good indication of its effect on a person, and this is what

Origen was looking for—a completely compliant yet ambulatory prisoner.

The drugs took hold quickly and soon Dekker was shuffling about in a fog, like a zombie, if he could have seen himself. Once deposited and locked in the closet he was left alone. In the small, dark room Dekker began to hallucinate. The hallucinations were vivid and terrifying: He kept seeing the golden mask of Abaddon with flaming eyes and wicked laughter. He relived the death of Kara Triberg, crushed beneath the stone pillar in the temple below Krugerschloss. He saw himself sliding down a long, dark chute, ending in a flaming landscape straight from Dante's vision of Hell. He knew Satan would rise up from the boiling lake of fire to grab him, taking him to his doom.

Dekker wanted to scream, but could not; he wanted to wake, but could not. He saw his last night with Kelly, her soft, warm embrace turned to stone, and then Abaddon reaching down to strangle the life from her. Dekker cried out at his inability to help Kelly, to save her. He felt like he was bound tightly in rolls of bubble wrap that allowed him to see Kelly's desperation and last breath, but prevented him from taking any action. He cried out in an agony so deep, and a pain so bitterly hurtful, he was certain he would himself die.

And the thought appealed to him. If he could just die, it would all end.

As the effects of the drug diminished, he was left with a haunting, laughing voice taunting him, admonishing him for the stupid mistake he'd made. He had walked right into a lion's den, his hated enemy's lair. Dekker regained some level of consciousness and tried to think. He had been in tight places before, but he'd never been filled with such an intense sense of defeat. Maybe he was too old, past his prime. It was discouraging, and the more he dwelt on these thoughts, the deeper he sank into a pit of self-pity.

He spent many dark hours in this mental state, a place from which he did not know how to escape. He felt his hands and feet bound, but oddly, he was not uncomfortable. He knew he had been captured and there was no avenue for escape, and for some reason the drug interfered with his use of the Flows. Dekker had let anger and his absolute commitment to retribution cloud his judgment and actions, and now he was suffering the consequences.

Let that be a lesson, and let me not do it again.

Somewhere in the very early morning hours as his mind began to clear, he made the decision to cast off the load of self-pity he carried since Kelly's death. He would use his skills and intellect to get out of this situation, and more importantly, move him toward his goal to end the threat of Abaddon forever.

His spirit felt calm again and he fell into a deep sleep. He dreamed, but not the violent, red-tinged, drug-induced dreams, or even those of recent weeks that woke him at night. Instead, he dreamed of beautiful things and the people he loved and admired. He even dreamed of Kelly, and instead of sending him into a fit of rage, he enjoyed the good memories.

Despite spending the night locked in a closet, Dekker awoke feeling rested, and more importantly, free. He knew that Lord Geoffrey and Origen held him in captivity, but that wasn't important: He perceived the mistake of his earlier actions might actually get him closer to his goal. He was being held in a closet somewhat near the front door of the estate, a location he discerned from the growing foot traffic and door closings.

Dekker listened, since it was the only sense still available in the dark closet. The more he knew about his captors and their resources, the better his chance of escape. He heard one muffled exchange between two of his captors, the one telling the other to get ready to prepare the prisoner for a trip.

"We're going to have to keep him drugged, for sure. He's dangerous, and we don't want anything to happen to his lordship on the flight."

"Are we going to knock him out?"

"Nah, he's got to be conscious enough to walk and answer a few questions from Customs and Immigration."

"So it's going to be scopolamine again?"

"Probably."

There was a muffled knock at the front door. "Now, who's that?" asked the guard.

Dekker learned a great deal from the earlier muffled conversation outside his closet door. He knew they did not intend to kill him, that Lord Geoffrey was taking him on a long flight, presumably to England, and they were going to drug him again. He heard one of the men open the front door and exchange words with the visitor, although it too was muffled. The only phrase he picked up was the visitor saying, "Government." What was going on? Dekker had no way to know, only that it seemed someone from the government was there and that gave him hope.

The visitor was asked to wait in the foyer while the guard went to get his superior. A minute later there were footsteps and a quiet discussion until they reached the front door. Dekker strained to hear the conversation, hoping they would invite the visitor in. They did so, and by placing his ear to the door Dekker made out the better part of the conversation.

"I am Special Agent Strickland of the NCTC, and I'm sure your man told you I'm searching for a missing person."

Dekker was elated—Rusty somehow found him!

"And what is the NCTC? I've never heard of it."

"It is part of Homeland Security," answered Rusty.

"How is it you came to my door, Agent Strickland?" Origen asked, completely ignoring what Dekker considered the obvious question.

"Your name and address came up in a curious way during my initial investigation, and I wanted to check it out personally."

Origen still refused to ask the obvious question. "If you wish to search my house or property, you will need a warrant. Do you have such a document, Agent?"

"No, sir, I do not. This is simply a courtesy visit."

"Thank you. When you return with a warrant we will be happy to let you look around." Strickland made his apologies, promising to return, and left.

Origen, so cool and controlled a moment ago, exploded in anger. "Someone get Lord Geoffrey. Tell him he is leaving right now. And you," apparently addressing one of the men standing at the door, "get the prisoner out here. I'm getting this problem out of my hair today!"

Dekker's mind swirled with questions. If he could somehow signal Rusty and let him know he was here, maybe the tables could be turned on Lord Geoffrey. He heard everyone clear out of the hallway, but the atmosphere of the house changed in an instant. Now there was anxiety, turmoil, and confusion. These were elements Dekker could use to his advantage. Since they were going to drug him again, he wanted to be prepared. If they held him down and injected him there wasn't much he could do, but if they used pills, they would have to force them into his mouth. In that case Dekker could hold the pills under his tongue until he could spit them out. He would have to wait and see what course his captors took.

RUSTY WALKED AWAY from the manor house convinced they were hiding something—or someone. The owner never asked Rusty who he was looking for, or why he'd zeroed in on this particular house. If Dennis' information about Dekker's whereabouts was correct, he would have to move carefully to free him from the house. If he went seeking a search warrant there would be questions he would rather not answer, and it would all take time, and he was certain time was something Dekker did not have. His only remaining option was to keep an eye on the house and see if Dekker appeared. The problem was, where to set up surveillance?

The house was isolated and surrounded by thick forest, and only one road led to the property. Parking on the side of the road would be suspicious and would indicate his visit was more than casual. He'd have to hide his car, hike in through the woods, and set up in a place he could watch unobserved.

Rusty's solution wasn't elegant, but it served his immediate need. Patuxent River Road ended at the Origen house, but a quarter mile back there was a small cul-de-sac serving three homes, all set back in the trees. It wasn't a suburban-style cul-de-sac; it was intended more as a turn-around point, a wide spot in the road. One home on the East side had a number of cars in the drive and even one parked in the cul-de-sac, which was a perfect cover. The home must have multiple teenagers or college-age people, each with their own car, so Rusty trusted one more car parked in the cul-de-sac would go unnoticed.

Once parked, Rusty went into the trunk to retrieve some gear. He hadn't expected to be doing a stakeout or conducting surveillance, so he wasn't provisioned with food or proper equipment. "Can't do anything about it now," he said as he grabbed the few things he always kept on hand: Binoculars, a camp chair, and some energy bars.

One thing he was happy for—his gym bag. In it he kept a pair of athletic shoes, socks, a sweatshirt, and a pair of cargo pants—the kind with leg pockets and a zipper allowing you to take off the bottom half of the legs.

He stepped behind a tree and, with as much discretion as possible, changed from his business uniform—a suit and tie—and into the casual clothing. He returned to the car, stored his suit and street shoes, grabbed the binoculars and other gear, and set off for the house at the end of the road. Rusty ducked into the trees before coming within sight of the house, so the rest of this hike was "off road" to avoid detection.

He assumed the house had some sort of surveillance. *There might even be patrols,* he thought.

Moving through the thick woods and underbrush, Rusty looked for signs of electronic surveillance—cameras or motion detectors, but found none. His route through the woods swung around the entry area, giving him a good view of the house's north side and the front entrance. He wanted to be in this position because this side of the house had a small portico and door that was plainly the non-formal entrance area, and probably where Dekker would appear. He unfolded his camp chair and settled in to watch.

GEOFFREY WAS UPSET by the news of the government man's visit, and agreed Dekker must be moved as soon as possible. Origen had the limo brought to the North service entrance while he gathered up his things.

Two of Origen's men were sent to bring Dekker to the car, but in the urgency of the situation, neglected to get more drugs. "We gave him enough last night to carry him through twenty-four hours," said one of the guards. "Let's just grab him, toss him in the car, and get him to the plane."

Origen's men opened the closet door with cruel remarks about having a restful night, and would he like his bed made. Were Dekker not bound and gagged, he was certain they would not mock him. He knew what was coming and played like he was still under the drug's influence. To a great extent it was true, but he now had clear thinking, and that made all the difference.

One of the guards had a motion sickness patch, so he stuck it on Dekker's arm. The patch assured a continual, though smaller, dosage of scopolamine that would maintain his present state. The men hoisted Dekker to his feet, dragging him to the service entrance.

RUSTY NOTICED THE activity at the portico and watched as a black limousine pulled under the slate roof. He saw a stately looking gentleman come out the door followed by one of Origen's staff who carried luggage. The luggage went into the trunk and the gentleman took a seat in the front.

Odd, Rusty thought. *Usually a dignitary sits in back when he is chauffeured around.*

The reason became clear when the door opened and two big men dragged another outside. It was clear the man was drugged and one of the men bent down to cut the binding from his ankles. When the men finally moved out of the way Rusty recognized Dekker. He wasn't immobile, but apparently incapacitated by some drug. They put Dekker in the rear seat and stepped away to confer with someone hidden from view in the doorway.

The gentleman in the car became impatient waiting for whatever was going on in the doorway. He got out of the front seat, making sure the prisoner was immobile behind the privacy window, and moved around the car, telling the guards to hurry up. This was Rusty's chance—if he didn't get Dekker now, who knew when another chance would present itself? With everyone distracted by the conversation in the doorway, Rusty dashed up to the limo, opened the right rear door, and pulled Dekker out. Lord Geoffrey, who stood away from the limo and faced the doorway, did not notice what was happening.

Rusty was surprised Dekker was able to move as well as he did, but had to wait until they had reached the cover of the trees to begin to talk. He whispered into his hostage's ear. "Dekker? Let's get out of here."

"Scopolamine," was all Dekker could reply, but it was enough. Rusty understood Dekker had been drugged with scopolamine. Dekker also scratched with his free hand at his upper left arm. Rusty stopped for a moment under the trees to see what the problem was with Dekker's arm. He saw the patch and tore it off. "Thank you," said Dekker with a thick voice.

Rusty ran through the woods as fast as possible while supporting another man. Dekker moved his feet as best he could, but it certainly was not at a speed great enough to keep up with his colleague. *Zombie drug, indeed*, Rusty thought. It was just what they didn't need. At a time when speed and agility were called for, Dekker was moving like the living dead.

So far they were good. No alarm had been raised and everyone was still unaware of the prisoner's escape. No sooner had Rusty congratulated himself on a great rescue, then they heard a shout. The escape had been discovered and Rusty reasoned the best they could hope for was to find a hiding place in the woods. If he could get them behind the searchers, he could backtrack and get around to the cul-de-sac where his car was waiting.

CHAPTER TWENTY

GEOFFREY WAS LIVID ABOUT DEKKER'S escape and shouted orders at anyone who came into his field of view. Origen mobilized every staff member in the house, about twenty in all, all while withering, recriminating accusations of incompetence were thrown his way by the Englishman. He dispatched men into the woods where he assumed Dekker would go, but also sent some down the road to get around the prisoner and cut off any escape.

Rusty found a decent-looking hiding place and sat Dekker there. "Look, Dekker, I'm going to leave you here for a moment and do a little recon. Do you understand?" Dekker nodded his head and waved his arm more or less in front of him, indicating Rusty should go.

Rusty dashed into the woods and was soon hidden by the trees and underbrush. He intended to find out how many men were searching for them and then plan a way out. He moved quickly and soon found himself at the road, not far from the cul-de-sac where his car was parked. This was good, because he could simply retrace his steps, get Dekker, and get the hell out of there. His hope was short lived, however, when he spotted four armed men come around the curve, heading his way. They were the team closing the back door to entrap Dekker, and from the sound of their conversation it seemed they were unaware Rusty was part of the escape equation. He slipped silently back into the woods, waiting to see what Origen's men would do. Rusty prayed they did not go all the way to the cul-de-sac and discover his car, but he would have to wait and see.

DEKKER SAT QUIETLY against a tree. What else could he do? He listened to the sounds of the men searching in the woods. They seemed to be moving past his location, heading left toward the main road. He tried to concentrate and use his proximity sense to "listen" to the searchers, but he found his ability to reach out or to tap into the Flows was blocked. *It's the drugs*, the thought, and was strangely troubled by the loss of a skill he relied on in tight spots like this.

"I'm really on my own," he mumbled to himself, and hoped Rusty would return soon.

Time went by, how much Dekker couldn't say—another side effect of the drug. It was quiet around him, although he could hear some rustling and conversation in the distance. He continued looking for Rusty and thought he heard him coming. The sounds were certainly only one person, not a group like those hunting him. Eagerly he looked for Rusty, hoping he would soon be out of this trap.

Dekker watched as leaves began to move slightly off to his right. Finally! But his hopes collapsed when a stranger pushed through the growth and spotted him. The man let out a shout. "I found him!"

Dekker's hopes were crushed.

Soon several other men responded to the call and came pushing through the woods, circling Dekker still seated against the tree. The original discoverer held a short, nasty-looking machine pistol on Dekker, and the new arrivals crowed around their captive, taunting him over his misguided escape. The guards secured his hands with heavy plastic zip ties and lifted Dekker to his feet. He could do nothing but accept his re-capture. He would continue acting like he could hardly move, which wasn't a big stretch, and hope a new escape opportunity would arise. The group of armed men escorted Dekker back to the manor house.

RUSTY HEARD THE shout of discovery, just as he began moving back toward Dekker's hiding place. By the time he reached the spot, he saw a dozen men pushing and dragging Dekker back to the house. Rusty felt the sting of failure. He was so close to getting Dekker out, and now this—it would take him some time to recover from the disappointment. Meanwhile, he needed a new plan.

Rusty knew they intended to drive Dekker out of there, so he made his way back to his car. He heard the limo coming down the road and jumped into his car, laying flat on the front seat. The big car zoomed past, going much too fast for the small road. *They're sure in a hurry*, Rusty observed, and began his pursuit while fishing around for his cell phone.

The limo traveled north on Interstate 97, exiting on Highway 162 that lay behind BWI, serving Ultra Aviation Services. Rusty had no trouble following from a safe distance and he pulled into the private aviation parking area and waited to see which aircraft belonged to Dekker's abductor.

Thirty minutes later one of a half dozen Gulfstream jets was pulled to the loading area, and Rusty knew he had the plane. He took note of the tail numbers and waited. A few minutes later five men walked to the Gulfstream and boarded. One man shuffled a good deal and seemed to be keeping the group back.

That's Dekker, thought Rusty, *still playing zombie.*

With all passengers and crew onboard, the aircraft was sealed up and taxied to the end of the runway reserved for private aircraft. The Gulfstream lifted off and soared into the sky. Rusty was outmaneuvered. "Good luck, Dekker."

CHAPTER TWENTY-ONE

KAMENWATI WAS PLEASED TO RECEIVE Lord Geoffrey's message that Dekker had been captured and was en route to Strasbourg. He sent back a message stating that upon landing at the Entzheim Airport outside Strasbourg, Geoffrey was to take Dekker to a certain canal boat on the Danube River. Orders were acknowledged and understood, and Kamenwati began to organize his secret meeting.

An acolyte burst into his office, out of breath, and with a terrified look on his face. "Sir, the Master wants you immediately!"

Kamenwati had no idea what was on Abaddon's mind and that concerned him. He opened the bottom desk drawer that held the box holding the Succubus' ashes, placed his hand on the box, and was comforted. After dismissing the acolyte he took the box and transferred the ashes to a small leather bag he tied up and put into a pocket. *In the end, I have the power*, he thought. He left instructions with his key Adept to continue with the Strasbourg meeting arrangements.

"Why have I been unable to reach Lord Geoffrey?" Abaddon was back into his micro-managing mode, it seemed. "I have been sending out calls on the Flows and have received no reply. Can you explain this?"

"Yes, I believe I can. He is investigating the Dekker matter and has obeyed my order to withhold any communication until he has our man in-hand."

Abaddon gave him a searing look, as if he wanted more information. Kamenwati unconsciously reached into his pocket seeking the comfort of the Succubus' ashes. "If Lord Geoffrey were to use the Flows freely, anyone sympathetic to Dekker could intercept it and thwart the capture."

Abaddon thought about the Egyptian's strategy for a moment and then nodded his head. "Yes, I see the wisdom of your order. Do you have any word?"

"Only that Geoffrey was on a promising lead in America. We should get news soon." Abaddon seemed appeased.

"Finally. Now, what about our efforts in Europe?"

Kamenwati hoped his relief at dodging the Dekker pitfall did not show, as he strove to keep his emotions under control. This was an exchange that could have exposed his plan, and more ominously, his subterfuge. Abaddon was not stupid, but he was distracted, and that worked in the Egyptian's favor. Kamenwati went into a detailed report on the status of their European operations, both the religious-oriented Brotherhood cells and the more secular Consortium groups.

"In summary, the Brotherhood is regaining strength throughout Western Europe, but developing more slowly in Eastern Europe. We have brethren all over, but enticing them back into the fold has proven more of a challenge than I expected."

The Master traced a finger across his desk, nodding his head in affirmation of each point Kamenwati made.

"And yet, we have been able to restore key influence in several governments. Not to the level we once enjoyed, but influence nonetheless." Abaddon looked up, the inscrutable golden mask frighteningly unreadable. "And what of the Far East?"

"There, too, we have a mixed report. The Chinese in particular have been resistant to reintroducing the Brotherhood into their system. They don't mind the Consortium activities, since they receive a healthy piece of that business, but the reintroduction of our faith-oriented worldview simply grates against their ingrained Communist ideology." Kamenwati stopped to take a breath and gather his thoughts. "They have little tolerance for the vision of a world restored to its original reverence for Magick."

"The Chinese always were a problem," Abaddon said. "And I perceive the times are different now. The people, once steeped in the worship of their dead ancestors, now seem only to worship at the altar of capitalism."

"So true, my Master. Yet the core belief in supernatural powers is still buried deep in their hearts. That is what we must unlock and redirect to the Brotherhood."

The conversation moved to the Americas where Kamenwati had several areas of good report, especially in Central and South America where the principles of Magick were not so foreign. Also, in certain countries, like Brazil, their reach within the political establishment was deep. When the Brotherhood's man at the top in Brazil was exposed and jailed, the next in line was ready to carry out the mission. Unfortunately, venal, power-hungry dictators seemed to be the best the Brotherhood could hope for in the rest of the region.

Abaddon was not overly concerned with the South American initiatives. "They will go along with whatever their neighbors in North America do."

Abaddon stood and walked to a wall map, pointing to the general European sector. "I want to concentrate our efforts on this region. We need to reestablish our foothold as quickly as possible, and once solidly in place, we'll be able to influence the other regions of the world." Abaddon went back to his desk, shuffled through paperwork, and extracted the document he sought. "These are the target countries I want you to focus on."

Kamenwati looked concerned. "This is a great deal to manage at one time. We have only limited resources."

"Enough!" Abaddon shouted. "I say it can be done and must be done."

Kamenwati dropped his eyes and wondered how he would achieve such a goal. He would have to study the Master's document and get back to him. "As you wish, my master." Abaddon always responded well when his highest lieutenant bowed to his wishes. "Allow me some time to develop a plan and return for your approval."

Abaddon dismissed the Egyptian with a wave of his hand and did not look up when Kamenwati stood and left. It wasn't until he reached his office in the administrative center that Kamenwati let his emotions show. "Damn fool!" He tossed the piece of paper on his desk with more than a little disdain. "He thinks we can simply snap our fingers and undo the damage done when governments became aware of our existence, and more to the point, our influence."

He thought about the tedious process of recruiting, subverting, and compromising rising officials. "And once they are on our team, getting the proper laws and regulations in place can consume years of effort. No, this is not something that can be mandated to happen on a given date; it must develop at its own pace. Some will be ready quickly, others not for years, and Abaddon does not want to hear that excuse."

The Egyptian decided to put off the report he knew Abaddon wanted. After all, one day in the not too distant future this would all be his.

Kamenwati smiled at the thought of his own ascendency.

CHAPTER TWENTY-TWO

RUSTY WATCHED THE GULFSTREAM JET fly into the distance as he thought about his options. Dekker was clearly a captive and they were spiriting him out of the country, but his—and Dekker's—status precluded taking any overt, official action. He needed information to plan his next move, and knew just who to call: Dennis Allende. He would have access to all sorts of information and could probably tell him where the Gulfstream was going. He called. Dennis picked up almost immediately, diving into his own questions about Dekker. Strickland calmed him down and explained what he had been doing.

"Do you mean they've taken Dekker out of the country?" Dennis was incredulous.

"I'm afraid so, Dennis, and that's why I'm calling. I need you to track a tail number and tell me where it's headed." He gave the tail numbers to Dennis.

"Sure thing, but what do you plan to do?"

"I don't know, but the first step is finding out where Dekker is headed."

"Hold on," Dennis said as he began searching FAA records for the aircraft. "Got it. The plane is owned by the British government, so it passes through inspections on the diplomatic immunity provisions of international law."

"Does that mean you can't find out where they're going?"

"No, just they didn't have to disclose the names of the passengers or descriptions of cargo. All I can tell you is four people, plus the crew, are on board, and they're headed for Strasbourg, France, specifically Entzheim Airport."

"ETA on that?" Rusty was trying to calculate the head start they'd have on him.

"They should be landing tonight, about eight o'clock local time."

"That's not good. Any ideas?"

"Yes, but it's not by following them. I have a better way." Dennis laid out his plan, which also included himself.

Rusty headed back to McLean and the NCTC headquarters.

BY FOUR O'CLOCK in the afternoon Rusty and Dennis were sitting in the NCTC executive office waiting area for a meeting with Jim Lynch. Marilyn Stamm invited them into Lynch's office, and was about to leave, Lynch stopped her. "I'd like you to stay and take meeting notes, Marilyn." They all sat around the small conference table in Lynch's office, ready to begin.

"Okay, Dennis, you called this meeting. What's on your mind?" Dennis was familiar with presenting to his NCTC boss and knew how he preferred to receive information. He laid out the core of the problem and turned it over to Rusty for the abduction portion of the story. Much of this was new to Lynch and it certainly got Marilyn's attention as she wrote notes.

"You mean to say this Origen fellow has been operating right in our back yard and we had no idea?" Lynch was incredulous and not a little embarrassed.

"Yes, sir, and I believe his moles in the FBI and other intelligence agencies keep him well protected," said Rusty.

"That's a hole we will have to fill, don't you think, Rusty?"

"Yes, sir, but right now this is about Dekker—and Abaddon." Marilyn stopped writing with the mention of the madman's name and looked up with an *oh-no* look on her face.

"Go on," said Lynch.

Dennis took over once again and laid out his proposal for a plan of action. "Dekker needs help. First to escape from the Brotherhood, and then to capture Abaddon and put him in a real prison."

"We can't use agency assets," Lynch said. "Too easy for Abaddon to spot." Thinking for a moment, he continued.

"Rusty, I want you to investigate this Origen character and shut down his operation." Rusty began to protest, but Lynch cut him off. "A Brotherhood cell operating right here in Washington is a big problem, and with Dekker out of the picture, I need you to do the job."

"Yes, sir," said Rusty.

"And Dennis, you need to go to Iceland and convince Galdur to go to Krugerschloss and save Dekker."

The pair left Lynch's office and went down to Dennis' office—his "domain" as he termed it—to discuss a plan. "This is all going to boil down to infiltrating Krugerschloss and somehow freeing Dekker," said Dennis. "Not to mention facing Abaddon."

"You make this guy sound like an alien monster, Dennis. Is he really that bad?"

"Let me put it this way: The reason Jim is onboard with us is because he does know the scope of the problem. If he hadn't been through the last confrontation with Abaddon, I'm pretty sure he'd only be willing to rely on technology— passive searches and observation."

Rusty seemed confused by Dennis' last reference.

"We're never going to capture or defeat Abaddon with our technology, Rusty. He operates on quite another plane of existence. You'll have to trust me when I say we need some supernatural help, and that's where Galdur comes in."

"I'm not sure what all that means, but I'm willing to accept that you know more about our opponent than I do." Rusty looked askance, though, when Dennis said he would be off to Iceland on the next flight to find the old mystic named Galdur.

"This falls into the 'fighting fire with fire' category. We need a mystic to catch a mystic." Rusty couldn't help but wonder what he had gotten himself into.

CHAPTER TWENTY-THREE

DEKKER WAS CONSCIOUS OF WHAT was happening around him but he was still unable to move. The sensation was very odd, and for a man accustomed to being in control of his every action, it was unnerving. He tried a few experiments. He commanded his feet to move back and forth, which they reluctantly did; he tried lifting a hand, but found it bound with white plastic. *How did that get there?* He attempted to shift his position. *Am I standing or sitting?* He felt a heavy hand on one shoulder that shoved him back into a seat. *Well, sitting, at least.*

"Where do you think you're going?" The voice was rough and sneering. Dekker found he could not move out of the seat and had to let things develop.

"That's better my little zombie. You just sit back and enjoy the ride, we'll be there soon enough."

Dekker was annoyed he had no control. He remembered the scopolamine and knew it was the effect of the drug, but it didn't make him feel any better because his mental skills could overcome mindless obedience to outside orders. Could he tap into the Flows and the greater powers of Magick? That reminded him of Galdur and Kara's training, and to a lesser extent his Native American friend Eagle Claw's guidance; he grieved his neglecting of spiritual power and awareness. Had his grief wounded him so deeply that he'd forgotten all he once knew? He tried to recall when he'd lost touch with that world, but could not. He recognized that he had sunk deeper and deeper into a pit of grief and self-pity, and that he seemed unable to escape.

Not true! The only one keeping me down is myself. If I had the power to imprison myself, I also have the power to be free. The thought was invigorating and helped clear his mind.

He concentrated on images and memories that would put him into a deep meditative state and soon found he was floating in a warm limbo. In this state he could see himself from above. He was sitting in an airplane, his hands bound before him, laying quietly on his lap. Two men with dour expressions flanked him, and both bored with their duty of guarding an all but catatonic prisoner.

Dekker's consciousness soared upward and outward, depositing him in the Shamans Meadow hidden deep in the mountains of New Mexico. There, in the enclosed field of evening primrose, he looked around. He saw it as it had once been: primeval, undisturbed, and quiet. Then he sensed another presence, one that made his spirit soar. Kelly! How could this be? He saw a shape form in the cave across the field and knew it was she. His joy was hard to contain and he struggled to run through the evening primrose to get to her. But he was strangely immobile, his feet stuck where he stood. He called out her name and she waved to him. He tried to shout an explanation why he couldn't come to her, but before he could, she vanished back into the darkness of the cave.

He was angry with himself for losing Kelly again, but before he could engage in self-admonition he was again whisked off, this time standing before an ancient cottage set below a cliff. Small, wood-framed windows with homemade glass punctuated the whitewashed walls. There was a simple porch with a sturdy-looking wooden banister and a single door. This was a familiar place, one he found very comforting. He moved to the porch and was glad to find this time he seemed able to move. He opened the door and floated inside. There was an old man sitting in a worn chair, sitting before a large fireplace providing not only warmth for the cottage, but a cooking hearth as well. The old man looked around the edge of his chair and seemed to spot Dekker, and invited him in. Dekker floated around before him, settling on the great stone hearth.

"Galdur," was all Dekker could say.

"Yes, and I cannot tell you how long I have awaited your return, Adam."

Dekker was sorry he remained away for so long. "I forgot the way, Galdur. So much has happened."

"I know, Adam, but I have never been far from you during the trials you have been going through. I am acutely aware of your loss, and I, too, grieve her passing. I also know who did this terrible thing to you."

"Galdur, I am being held prisoner. I have been drugged and have no control of my will."

"Nonsense. The drug only dulls the will and inhibits your ability to act independently. You have the power to overcome the drug's effects. You have the power to free yourself from its control." With that thought Dekker was swept up again and deposited back into his body on the aircraft. With renewed awareness, he set about neutralizing the psychotic effects of the scopolamine.

He kept his eyes closed, so not to alert his captors of his consciousness. Dekker concentrated on his proximity sense, and even with his eyes closed he could clearly sense the position of everyone on the aircraft. The two guards sat on his left and right, Lord Geoffrey sat alone toward the front of the cabin, the cabin steward straightening up things in the galley, and the two pilots in the cockpit.

A soft chime sound seemed to be signaling the steward, who went forward into the cockpit, emerging a moment later. The steward went to Lord Geoffrey to deliver a softly spoken report that the aircraft was one hour from landing. Geoffrey looked at his expensive Rolex watch, grunted approvingly, and asked the steward to bring him a drink. The young steward straightened up and headed back to the galley to fill the order.

The guard on Dekker's left stood, stretching his muscles. The other guard seemed reluctant to leave Dekker's side even though there was nowhere for him to go, even if he were conscious and fully capable.

"Don't worry, my friend," said the standing guard. "He's down until well after our scheduled landing time."

"I hope so. Something doesn't feel right about him, and I'll be glad to get him off our hands."

Lord Geoffrey got up and walked back to inspect his prisoner. "Is everything in order?" The two guards nodded while Geoffrey grabbed Dekker's chin with one hand, moving his head back and forth with no apparent reaction. "Did you boys give him too much juice?"

"No, sir, just what was ordered."

"He will need to deplane on his own, so you two make sure he's ambulatory. We land in an hour."

Dekker took in the whole conversation and began to formulate a plan. It would require precise timing, and more importantly, having his fully working mental and physical abilities.

The hour passed quickly as Dekker concentrated on neutralizing the drug in his system. He was amazed that Galdur could know about this and advise him to counteract the drug with his mind. He could almost see the drug coursing through his veins and into his brain. He watched as molecules attached themselves to the neural receptors and collected like a pools of water in the areas controlling will—essentially "drowning" the brain functions. He was able to create small "canals," allowing the drug to drain away, leaving the affected areas clear. The more drainage canals he "built," the clearer his mind became, but it was slow going and he was running out of time.

Dekker felt the landing gear lower and lock into place, indicating there were only minutes before landing. One of the guards cracked an ammonia capsule and waved it beneath Dekker's nose.

"Wake up, sleeping beauty. We're landing." Dekker reacted violently to the aroma, swinging his head away to avoid the ammonia.

"There you are, like new." The guard laughed at his own joke and made sure Dekker was strapped into his seat. "Don't want to have any accidents, do we?"

The Gulfstream landed and Lord Geoffrey issued an order before deplaning. "Make sure he gets to the car without incident."

The guards gave each other weary looks and watched Geoffrey leave the plane. "Yes, your worship," one said softly. The other smirked, and then turned to Dekker. "Up you go, buddy. Time to take a walk."

CHAPTER TWENTY-FOUR

DEKKER HAD NO OPPORTUNITY TO escape his two guards as they guided him to a waiting car; he was no longer under the sway of the scopolamine, but needed to keep up appearances. He watched out the window as the car moved smoothly from the airport, through the city of Strasbourg, and onward toward the Danube River. The car turned onto Rue du Havre, following a wide canal Dekker knew would eventually empty into the river.

They reached the end of the canal at a set of locks to control flooding. There were several boats, barges, and fishing vessels lined up in the lock, waiting for the re-leveling of the water and passage into the Danube. The car pulled into a quay below the lock where a nondescript barge was tethered.

"Here's our hand-off point," one guard said to Dekker. "I hope you don't get seasick. Wait, you're full of scopolamine, so that won't be a problem." The other guard laughed at the joke. Dekker did not.

The ride gave him a chance to orient himself, and various road signs told him he was in Strasbourg, France. He knew across the river was the Black Forest and Krugerschloss, and he expected the ride to continue into Germany. But the announcement he was to be transferred to a river barge was confusing. Why put him on the river? There was no direct water route into the Black Forest, much less to Krugerschloss. What was going on?

He would find out very soon as they pulled to a stop in front of the barge with the name *Simone* painted on the low superstructure typical of European river barges.

The guards hustled him out of the car, binding his hands behind his back. A man emerged from the boat, followed by four young men dressed in gray robes. The man, clearly the elder and their leader, was tall and very lean. His skin was somewhat dark, set off by the white robes he wore.

The man issued an order to his four assistants and they came to the dock and took custody of Dekker.

"He's all yours now, Kamenwati," shouted Lord Geoffrey up to the man on deck.

The four new men surrounded Dekker and led him up the short gangplank to face his new captor. Dekker inspected his new jailor and saw he was old but still very spry. His eyes were bright and more than a little menacing, and Dekker knew in that moment this man could be every bit as ruthless as Abaddon.

Kamenwati spoke no word but inclined his head toward the doorway leading to the main cabin. The four new guards pushed Dekker inside and seated him in a comfortable, upholstered chair in a surprisingly well-appointed room. This was clearly a cruising barge rather than the traditional cargo- and livestock-hauling variety that plied the rivers and canals of France. Kamenwati descended the ladder into the salon and sat across from Dekker, ordering his men to release the bonds.

"Mr. Dekker, my name is Kamenwati, and I brought you here to consider a proposition." Dekker looked at the man, not sure what to make of such an opening line. "We have a common adversary; I wish to help you reach and kill him."

"And who would that be? I've had many adversaries over the years."

"I'm sure you have, Mr. Dekker, but this one had your wife killed. It is Abaddon."

"Abaddon," Dekker repeated softly.

"I sense your confusion and your questions. You see, I am what we call a 'deep practitioner' of Magick. My skills are equal to Abaddon's, and he has kept me down for many decades through his ruthless rule of the Brotherhood. I watched from afar your previous encounter with him, and celebrated when he was bound in the stasis, thinking his tyranny was finally over."

Carefully omitting his part in Abaddon's release, Kamenwati continued, "But confinement was not to be for Abaddon. He managed to escape and has been calling the faithful back to him in hopes of regaining the momentum you so inconveniently stopped five years ago; he still thinks he can rule the world if only all modern contrivances can be neutralized."

"What do you want from me? I'm no deep practitioner of Magick and can't fight him that way."

"No, but with my help I believe we can constrain or distract him long enough for you to enact a more permanent solution. Abaddon is quite obsessed with you. He sees you as the source of all his problems, and as long as you are alive you remain a threat to his ultimate goal."

"How did Abaddon get free?"

"I am not certain, but as long as there is life in Abaddon, regardless of his physical state, he is a threat to the world."

"And I suppose you want to take his place and lead us all to a benign future?"

"Oh, no. I wish to rid the world of an evil that can, and will, infect everything it touches."

"Why do you need me? It seems you have all the answers—and the power. Why not simply get rid of him?"

"I wish it were that simple. As I said before, Abaddon is deeply schooled and experienced in Magick and can sense or see any threat long before it might get to him. That makes plotting and moving on him impossible."

"Why not use the time-honored technique of poisoning his food?"

"He has the ability to sniff out any such subterfuge, and even if something could get through, he can neutralize the effects to his body."

Dekker recalled his own recent experience dissipating the scopolamine in his body and had come understanding. "You make him sound invincible."

"Yes, invincible, yet not invulnerable. He has a weakness, a blind spot, if you will."

Dekker raised an eyebrow in an unspoken question.

"You, Mr. Dekker."

Dekker was quiet for a long while, trying to think through this situation while wrestling with his emotions. Was it possible this Kamenwati could be trusted? It all sounded too good to be true, but then, should he spurn an opportunity to finally stop Abaddon? He churned through these thoughts, always ending where he started: in deep distrust. What was the old proverb, "Beware Greeks bearing gifts?" Could he maneuver Kamenwati to work for his advantage? Why not use the tool placed before him?

Dekker felt as if he were making a deal with the devil. He knew nothing of Kamenwati or his history with Abaddon. It was an impossible situation and Dekker knew he needed help to make this decision. He would have to stall for time to consider all the implications. "How do you see this working?"

"I am Abaddon's chief of staff and the only one who can get you into his presence."

"Sounds cozy. How do I know you haven't been sent to mislead me to get me to step willingly into the lion's jaws?"

"I have already taken a huge risk by diverting Lord Geoffrey and talking with you. If Abaddon knew, he would surely kill me in a most brutal manner."

"Let's say I go along with you. What's your plan?"

"Simplicity itself, Mr. Dekker. I'll take you near Krugerschloss, where you'll be released. We will create multiple sighting reports and inflame Abaddon's mania. I will 'capture' you and bring you to Abaddon."

"And how will I defeat him? Surely you don't expect me to use Magick to defend myself."

"Oh, no, Mr. Dekker. I will be right there giving you the aid needed. Besides, once in his presence, a knife or a gun will defeat any mind tricks he may use."

Dekker thought it was more likely his hands, squeezing the evil life out, just as he did to Kelly. "It all sounds too easy. I can't believe Abaddon would be so foolish."

"On the contrary, Mr. Dekker, he will be so filled with hate and revenge he will throw caution to the wind, and thus give you your opening."

"And if he doesn't react the way you plan, what then?" Kamenwati smiled at Dekker, but it was not a friendly smile.

CHAPTER TWENTY-FIVE

DENNIS WATCHED THE FLAT COUNTRYSIDE of Iceland pass by his window. His parting with Rusty left him feeling the NCTC agent was disappointed to be left out. But Lynch's orders were orders, after all, and he knew Rusty would make short work of Origen and his network.

The BSÍ bus he rode in was a fuel cell vehicle that ran quietly, without the typical clatter, smoke, and noise of a diesel engine. He was traveling north to the last stop on the route—Dalvik. Dennis saw the rise of mountains in the distance and wondered how Galdur could live in such a lonely place—he certainly never could. It had been a long time since he'd last seen Galdur, but his fondness for the man hadn't faded. He recalled his numerous arguments to convince the old mystic his quaint beliefs in supernatural powers were nothing more than the age-old tricks of psychics and shamans.

Galdur agreed the world today knew only of tricks, deceits, and slight-of-hand, all pale reflections of the truth. Dennis simply could not accept there were other modes of thinking, other "truths" beyond those defined by science and technology—until that final day in the Black Forest when he witnessed something he still could not explain, much less understand.

As the mountains grew closer, Dennis nodded off to sleep, then started awake when an overhead speaker in the bus announced their arrival in Dalvik. Of course, the announcement was in Icelandic, but Dennis understood the intent: End of the line, everyone off the bus.

Dennis stood and pulled down his bag from the overhead compartment and waited in the aisle. *I've got to find transport to Galdur's home* he thought.

It is fortunate most Icelanders speak English. After leaving the bus Dennis was able to find an inn where he could get directions, and hopefully, a ride to his final destination. It was midmorning, but the inn's pub was bustling with local fishermen. Their workday was over, having begun long before sunrise, and they made a habitual stop for a drink and some smoked fish while their nets dried.

Dennis could not have faced more exotic choices for breakfast, so he ordered coffee and Skyr, a local dairy product similar to yogurt. The coffee was rich and thick, almost an espresso. When the innkeeper brought a selection of breads to accompany his coffee, Dennis gathered up the courage to ask for help.

"I wonder if you could help me, sir." The weathered face of the innkeeper stared down at him, but made no reply. "I'm looking for an old friend who lives around here. His name is Galdur. Do you know him?"

The fellow's eyes crinkled, as if the innkeeper were evaluating his intent. "*Yao,* I know Galdur. What do you want with him?"

"As I said, he's an old friend and I happened to be in Iceland and wanted to look him up."

"He doesn't come into town much, but that man over there," he pointed to a table at the far side of the room, "he may be able to help you. His name is Andrésson."

Dennis went to the man's table and introduced himself. "Mr. Andrésson, my name is Dennis Allende and I am a friend of Galdur. I was hoping you could tell me where to find him."

"A friend of Galdur's, you say? You're American, yes?" Dennis nodded. "I only saw Galdur in the company of one other American, and you're not him," said Andrésson, looking Dennis up and down with suspicion.

Dennis was afraid he would lose the man, so he tried a new tack. "You must mean Adam Dekker." Andrésson's eyes opened in surprise and he invited Dennis to sit. "You are Dekker's friend?"

"Oh, yes. In fact, we work together. That's how I know Galdur."

"I heard some wild rumors after Galdur and your friend disappeared, then just as suddenly Galdur was back."

"Yes, well, it's partly about that time that I want to see Galdur."

"Tell you what, young man, finish your food and I'll take you out to him. You'd never find it on your own." Pleased and grateful, Dennis accepted Andrésson's invitation.

Dennis was surprised when he saw the transportation to be used: An old wooden cart with large, iron-banded wheels, hooked to a pair of horses. The bed of the wagon was empty, and Andrésson explained he just delivered an order of vegetables and ground provisions to the inn. There was plenty of room on the wide wooden bench, and the two men climbed up and began the trip from town.

The ancient cart followed a plain dirt road heading toward the mountains creating a picturesque backdrop to the coastal town of Dalvik. Andrésson took a side track leading around a cliff, and Dalvik was no longer visible. Dennis wasn't prepared for the vista unfolding before him—a wide valley, green with heather, and bisected by a glittering stream running down the middle. The hills sweeping up left and right were brilliant green, and it created the impression of a primeval world untouched by modern man.

"It's like we stepped into Middle Earth," said Dennis.

Andrésson looked at Dennis questioningly. "Don't know what that means, young man, but it is beautiful."

"More than that, it is tranquil and other-worldly, like something from a fairy tale," Dennis said. *This route has been used for years, maybe decades*, Dennis thought, *perhaps centuries*.

The trip was slow but somehow appropriate, with only the sound of horse hoofs and wagon wheels, and an occasional burst of birds startled from nesting areas. He asked about the history of Iceland and Andrésson was only too happy to take on the role of teacher.

"Iceland has had its ups and downs, like all countries. Back in the eight hundreds, a Viking named Ingolfur Arnarson landed here and made his home near present day Reykjavik. Tribal chiefs ruled the land for many years until they united and established the Althingi, the oldest parliament in the world. Eventually Iceland entered a treaty with the Norwegian monarchy, and was then passed to Denmark when the Althingi was disbanded. Patriotism caught on again in the nineteen hundreds and the Althingi was re-established. World War Two was a difficult time for us because Germany cut off communication between Denmark and Iceland; we had to assume control over our territorial waters and foreign affairs. The British occupied Iceland in the nineteen forties, but responsibility for Iceland's defense went to the United States. We became a fully independent republic in nineteen forty-four, and our Independence Day is June seventeenth."

"What about those famous sagas? The ones with all the great heroes and monsters?"

Andrésson lit up with the question. "Our greatest cultural heritage. The Sagas are our best-known literary accomplishments, and really have no match in the Nordic world. The Sagas glorify the virtues all Icelanders cherish; courage, pride, and honor."

Dennis was intrigued with Andrésson's answer. "Do you know any of the Sagas? Could you tell one?"

"I do, but unfortunately, there is no time to tell you a full tale. We are coming close to Galdur's cottage, and I wouldn't want to leave you hanging."

The wagon was taking a small sidetrack from the central valley onto a smaller vale. Before long they could make out a sod roof set against the hillside.

"Is that Galdur's place?" Dennis asked.

"It is. And unless I'm mistaken, he will be expecting us. It is very hard to sneak up on old Galdur."

Galdur's home was made of bright, whitewashed walls with small, shutter-covered windows and a carved, brightly painted door in the middle. Galdur was standing in it, and to Dennis' eyes, he hadn't changed a bit. His white hair was longer now, and gathered at the base of his neck with a strip of leather. His clothes were simple, a plain tunic over baggy trousers, but he had modern hiking boots on his feet.

Galdur smiled at the sight of his young friend and greeted him warmly.

Dennis thanked Andrésson for the ride from town as the cart turned around, heading back out of Galdur's valley.

"I'll be taking another load of produce to the inn tomorrow," Andrésson said. "Would you like me to stop by?"

"Yes, please," answered Dennis. "I'm pretty sure I'll be ready to go."

He watched Andrésson's receding figure against the warm light cast on the hillsides. Turning to the cottage, Galdur invited him inside.

The cottage was rustic but warm and comfortable. Because timber was not readily available, the thick walls were constructed of hay covered with mud plaster. The material provided wonderful insulation through the winter and the damp days of spring. In the summer the walls maintained a cool and comfortable temperature, while the sod-covered roof was an additional layer of insulation.

Dennis asked about the unusual wall and roof materials, and Galdur could only laugh. "We've been building our houses this way for centuries and we don't seem to need steel beams or electricity to live."

"What about fire? It seems all this dry and compressed hay is a hazard."

"True, fire is a danger; we simply have to be vigilant," Galdur patiently explained, showing Dennis to a chair.

The cottage was basically one large room with a stone fireplace on one wall and comfortable seating before it, on a wood plank floor. A kitchen was built against another wall with a small table and chairs set on a woven rug for an eating area.

Dennis asked, "Do you get lonely here?"

"Oh, no, I have many pursuits and many friends to keep me occupied. Then there is the occasional 'adventure,' as I am sure you recall."

"Yes, it was touch-and-go for a while."

"And we would have failed except for Kara Triberg." Galdur looked down, expelling a small breath. "If not for her, I don't think we would have succeeded in our plan."

Dennis leaned forward. "That's what I'm here about. It seems Abaddon has gotten loose and is hunting for Dekker. We need someone with your tools—your skills—to do the job."

With a sigh, Galdur stood. "You are quite right about Abaddon. It caused quite a shockwave along the Flows. I've been investigating it for weeks and finally came to the conclusion it could only be accomplished with the help of a deep practitioner, someone with great powers in Magick, to release him from that confinement."

"Who would do that?" Dennis was incredulous. "Are many people capable of such a thing?"

"Very few, Dennis. And those that could do it would never want to."

"Never is a big word."

"So it is, and so it seems the evil spirit that inhabits Abaddon has won its release and is now free to continue its plan."

"I know about Abaddon's 'plan.' But I thought that was crushed five years ago."

"Yes, his plan was to turn the world on its head, to strip away man's dependence on the technology you are so passionate about, and end the international monetary system he thinks has been the downfall of man. He seeks to return the world to a state of reverence and dependence on Magick, where all men look up to practitioners such as himself for guidance through life.

"Not all of us want this new—or I should say, old—world order. The world, and mankind, has moved on. There are new realities now and they are to be respected as much as the Old Truths. There is a convergence happening, a blending of the natural order and technology. Man is engineering this with advances in science, medicine, communication, and even the arts. Eventually, it will all blend and there will be a new harmony between man and the world. But that harmony cannot be forced, it must be given the chance to evolve and find its new level, its new rhythm."

"Can Abaddon be stopped, or re-imprisoned?"

"That is the question." Galdur dropped himself back into the large overstuffed chair before the fireplace and let out another sigh. "I'm afraid youth is behind me. The struggle in the stone temple below Krugerschloss took more out of me than you might think, and yet, I too am angry at this turn of events. As I said, Abaddon could not have escaped without help from a deep practitioner with considerable power."

"Who would reach out to help resurrect Abaddon?"

"That is a very good question, one we'll not find the answer to here in the Iceland." Galdur stood again with resolve. "I must consult with Salim; I cannot hope to answer these questions without him. So I must contact him in the ruins of ancient Babylon."

"You are suggesting going there alone, or can I go with you?"

"I'm afraid not, Dennis. Your presence would be disquieting for Salim, and he will meet only with the deepest of practitioners. I am sorry."

"Why do you have to go there? Iraq is not exactly open to tourists."

"It is the location of the Great Nexus, the point of origin for all Flows, and Salim is the keeper of the Nexus and head of our order."

Dennis knew about the rivers of energy that crisscrossed the world. Galdur had even instructed him in their use for communication between those schooled in tapping into their power. "Can't you just contact Salim through the Flows and ask him to meet somewhere more hospitable?"

Galdur considered the question. "He rarely leaves his temple area, but I may be able to entice him to meet close by."

"Great. So while you're off to secret meetings, am I supposed to sit around here?"

"No, you must go home. What Dekker is facing cannot be helped with your technology." Dennis raised an eyebrow in question. "And I communicated with Dekker just hours ago."

"You spoke with him? Where is he? How is he?"

"Dennis, you must remember that the Flows do not work like your telephones. One can only send impressions, feelings, and images of things. What I can tell you is he is very conflicted. Abaddon has dealt him a great blow, one I'm not sure he will survive."

"His wife, Kelly," Dennis said softly. "She was murdered by what Dekker said was the Brotherhood, and he's been out for blood since."

"Yes, I know, but I also got the impression the Englishman you encountered before is the key to this whole thing."

"You mean Lord Geoffrey Stapleton?"

"The very man. He is more dangerous than you might think." Dennis considered the warning but Dekker was going after Abaddon alone, and in a state of mind that was not necessarily clear-thinking. It was a dilemma he would have to think about.

CHAPTER TWENTY-SIX

ANDRÉSSON PICKED UP DENNIS THE next morning, and continued on by bus to Reykjavik.

While en route Dennis thought more about Lord Geoffrey Stapleton. "He is a nobleman and a member of the English House of Lords. His family owns huge tracts of land in southwest England, including most of the Salisbury Plain where Stonehenge is located." It occurred to Dennis that Stonehenge was probably the source of the family's involvement with Magick and the Brotherhood.

"Why in the world would a prominent family get involved in all this superstitious bunk," Dennis wondered. But he quickly answered his own question. "The belief in supernatural powers—witches, spells, and the like—are deeply embedded in the English consciousness, especially in the countryside outside London. That's where all this Magick stuff comes from."

Dennis considered the origins of the Brotherhood, a topic he researched deeply soon after their last encounter with Abaddon. The belief system and its apparent ability to manipulate people and circumstances began at the dawn of civilization. The Druids, who dominated in Britain for centuries, were latecomers to the game. What he knew as the Brotherhood was actually descended from a well-established priesthood in the ancient world. They are even in the Bible. In the Moses story, the priesthood was there, duplicating all the miracles Moses performed. It's not questioned today, as people just accept it as told. But turning a stick into a snake or turning water into blood were no small feats.

That was the sort power Dekker faced in Abaddon. He decided he couldn't let his friend tackle it alone. Despite Jim Lynch's directive to come back to Washington, he would instead go to Krugerschloss.

CHAPTER TWENTY-SEVEN

DEKKER WAS DEEPLY DISTRUSTFUL OF Kamenwati and his offer, but the chance to get close to Abaddon was tempting enough to overlook his misgivings. If he accepted, Dekker knew he was getting into bed with the devil and the trick was controlling him, making him work toward his goal. He would accept Kamenwati's help, but on his own terms.

The first thing was to do is get on a correct footing with Kamenwati. Dekker had been captured, drugged, and transported against his will to this barge, and he needed to assert his position. He would start by protecting his mind and emotions from the psychic snooping of others.

The Egyptian mystic sat quietly as Dekker debated with himself. He reached out with his mind to discern what his captive was thinking but oddly found his probes ineffective. *How very interesting,* he thought, *this man has more depth than I expected.* He sensed a conflict in Dekker, which, given the circumstances, was to be expected. But he could discern no specifics, nor how the internal debate finished.

Dekker stood and walked to one of the salon's small rectangular windows. "I accept your help, but you must release me from here and promise not to follow me."

Kamenwati had his own internal debate, weighing the benefit of having Dekker working with him, versus the danger of letting him loose. What might he do, unsupervised and unguarded? That was the question, because in any iteration of the future, Dekker posed a threat to himself and his plan to take over Abaddon's empire. In the end had to accept Dekker's demands, at least for now, because he was certain he could surreptitiously keep track of the American.

"Very well, Mr. Dekker. You may leave whenever you wish. But tell me, what is it you plan?"

"I guess I plan to go to Krugerschloss. That's where I'll find Abaddon, right?"

"Yes, that is right, but I would caution against rushing headlong into the lion's den. It is where he has the most resources and is strongest."

"Okay, then, what would you recommend?"

"He must be lured to a place where you will at least have a fighting chance to defeat him."

"And where would that be?"

"Perhaps the Alder grove outside the caverns, or even here on this barge."

Dekker considered Kamenwati's strategy, weighing all angles, trying to determine the trap he might be stepping into. "Will Abaddon come to me? What is it that will tempt him enough to come out?"

"Setting him up to spring without thinking is my task; as to the bait, well, it's you, Mr. Dekker."

Dekker thought about that for a minute, considering the Egyptian's offer to make him the proverbial bait on a hook. And then he remembered the bait was never meant to survive, only to draw in and snag the intended prey. This was a very dangerous game and Dekker needed all his wits and skills if he hoped to survive.

That's interesting, he thought. *A short time ago I didn't care if I lived or died—now I'm thinking about survival.* Dekker looked the Egyptian straight in the eye. "You're on, Kamenwati. Now, how do you plan to get Abaddon out of his rock castle?"

Kamenwati gave Dekker a nod of acknowledgement, but inside he was relieved. Executing what was shaping up as an excellent plan could not work without Dekker's cooperation. He would provide a diversion to stage this coup—the most exqusite advantage being his hands will be clean because he can exploit Dekker's obsession to kill Abaddon.

The Egyptian outlined his plan to Dekker, making sure he kept an altruistic tone. Dekker took it in, looking at the elements from the standpoint of how it would benefit Kamenwati. He didn't trust the Egyptian; he was certain there was another objective, and indeed there was. Kamenwati did not tell Dekker he never intended to get Abaddon out of Krugerschloss, that his plan was to sabotage both Dekker and that fool Geoffrey before the assembly of Brothers and take control of Abaddon's empire.

Kamenwati asked what Dekker's next steps might be, and how he could interlock with the plan. "I'm not sure. I need to think this whole thing through," said Dekker. He needed to think about it, but not for the reasons Kamenwati suspected.

As the Egyptian took his leave he had a final thought for Dekker. "I'm late getting back to Krugerschloss, but you are welcome to use the barge as long as necessary. In fact, this will be our meeting place in the future." Dekker watched the Egyptian and his guards leave the barge, relieved; there was an oily feeling to his presence that was perceptible only when Kamenwati was gone.

Now was the time for action, and his first order of business was contacting Galdur. Was he strong enough—centered enough—to access the Flows and reach his friend? He sat in the barge salon thankful it was empty and quiet. He went through his relaxation routine and felt layers of stress and self-doubt peel away. He reached the meditative state where his mind was in tune with his body and remembered

Galdur's first lesson in accessing the Flows, a lesson learned on the edge of a fjord in Iceland. He approached the Flows carefully, almost timid about the process.

He remembered a time as a child when his father took him to a cabin on a lake to fish and swim. He recalled how cold the water was in the morning and how timid he was about getting in. His father told him he would get used to the water temperature faster if he jumped in, but at eight years old he simply could not do that. Instead, he stuck his feet in, then slipped in up to this knees, and so on. Eventually he made it into the water but vowed he would do it differently next time.

Dekker firmed his resolve and moved directly into the Flows, his consciousness swept up in the current of its passage. He did not want to wander too far, knowing he could get lost, and so found an anchor point to begin. He turned his intention to Iceland and his friend Galdur, and soon found his consciousness hovering outside the familiar cottage. He was very pleased when Galdur stepped out of the door and, standing on the porch, once again inviting Dekker inside.

The process of communication within the Flows is nonverbal; it relies on images to convey a message that is non-specific and often confusing. Only an experienced person using this technique on a regular basis could carry on a cohesive conversation. Dekker was certainly not an experienced person, but Galdur was. He was received with warmth and acceptance; the greeting of an old friend. It was a good feeling and there was no judgment from Galdur, only warm understanding.

Galdur knew nothing of what happened since his last communication while Dekker was drugged and bound. Dekker began with a series of images to show him what he'd been through, ending with Kamenwati enlisting his aid to defeat Abaddon. Galdur's reaction was immediate and was clear: the Egyptian was not to be trusted. *"Kamenwati has embraced the worst aspects of Magick, the most evil and destructive,"* said Galdur. Dekker was pleased to have confirmation of what he already believed. He would be vigilant for signs of treachery and keep his guard up.

Dekker outlined as best he could through the Flows, his plan to stop Abaddon, but he was unsure a physical attack would work. Galdur responded with a series of images showing Dekker that a frontal assault was the wrong approach. *"It might be appropriate in your world of special operations, but in the supernatural, mystical world, it will fail miserably. You must approach this attack with much more subtlety."*

Dekker asked, *"What steps must I take?"*

"Meet me in Baden-Baden, at the same hotel we used before." Dekker gratefully accepted the invitation, knowing he was less than an hour away from the famous resort area in the Black Forest.

Galdur indicated where they were to meet and Dekker began plans to reach the hotel.

CHAPTER TWENTY-EIGHT

KAMENWATI EMERGED FROM ABADDON'S chambers well pleased with the first part of his plan. He went into the audience knowing it was possible Abaddon would be alerted to his plot to overthrow him. The Egyptian had to offer up a candidate for subversion that was believable, diverting attention away from himself, and he did so masterfully.

"Master, Lord Geoffrey is planning some subversion. I met him as he returned from America. He had Dekker with him and claimed he was bringing him directly to you. That was two days ago."

Anger built quickly in Abaddon and he began lashing out. "Where is Dekker? And what has happened to that Englishman?" He crashed his fist on the desk. Kamenwati made no excuse for Lord Geoffrey and was happy the bait had been taken as presented. Abaddon dug no deeper and asked no more questions. The Egyptian let Abaddon rant for several minutes before suggesting he, Kamenwati, should summon Lord Geoffrey back to stand before him.

"Bring him to me, and the American as well. We will end this thing now!"

"As you wish, my lord. I will see to it."

FURY KNEW NO bounds in Abaddon's mind. How hard could it be to bring one man in? And what was Kamenwati up to? Abaddon was having trouble seeing the Egyptian's intentions, but he remembered the talisman he carried, the ashes of the Succubus. He shook off the thoughts as he remembered his present efforts.

Salim, the head of the Order in ancient Babylon was a long-standing thorn in Abaddon's side. Salim had great influence, not only because he presided over the convergence of the Flows, otherwise known as the great nexus, but also because he had the ability to control—even suspend—the function of the Flows. This capability gave Salim great leverage throughout the Brotherhood, and more specifically, over Abaddon, a shortcoming he would soon correct.

His first step was to contact the Consortium's secular arm in Baghdad, which on the whole, remained unscathed through the collapse of the Brotherhood. The members of the Consortium cell were not driven by fervor or ideology, they simply responded to greed.

The Baghdad organization was not large but they were loyal to Abaddon, so there was immediate cooperation when he contacted their leader. He did not question why Abaddon wished to remove the head of the Order; he accepted the Master wished it, and set about pleasing the one who could call down death upon them. The Baghdad Consortium leader, for his part, knew he must take care with this operation, for Salim, despite his mild-mannered ways, could call destruction upon them as quickly as Abaddon. So he planned a kidnapping, a proposition Abaddon very much liked. He ordered the cell to wait until the new moon, a time they could hold a ritual sacrifice without danger to themselves.

THE TELEPHONE ON Lord Geoffrey's desk rang. It was the private, unpublished number he used only for Krugerschloss business. "Just wonderful," he said under his breath. In his experience this telephone rang only when there was trouble, and he had half a mind to ignore it. But ignoring the call wouldn't make whatever problem there was go away. He had to face it.

"Hello?"

"Lord Geoffrey," said Kamenwati, "the Master wishes your return to Krugerschloss."

"When?"

"Immediately. When shall I tell him to expect you?"

Geoffrey looked at the antique clock on his desk and calculated the time it would take to get there, plus the one-hour difference. He gave Kamenwati the estimated time of arrival.

"Very good. By the way, I will not be in attendance. Other duties require my presence off site." Lord Geoffrey was uncomfortable with that arrangement and said so. "I'm afraid it can't be helped. The Master himself gave the order."

"And what is it I am being summoned for?"

"I don't know. He confides little in me, so I can only speculate."

"Please, speculate."

"I guess it has to do with the American."

"I left him with you, Kamenwati. Is there a problem?"

"Umm, yes. He seems to have gone missing." Lord Geoffrey could not believe what he was hearing. Could this day get any worse?

KAMENWATI LEFT TWO of the Brothers to spy on Dekker. They were to observe and follow, but not intercept or disrupt.

They had been in their positions for only an hour when Dekker appeared on deck. "There he is," said one guard. "Wonder where he might be going?" They watched Dekker look around the boat and step onto the gangway. He looked around again at the bottom of the gangway and walked across the dock area to a small building serving as the harbormaster's office and a captains' lounge.

Inside the office Dekker found an old man napping behind a desk that looked like World War II salvage—pitted, stained, and slightly off-level. He rapped on the wooden surface, wondering if hitting the old desk might cause it to collapse. It didn't, and the man woke with a start. The worn French seaman's cap on his head hardly covered the mass of white-gray hair, matched by extraordinarily bushy eyebrows. The old man was not the least bit embarrassed by his napping, and asked Dekker what he needed.

"I'm sorry, I don't speak French. Do you speak English?" The old man squinted at Dekker and told him he did speak a little English. "*Oui.*"

"Can you tell me where I am?"

The strange question was new one for the old man, and he gave Dekker a curious look. To answer the harbormaster's obvious question, Dekker made up a quick story. "I came in on a boat and lost track of time and place."

"*Êtes vous en* Strasbourg."

"France?

"*Oui.*"

"This is the Danube River, then, and on the other side is Baden-Baden?"

"*Oui*, but you can't sail there." The old captain laughed at his own joke.

"How might I get there? Are there buses or tours?"

"*Oui*, there are several but I have never been there myself. That's a place *le elite* go for holiday, and I don't much like the rich."

"Do you have a telephone I can use?"

"Local only, *non* calls to l'Allemagne." The old man lifted the ancient rotary dial telephone over to the edge of the desk. "And you'll ask for this next." He opened a drawer, lifting out a dog-eared directory and dropped it unceremoniously next to the telephone. It was in French.

"Can you help me find a bus service to Baden-Baden?" With a great effort the old man sat up and opened the telephone book. After thumbing through for a minute the old man slapped his hand on a page. *"Voila,* here are several."

"Merci," said Dekker, taking the book.

After a few minutes of looking at listings Dekker decided he liked the sound of *Voyage La France et l'Allemagne.* He called, requested an English-speaking attendant, was transferred, and reached a nice lady who booked him a seat on a bus leaving in an hour. He gave a memorized credit card number to hold the seat and asked where to meet the bus. It turned out they made several stops throughout the city, one of which was at the Aerodrome de Strasbourg-Neuhof, a private aviation field quite close to Dekker's location.

"Merci, madamosielle. You have been a great help." He replaced the handset and looked at the old man. "And you, *monsieur,* have been a great help as well."

"Humph," was all the old man had to say, sat back in his chair, and placed his feet up on the desk as Dekker found him, satisfied to go back to his nap.

Dekker set out on an easy walk following railroad tracks for a short distance and then cutting through some trees to the Rue de la Musau, leading straight to the airfield. A Saudi organization maintained an office in the main building, and Dekker was not allowed to enter without a reservation. So he sat on a bench outside and waited for the tour bus.

KAMENWATI'S BROTHERHOOD GUARDS watched Dekker leave the rickety building and head into the woods beyond. They followed. When they saw the small airfield, they assumed Dekker had arranged a charter flight, but then watched with surprise as he sat on a bench outside the terminal building.

Soon a tour bus pulled up to the building and Dekker spoke a few words to the driver, and then boarded. The guards looked at one another, certain this was not part of Kamenwati's plan. The doors closed and the bus pulled away long before the guards could hope to catch it. They would simply had to go back to the barge and wait. The only good thing was the tour bus name, *La France et l'Allemagne,* suggesting Dekker was heading to the Black Forest resort town of Baden-Baden.

Kamenwati did not react the way the Brotherhood guards expected when they reached him by satellite telephone. They expected he'd be angry and lash out at them. Instead, the Egyptian took their report with equanimity, even a little pleasure, and told the men to stay with the barge. He summoned a new group of four Brothers, instructing them to search for Dekker in Baden-Baden and hold him in place. The adepts were puzzled by his orders but did not want to question such a powerful man. Their unspoken concern was the orders were at odds with the Master's. Why hold the American? Why not bring him immediately to Krugerschloss? The Adepts surmised something else was going on, but followed their orders, not wanting to be in the middle of some struggle between Kamenwati and Abaddon.

THE BUS RIDE was uneventful, giving Dekker the opportunity to re-center himself, now that he knew where he was going. Galdur would be waiting for him at one of the older inns, the BKH Baden-Baden, located outside the main town on Waldenstrasse. He was looking forward to seeing Galdur and enjoying the calm surety of his presence, and most importantly, hearing his advice about Kamenwati.

Dekker needed to buy new clothes; he had been in his present clothes for several days, and he stood out as an American. The resort town was full of shops and boutiques, each with a specialty. He wasn't looking for fashion, just utility. Walking along the sidewalk he remembered the first assault on Krugerschloss, when his friends were with him and his world was still right. He thought about Dennis; he knew the young man would be doing something rash and probably misdirected to help him, and he smiled. And Jim Lynch, Dekker's old friend and the Deputy Director of the NCTC, who saw him through many tense missions and celebrated his victories. He wondered how this one would turn out; he wasn't giving it much of a chance for good.

Dekker's thoughts turned dark again thinking about his present situation. He was going to face a madman who'd ordered the killing of his wife, and then what? What did he think would happen? If he got lucky, the surprise of seeing Dekker would give him the time, the split second, necessary to attack and kill the freak. On the other hand, if his plan was discovered or revealed, Dekker might not make it beyond the front entrance of the mountain castle. He shook off thoughts of failure; he focused instead on the grim satisfaction he would have defeating Abaddon.

After buying clothing and boots suitable for hiking through the forest, Dekker found a taxi that to drive him to the hotel, one he remembered well from the last encounter with Abaddon.

When the taxi dropped him at the main building he discovered Galdur had yet to check in, but he left a message that Dekker should take a room; he would be along.

CHAPTER TWENTY-NINE

ORIGEN FELT UNEASY AFTER LORD Geoffrey's departure. He was happy to see him leave with the captive, yet this episode left him anxious.

He thought again of his roots in Europe, in and among the Romani. It was a society apart, living by its own rules, a people who would let him disappear. He determined the Consortium enterprise was no longer worth the risk, and he must take precipitous action to avert a storm.

The coming of the Englishman to oversee the capture of one man was far beyond the ordinary. Coupled with the calls from the newly resurrected Abaddon, he felt the Consortium system crumbling. Origen realized he was afraid—fearful of the implosion of a system that would surely crush him in its collapse. The trick was going to be extracting himself without anyone knowing—especially Lord Geoffrey, and most especially, Abaddon.

His decision made, Origen contacted some well-placed individuals to call in favors. He would get out, or at least get far away, until the storm passed.

RUSTY AND HIS surveillance team approached Origin's manor house on Patuxent River Road. He was unsure of Origen's psychic or paranormal abilities, and he had only a sketchy idea of what an Abaddon mystic could do. He decided to move in with a small force—only four men—to accomplish Jim Lynch's order.

The team was arrayed in a line through the woods, each man within the sight of the next, Rusty in the center. They proceeded slowly, trying not to make noise in the deadfall that covered the forest floor. Each man carried a small backpack over his camouflage jumpsuit, a sidearm strapped to one leg, and a short-barreled assault rifle. Rusty was taking no chances.

Origen kept a sizable security squad at the manor, and Rusty had seen all of them armed during his previous, and unsuccessful, effort to rescue Dekker. As the team approached the tree line, Rusty stopped, holding a fist up. He watched an automobile leaving the side portico, kicking up gravel as it raced up the main road.

"Nuts," Rusty said. "Someone got away. I wonder what the hurry is?" He knew there was no way to get back to their vehicles and follow; instead they would continue the operation.

Rusty would soon find it was Origen who escaped their carefully planned trap.

CHAPTER THIRTY

GALDUR WAITED PATIENTLY AT A rooming house in a poor neighborhood of Baghdad, expecting the arrival of Salim, the head of his order and the guardian of the Great Nexus. Galdur was disturbed by Salim's silence on the Flows, and he had a growing suspicion something was wrong.

Earlier appeals persuaded Salim to help his Icelandic brother confront and defeat Abaddon once and for all. They arranged to meet in Baghdad to make plans in person, since anything communicated through the Flows was open to interception. Salim indicated there was not a day to loose, that time worked in Abaddon's favor and against them. The urgency of Salim's request was not lost on Galdur.

As the sun went down, Galdur listened to the Islamic call to prayers issuing through loudspeakers on the tower of a nearby mosque. He did not follow Islam, nor did Salim or any of his order. The beliefs of the Brotherhood were based on a far older system, predating even the Jewish beliefs—although many of the Jewish tenants and traditions, particularly the mystical as codified in the Kabbalah, came from ancient Brotherhood beliefs.

Galdur received a sharp call in the Flows. It was Salim. *Yes, my brother?*

Galdur, I have been betrayed and am held captive.

Can you tell me where?

Not exactly, but I can hear the mu'adin *calling salat.*

I will find you.

Take care, Galdur. They are listening and will be looking for you.

Salim cut off the communication, but at least Galdur had a place to start. If he heard the *mu'adin*, then his old friend was close. He needed to concentrate on identifying Salim's life force, his aura, to track him. It required some skill not to give away his hunt for the mystic, something he had not done for many years. Galdur prepared himself mentally and spiritually, and then set off into the darkening night.

Evening prayers were complete and the streets were once again full of people and noise.

He began by finding the mosque that broadcast the prayers. It turned out to be a modest structure with a small, walled courtyard and a tall spire. Galdur concentrated on his external sense, pushing it outward to "feel" the crowds and environment to search for Salim. He moved slowly around the mosque, hoping to get a sense of his friend. His circuit of the mosque revealed nothing, so he moved outward by two streets, perhaps one hundred yards, using the mosque as his center point, and began another circuit.

It wasn't until his fourth circuit, placing him about a one-half mile from the mosque, that he sensed Salim. He couldn't make a direct appeal through the Flows since that might give him away to those holding Salim. Instead he was forced to rely on a laborious search process to zero-in on Salim's location.

After an hour of searching and probing, Galdur spotted the building. It was a squat, low structure that looked like a storage shed or livestock barn. He watched it closely for some time, looking for activity inside. There were no lights, but Galdur sensed the presence of several people inside, including Salim. How to get his friend out? This was an occasion when he could use Dekker's skills and experience; he would know how to approach this situation. Thinking about Dekker brought several stories to mind about his more harrowing rescues, and the lessons learned.

Galdur concentrated on remembering Dekker's words, something he'd never imagined he'd need. As Galdur searched his memory, a theme emerged: Dekker rarely went in shooting, relying instead on stealth, distraction, and diversion. This was a principle that resonated with the principles of Magick and something Galdur thought he could use.

Dekker told him once that he often used explosions for to divert and distract. It was the sharp report, the startling sound, and the unexpected activity that was key to a successful distraction. Often something small, but out of place, would do the trick, and Galdur thought this might be his best course. The question was, what would that be his best course of action?

Galdur sat in a shadowed area of a wall to watch and concentrate on the building. He had several distraction ideas, but discarded each for one reason or another, ending with the easiest deceit of all.

Concentrating on the men guarding Salim inside, he realized none were particularly skilled in the ways of Magick. Their minds were consumed with thoughts of the reward they would receive when the skinny old man was turned over. Galdur could not perceive whom these men reported to, but his assumption was someone within the Consortium. Who else would order this abduction? It was nothing short of blasphemy, an unimaginable offense to the Order. Only one person Galdur knew leveraged that sort of influence or generated enough fear to overcome ancient taboos: Abaddon. His reasoning led to the conclusion that Abaddon was conducting a quiet operation to seize, and most probably kill, all remaining Brotherhood leadership, leaving him the undisputed Master.

What evil possesses this man? Galdur wondered. *He wants to consolidate all power in himself.*

Galdur perceived the men guarding his friend were not going to hand him over to anyone or take him anywhere. They were waiting for an order to sacrifice their prisoner. Why were wait so long? It struck him the new moon would take place tonight, a celestial event creating the darkest of nights, suitable for the most evil of deeds.

SALIM SAT IN silence, knowing what was to come. His only act of self-preservation was contacting Galdur, and so he sat quietly waiting for the situation to develop. He knew his powers could easily overwhelm the four guards, but to use his abilities in such a way would dishonor all he stood for, everything he professed, in the last seventy years. His dilemma kept him immobilized in an endless rationale loop, debating what action to take.

The result of his internal argument was inaction, and that grieved him. His only hope was in Galdur, who was much wiser in the ways of the world. Perhaps he could see through his artificially constricted sense of self-preservation and offer a suitable solution.

Salim felt Galdur's approach. His spirit lifted, feeling his answer was at hand. The problem was the guards. How would Galdur get past the guards, and assuming he could do that, how would he attain his freedom? These were questions without answers that fed right back into his core dilemma.

He disengaged from the inward battle to watch something strange happening to his jailers—each was nodding off to sleep! In a few moments all four had slumped or slouched into more comfortable positions, and soon the sound of snoring filled the small building. Salim was going to call out but received a strong check to his spirit.

Be still. Wait.

He heard and obeyed.

After a few minutes a small door opened and Salim saw Galdur's silhouette outlined against the dark night sky. In a moment Galdur navigated around the sleeping guards and ritual sacrifice table, with its assorted knives, hooks, and gouges, to reach Salim. Galdur was fully robed and hooded, with only his eyes exposed. But in those eyes he saw the concern Galdur had for his safety. Overcome with joy Salim began to speak thanks, but Galdur stopped him, indicating he should follow.

Galdur retraced his route through sleeping men and equipment, and the two left the building. Galdur whispered a warning to his friend. "We're not out of this yet. Remain quiet and follow me." Salim did as Galdur asked, following him into the inky darkness of the city's back streets.

They stopped to avoid contact with people, but because the hour was late, there were few roaming the streets and alleys. They moved quickly, at almost a jog, changing direction often. Salim saw the spire of a mosque off to the right, and a little later it was on the left. Finally the mosque was behind them and there was a distinct feeling of release— the danger was, for now, behind them.

Galdur stepped into a doorway, stopping to rest.

"You found me, Galdur."

"Yes, and if I'm not mistaken, not a moment too soon."

"What do you mean?"

"You were to be executed tonight." He looked up into the dark sky. "It is the new moon." Salim followed his gaze and nodded.

Galdur outlined the plan for Salim. It was the reverse of his entry route into Iraq, one that avoided government interference. "It's not so comfortable and it will require many hours, but it will take us to Beirut and on to our final destination."

"How will we remain undetected by Abaddon?"

"He is distracted by other issues, so for the time being if we stay off the Flows we should have no trouble. My concern is crossing the desert frontier through Syria."

They moved carefully down the quiet streets, doing their best to avoid police or militia patrols. With their perceptive skills it was not hard to evade the many patrols and they ended at a large truck-marshaling yard.

"This is where we will find the Brother waiting for us."

"Here? In this sea of mechanical monsters?" Salim was aghast at the thought of so much machinery.

"Take it easy, Salim, not all our brethren are as strict in their beliefs and customs as you." Salim thought about Galdur's comment for a moment, realizing that inflexible orthodoxy would not help them escape—or defeat Abaddon.

Galdur got to his feet and asked Salim to stay where he was. "I must find Ali, our driver." Salim was content to sit for the moment and watched his friend disappear into the inky darkness.

CHAPTER THIRTY-ONE

RUSTY TRUSTED HIS TEAM TO execute the plan they discussed before deploying to assault the manor house. Two men would move around to the rear while he and the others entered the house through the portico doorway.

As Rusty approached the portico he saw a guard lazily step from behind a column at the front door. He dropped to the ground, as did the other two men with him. The guard was armed but clearly weary of his sentry duty, stretching his arms, yawning, and returning to his position behind the column.

Rusty thanked the heavens he happened to see the guard. With a hand signal he sent Mitchell, the man to his right, to take care of the sentry. Mitchell moved with surprising speed to the front, hiding behind the very column shielding the sentry from view. Rusty and Donaldson, the man on his left, continued toward the portico doorway.

As Rusty and Donaldson reached the door they heard a muffled struggle, and then silence. Rusty motioned to wait, and a moment later Mitchell joined them. He nodded to success of the take down, and the three men moved into the manor house.

In the rear, the remaining two NCTC operatives scouted the yard and into the trees for a short distance, but found nothing threatening. Rusty briefed the team on the light surveillance around the house, a peculiarity of their belief system. "But it works in our favor today," Rusty said, and the men were pleased to discover he was right. They approached the steps up to the rear door and entered the house.

Rusty and his two men found themselves in a short hallway, an elongated room, really, connecting to a hall leading off left and right. He was unfamiliar with the layout of the house but suspected the security center was in the rear. He dispatched Mitchell and Donaldson to handle the rear, while he searched for Origen in the front part of the house.

The two operatives entering from the rear found themselves outside the security center where they heard talk among the guards.

"This is bullshit," one voice said. "Are we supposed to just sit around and wait? Wait for what?"

"I dunno," another said. "The boss told us to sit tight. I don't know about you, but what the boss says, goes." There were sounds of agreement from the others in the room.

"Hey, kid, check on your monitors and see if Stanley is asleep out front." The young guard, the one who was now the hero for spotting Dekker, went over to his bank of monitors.

"Holy shit! He's down," the young guard shouted.

"Waddaya mean down? He's probably just taking a nap," the first voice said.

"No, I mean he's down in a heap. I think someone is out there." A general scuffling and sliding of chairs indicated the other guards were moving over to the monitors to see for themselves.

The two NCTC operatives looked to one another, nodded in agreement, and stormed into the security center. As they did, both Mitchell and Donaldson rushed the room from another door, pouring in after their teammates. The four operatives caught the guards completely by surprise, gathering them up and securing their hands with cuff ties. "This is sweet," said Mitchell. "You two stay here and guard these guys while Donaldson and I help Rusty."

Rusty was unaware of the action in the security center since he was going room-to-room in the front of the house. He was surprised to find the rooms empty; he expected to find some sort of activity. He reached the front entry where he spoke to Origen about searching the house, and where he was stopped by the owner's insistence on a search warrant. He now had the warrant in his pocket, but with the abduction of Dekker and the direct involvement of NCTC, the stakes had grown considerably. Now it was a matter of national security and the gloves were off. But there was no one here, nobody to take into custody.

Mitchell and Donaldson came down the hallway to the entrance area, finding Rusty looking around in disappointment. "Hey, boss, you'd like to know we've got the whole security crew rounded up in the back," said Mitchell.

Rusty looked relieved. "At least we've got something." He followed his two men back to the security center and began questioning the guards.

"Where is Origen?" There was silence and a few glances between the captive guards. Rusty, in frustration, stepped up to one and grabbed him by the shirt. "Where is Origen?" The man flinched but remained mute. He then went to the young guard. "Tell me where to find Origen."

The young guard whimpered and then said, "He's gone. He told us all to wait in here. I don't know where he went, he only said he was late for a flight." Rusty relaxed and knew there were only so many airports to cover. He made a call to NCTC and an FBI team was dispatched to take the guards into custody and further interrogation. Rusty left, heading for the nearest airport—BWI.

CHAPTER THIRTY-TWO

GALDUR FELT HE WAS SEARCHING for the proverbial needle in a haystack. He knew the truck he sought, but where in this sea of vehicles might it be? He would have to be patient and inspect every truck. "My goodness, there must be a hundred or more!" It took more than an hour, but he finally spotted the rig parked near the rear fence.

He knew Ali, the owner and driver, slept in a small compartment in the rear of the tractor. He almost never left the rig when he was on the road—it was the best way to prevent theft and vandalism. A quiet knock on the tractor door roused Ali, who was happy to see Galdur. "A blessing on you, master Galdur. I was beginning to wonder if you were going to return."

"I told you it would take time, but now I'm ready to go."

"And the man you came to find?"

"He is close by and also ready. May we leave?"

"The yard is closed right now, so we'll have to wait for dawn before we can get into the queue for Route 2." Galdur understood and told Ali he would return with Salim for the journey to Beirut.

WHEN GALDUR AND Salim returned, Ali opened the rear of the forty-foot trailer. The inside was loosely packed with crates, bales, and bundles, each stenciled in Arabic indicating their contents. Galdur did not read or speak the language, but Salim did.

"You will be riding with shoes and carpets," he translated.

"I hope we get the softer ones," said Galdur.

Ali explained they would have to be confined in the trailer for only a short while, just long enough to get through the government checkpoint, and then a little farther on there was an insurgent checkpoint to extort travelers for "safety fees"—a new take on the old highwayman game. Galdur and Salim would ride in two large crates in the forward portion of the load, accessed by cleverly disguised side hatches. Squeezing down the side of the trailer, they reached the crates Ali opened for them.

"No stops before we're clear, so here is some water for each of you. Good luck."

Galdur was pleased to find his crate filled with woven rugs and made himself comfortable. He rapped on the wooden wall of his crate to signal Salim and was pleased to receive a return signal. He was exhausted from the exertion and the tension of the night's activity, and fell right to sleep. Even the bump of the rig starting to move did not disturb him.

After some time Galdur awoke and felt the truck pulling to a stop; he heard the back door open, and then footsteps. The sound stopped right outside his crate and he watched apprehensively as the crate opened, the light of day hurting his eyes.

"You can come out now, master Galdur. We are through the checkpoints and are on our way to Beirut."

Galdur crawled gratefully out of his crate and helped Ali release Salim. They were both happy to be out and climbed into the cab, ready for the trip across the Syrian Desert.

CHAPTER THIRTY-THREE

DENNIS TOOK A FLIGHT TO Frankfurt where he cleared customs, and then on to Stuttgart where he went in search of a car rental agency. He selected a small German firm offering small, underpowered Mercedes sedans. He hoped renting from a local off-brand company would obscure his trail, hoping it might take a little longer for someone to track him down.

He set out on the roughly fifty-mile trip to Baden-Baden where he would begin looking for Dekker. As he approached the resort town he remembered their last visit when they planned and divided up roles and responsibilities. Back then no one knew they were coming, but now it was an entirely new circumstance. If he knew Dekker, he would be staying outside the town, probably in the same hotel they used before, in an effort to keep a low profile. He believed this is where Dekker would go before launching his infiltration operation, and it was his best bet to connect with him.

As luck would have it Dennis' arrival at the BKA Baden-Baden coincided with Dekker's check-in. Dennis called the room and was surprised by his friend's reaction—it was distracted and cool, not what he expected. "Come to the room, Dennis. We need to talk."

Inside the room he found Dekker surrounded by maps, walking trails, and a hiking guide. Dennis knew what was up, but looked at the scene with some dismay. "How are you, Dekker?" He didn't get up from the couch; he only looked at Dennis while putting down one of the maps he was studying. After a long moment Dekker addressed the young computer expert.

"You shouldn't be here, Dennis. There's nothing you can do, no way you can help."

Dennis stepped into the room, his resolve set. "You don't know that. I can be a great asset—you know that from the last time. Besides, Abaddon and everyone in Krugerschloss must know you are coming and you need someone unknown, me, to be there. You don't know what kind of help you may need, but if I'm not there, there's no one to provide it."

Dennis' passion broke through Dekker's argument, and his look softened. "You know what, Dennis? You're right. I need a wing man, and someone with a knowledge of this situation." Dekker let out a breath and sat back in the sofa. "You are a stubborn man, and I actually expected you to come up with something like this."

Dekker's anxiety increased as time passed with no sign of Galdur. He considered striking out on his own to reach Abaddon, but he was afraid to do so.

Afraid. That word had never been part of his life or thinking. His training and experience helped him ignore natural fears experienced by all soldiers, turning it into focus and resolve. But this unreasoning fear of Abaddon—where did that come from? Perhaps because he'd managed to reach right into his home to kill both his wife and his dog; perhaps it was Abaddon's ability to operate on a different plane, in a different reality. Whatever it was, Dekker was bound by fear, and it was the promised assistance from Galdur that seemed to offer him a way out of that pit. *But Galdur is not here,* he thought.

Dennis observed his friend with some concern. He misunderstood Dekker's anxiety, thinking it was about the NCTC. "We met with Mr. Lynch to explain the situation," he said. "Rusty and I told him you were not a fugitive, but a prisoner and that we had to help you."

"It all goes back to the attack on my ranch."

"It goes even further than that," Dennis said. "It started when someone brought Abaddon back. I have no idea who would want to do such a thing, but he's back and it seems you're the object of his obsession."

"Yes, I sort of figured that out on my own."

"Your flight on Stapleton's jet took you to Strasbourg. How did you escape, and why are you here in Baden-Baden?" Dennis asked.

"Those are some big questions. Let me start with my so-called escape. There is another player in this game, an Egyptian mystic named Kamenwati. He's a big figure in the

Brotherhood, and not necessarily an Abaddon supporter. But something happened, his own ambition, I suppose, and he came to Krugerschloss. I believe he is the one who set Abaddon free. My suspicion also includes Lord Geoffrey—you remember him. In any event, the deed was done and Kamenwati is now Abaddon's right-hand man."

"How do you know all this, Dekker?"

"Kamenwati told me. When the plane landed I figured I was on my way to meet my fate at Krugerschloss, but I wasn't. I ended up on a barge on the Danube, talking to Kamenwati." Dekker walked around the room, trying to decide how to phrase the next revelation. "He made me an offer I found hard to refuse."

"An offer?"

"You have to understand, I've not been myself." Dekker's voice caught and it took a moment for him to regain his composure. "Since the attack on Vallecito, I've been crazy with anger. I knew who ordered this terrible thing, and I had only one thought in mind: Vengeance."

Dennis remained silent, waiting for Dekker to continue.

"That blind anger cut me off from all the things that gave my life meaning, and I simply lost my way. Until I received a message from Galdur while still drugged on that plane. I'm not sure how he got through to me, I suppose it was the drugs lowering my resistance to an outside voice coming into my head, but he told me about the danger ahead, that I'd need help, and I was to meet him at this inn in Baden-Baden. I couldn't believe how close I was when we landed. The fire inside me was re-kindled, and when presented with Kamenwati's proposal, I jumped at his deal."

"What was the deal, Dekker?" Dennis asked, concerned.

"He said he could get me in front of Abaddon, and from there I could kill him."

Dennis looked at his friend with doubt in his eyes. "You trust this guy, this Kamenwati?" After thinking, Dekker hung his head, shaking it.

"No, in the end I don't trust Kamenwati. I think he sees me as a pawn to get what he wants."

"And what is that?"

"I think he wants to be the big man. He wants to replace Abaddon."

"What are you going to do?"

"Kamenwati left me on the barge with no real guards. He was confident I wouldn't go anywhere and he wanted to demonstrate that I was not, despite what it looked like, a prisoner."

Dennis leaned in to Dekker, a concerned look on his face. "And you decided to get out of there?"

"That's right, Dennis. I figured the longer I was under Kamenwati's influence, the fewer my choices would be. Kamenwati left only two men to watch me; I ditched them, hopped a bus, and ended up here, waiting for Galdur. How about you? How did you happen to end up at this inn?"

"Mr. Lynch sent me to Iceland to find Galdur. When I found him he was worried for you. He told me to go home, that this was not my fight. And I almost did go back, but I realized I was probably the only person in the world, other than Galdur, who knew what you were facing, so I changed my ticked and came here."

"Thanks, Dennis, but Galdur was right. The help I need is less temporal and more spiritual, and I was hoping he would show up for just that reason."

Dennis continued. "Galdur will show up. He said he would, so you can count on it. Something must have happened to him along the way, but he will be here. Meanwhile, we can get a jump on this, and I can help you."

Dekker saw there was no deterring the young NCTC analyst, so gave in. "All right, Dennis, I can see it won't do any good to argue."

Now that it seemed Galdur was a no-show, Dekker had to face Abaddon alone. He intended to leave Dennis in the room to wait for the Icelander, giving him instructions to fill Galdur in on his plan. He gave one last look around the room, and with an air of finality, closed the door behind him, setting his gaze on the forest in the distance. He was brought to a quick stop when a car came flying into the parking area, kicking up rocks and dust as it slid to a halt. Dekker ducked for cover and watched as four men emerged from the car. He returned to the room and collected Dennis. "Looks like we need to get out of here."

CHAPTER THIRTY-FOUR

ABADDON PACED AROUND HIS QUARTERS, his anger rising with each step and each unanswered call to the Consortium leader in Baghdad. The new moon passed and he did not feel Salim's death. He began lashing out at any acolyte crossing his path, and he sent a group of them running in fear when, in anger, he struck one of their number dead.

The Consortium leader finally made contact with the Master and began with a jumbled apology and explanation of what happened to their sacrifice. Abaddon heard enough to know that Salim received help and somehow escaped. But who helped? Where did he go? Could Dekker possibly be involved? Abaddon let the last question hang as he thought about how to respond. He had half a thought to go there himself and take charge, but he knew Salim was gone and most probably far away from Baghdad.

Abaddon was accustomed to having scores of loyal believers around, jumping to please his every whim. His numbers at Krugerschloss were growing, but slowly. There were still too few acolytes and fewer Adepts to carry out tasks. He longed for the days when his loyal believers would jump off a cliff, like so many lemmings, if he asked it. Now, such an order would be a foolish waste of manpower and Abaddon was reduced to considering taking direct action himself.

Abaddon focused his psychic energies on Salim, although he knew the use of a Word of Denial would deflect his search. He would have to go about this in a less obvious way. "I will summon Geoffrey."

A CONSORTIUM TEAM sent by Kamenwati to look for Dekker arrived at an open parking lot, rolling to a halt behind Dennis' rental car. The SUV driver let the others out. "Look around for him, he must be here somewhere. I'll wait out on the main road to see if he tries to escape."

The four men got out and walked as casually as possible to the inn's main office. They found a clerk and, in German, asked about a rear exit.

"Why do you want a back door?" The clerk looked more closely at the determined men and thought better of his answer. "It's through the kitchen." He pointed to a doorway and the pursuers hurried to the back. They found the kitchen staff busily preparing lunch; they moved through the kitchen, taking little care for the people or equipment they bumped into.

The Kamenwati's pursuers burst out of the back kitchen door and saw nothing. There was no one around, and no car hiding behind the inn. They went back inside and grabbed the first kitchen worker they could.

"Is there a back road into this place?" The tone was none too kind, and the staff person was afraid. He couldn't answer—only nod his head. "Where? Is there a road?"

The kitchen worker nodded again, but this time spoke. "B-behind the shed."

The pursuers ran back through the kitchen, out the front door, and back out to the parking lot. They explained breathlessly the fugitive had given them the slip using a rear access road. The SUV driver swore again and looked closely at his dashboard mounted GPS unit. "The maps don't show a road back there." The pursuers got back in as the driver spun the big vehicle around and headed back down the access road around the inn, to the back area where they saw a small road leading behind a storage shed. They took off down the road certain they would catch their man. Their confidence waned when they discovered the access road led into town. "He could have gone anywhere," said the man riding in the passenger seat.

"I think we're going to have to report this," said the driver. "The longer this goes on, the worse it will be for us."

What the team did not know is that Dekker and Dennis waited for their hasty departure hidden in the nearby forest.

WHEN KAMENWATI RECEIVED the report from Baden-Baden he decided to take matters regarding Dekker into his own hands. He didn't like the idea of the American running around the countryside outside his control, and wondered what had set him off. He believed Dekker was a willing part of his plan, even though he had no idea what that really meant. Kamenwati believed Dekker's anger and need for revenge would keep him blind to the reality of what was taking place. But now it seemed the American had taken advantage of the loose supervision and set out on a plan of his own.

Stupid man, he thought. *He needs me to get to Abaddon; there is no other way to get close.*

Kamenwati knew Dekker boarded a tour bus to Baden-Baden but he could not understand why Dekker would head to the resort town, since his starting point in Strasbourg was considerably closer to Krugerschloss than Baden-Baden. Something else was going on, and Kamenwati thought it more than coincidental Lord Geoffrey also had men in Baden-Baden.

CHAPTER THIRTY-FIVE

THE CROSSING OF THE SYRIAN desert was going well. Ali turned out to be a talkative and entertaining host, his jokes and anecdotes about local politicians and leaders keeping Galdur in stitches. Ali turned to serious subjects, like the emerging caliphate and how it was sweeping Iraq and Syria like wildfire. Salim did not understand the jokes but he did understand the politics of radical Islam.

They were well on their way to the Lebanese border and pulling up to the fourth and final desert checkpoint, expected their passage to go as smoothly as the first three.

As they approached the walled checkpoint it became clear this would not be a perfunctory search. Someone was looking for something, and Galdur feared he and Salim were that something. The joking ceased and Ali suggested the men get back into their crates. He pulled the truck off to the road and lifted the hood to appear he was fixing some mechanical problem. Galdur and Salim used the diversion to re-enter the hiding places in the rear. With his passengers safely returned to their crates, Ali got back in the line of vehicles waiting to enter the checkpoint.

Ali's truck finally made it to the front of the line, and dark-clad warriors—ISIS militants, not government soldiers—greeted them. Ali did not like the look of this crew and he tried to anticipate what they might ask. When Ali stopped for inspection he became frightened.

"What is your cargo?" One of the inspectors demanded.

Ali tried to buy some time to think with a diversionary question of his own. "Who are you? I was expecting to see my cousin. He usually works this checkpoint."

By way of an answer the man lifted his AK-47 to Ali's face. Ali jumped back in fear. "I'll ask again, what is your cargo?"

"Only textile goods. You know, rugs, blankets, shoes, and bags."

"Where did you come from?"

"Baghdad, in the terminal lot."

"Did you see two old men?"

"Two old men? There are many old men in Baghdad."

"One was a foreigner, the other we're not sure about. But we assume they would attempt to buy passage out of the country; were you approached about that?"

"I was not approached."

"Open the back. We will inspect."

Ali reluctantly got out, walked to the rear of the truck, and unlocked the doors. The so-called inspectors climbed inside and began tapping crates, looking for anything unusual or out of place. They checked the seals on many crates, especially those large enough to hide a man. Salim concentrated on creating a Cloud around their crates as the militants worked their way to the rear of the trailer. They found nothing.

"You may continue," said the man who questionrd Ali. Salim's Cloud had worked.

Several miles down the road, as the traffic thinned out, Ali pulled the truck off the road and let his passengers out of hiding. "That was close," he said. "Those were not government guards. And they didn't seem local. I believe they were ISIS militia."

"What do you mean?"

"They recruit from all over the world, and the one who spoke with me had a funny accent." Galdur nodded his head and climbed into the cab after Salim.

"We can't worry about that now. The good news is we got through."

"Yes, we got through, but it was very close," Salim said, still visibly shaken.

They drove on in silence until reaching the Lebanese border. Once through, the mood in the truck lightened perceptibly. Ali began telling jokes and stories again and everyone seemed to relax.

"How are we to travel on from here, Ali?" Salim was apparently calm enough to think more than an hour into the future.

"Have no fear. You are going on a small sea voyage."

"I pray we do not have to ride in a box."

"No, you will both have berths in the crew's quarters." Salim seemed to like the prospect of a proper bed and nodded in approval.

"My cousin has made all the arrangements and will connect you with transportation for your overland journey into Germany."

AT THE PORT of Beirut, the goods Ali carried were offloaded to a warehouse and awaited transshipment overseas. Galdur and Salim took their leave of the resourceful Ali, who gave them a small bundle of cash and a blessing. "I pray your journey will come to a successful end."

Galdur and Salim boarded a cargo ship heading for Genoa, relaxing for the first time in two days. Galdur felt safe enough to use the Flows to reach Dekker, but was Dekker in a mental state that enabled him to hear the call? He did not know, but he must try.

Galdur and Salim sailed without incident, yet there was still no contact from Dekker. Galdur had grave concerns, and expressed them to Salim.

"The Flows can sometimes be fickle," said Salim. "For example, there are forces that interfere with the atmosphere and its ability to carry messages. This often happens when there is a storm, or the sun is disturbed."

"Yes, that could be it," Galdur acknowledged. "But still, that it should happen now…is that too much coincidence?" Salim had no reply. Galdur could only wait patiently to connect with Dekker.

The merchant ship docked in Genoa and their trip was thankfully uneventful. The two mystics were escorted to a bus terminal where they purchased tickets to Stuttgart, with onward passage to Baden-Baden. From that point they would have to make their own way into the Black Forest, since no one knew exactly where Krugerschloss was located.

CHAPTER THIRTY-SIX

RUSTY LISTENED TO THE CAPTURED guards with increasing concern. How would he find and stop Origen now? BWI was the obvious point of escape, but would Origen do the obvious? He couldn't leave the guards unattended, so he decided to leave his small squad in place to await the arrival of the FBI and pursue the fugitive.

He began by requesting a "no fly" order for Origen from any DC area airport, but with a good hour head start, Rusty knew his man could be anywhere by now. He had to put himself in the fugitive's mindset: how would he react to the situation at his house? He saw Origen leave, but where did he go? Would he chance an airport, knowing someone could easily alert TSA? These were questions he rolled over in his mind as he returned to his car and began a pursuit.

ORIGEN'S FIRST INCLINATION was to get away as fast as possible, thinking a flight to a non-extradition country was his best course of action. But as he calmed down, he thought better of that idea.

He approached the interchange for Interstate 95 and made his decision. He wouldn't do what the Feds expected. "I'll drive to Miami where I can get a boat and head for Cuba or Jamaica." Origen took the southbound entrance to the freeway, heading for the 495 Beltway and onward through Richmond, and then to Miami, a nine hundred seventy-mile trip.

As Origen approached Richmond he began to relax. There were no patrol cars or helicopters and he believed his deception worked. He continued on to Jacksonville, Florida, where he pulled in to a Quality Inn. It was very late and he needed to rest.

RUSTY PULLED OFF the road to think this situation through. "I've got TSA monitoring flights out of the country, so I don't have to go to an airport. I can receive their reports on my cell phone. So, which direction should I go, north or south?" He was not far from the Interstate 95 interchange as he pondered the question.

In Dennis' research into Origen's background he remembered a small piece of information. Before changing his name Origen was known as Dmitri Kosygin and emigrated from Europe. His point of entry was Miami International Airport. Rusty reasoned his fugitive would exit the way he entered—he was headed to Miami.

Rusty could beat him there because he wasn't limited to driving. He turned around and went to BWI where he could catch the next flight to Miami and head off his fugitive.

CHAPTER THIRTY-SEVEN

"THE MASTER IS IN ANOTHER rage," warned the acolyte sent to find Kamenwati. He was just about to leave to take charge of the search for the missing American, when this announcement came. The Egyptian had no choice except to drop everything and respond to the call from Abaddon. But as Kamenwati was leaving his office, Lord Geoffrey made an unexpected, and unusual, appearance.

"Lord Geoffrey," said Kamenwati. "I didn't expect to see you here. I need to warn you of a troubling situation." Lord Geoffrey had a haunted, hunted look in his eyes. *He's afraid*, thought Kamenwati, wondering what could cause such a reaction in one so highly placed in Abaddon's hierarchy. Before the Egyptian could say more, Geoffrey rudely pressed on with his need.

"I have reports of spies looking for Dekker." Kamenwati did not want to admit he lost his prisoner, and Geoffrey interpreted his silence as an invitation to continue.

"It seems someone else found out I was coming here and figured out why. My people have been looking over half of Europe and finally found an NCTC man entered the country in Frankfurt, rented a car, and headed, I believe, to Baden-Baden." Lord Geoffrey stopped for a breath and then continued on. "Can you help me?"

Kamenwati knew Dekker took a bus to the same town and now knew it was much more than coincidence, but he was not prepared to take the Englishman into his confidence. Misplacing the man Abaddon wanted above all others was a significant problem, especially since he'd ordered the Englishman to release the American to his care. It was an embarrassment Kamenwati was not prepared to face. He must find Dekker and set him back on the path prepared for him, and he must also consider someone else who may be in a position to change Dekker's mind, or at least his course of action.

"Where are your people now?" asked Kamenwati.

"They are driving around to each hotel in the area, searching. They will flush them out eventually, but I need more resources."

"There is a small Brotherhood cell in that area, perhaps I can engage them in your search." The Egyptian was thinking more about their ability to seek out Dekker and help Kamenwati tie up that loose end, but to Lord Geoffrey it looked as if he was getting the support he asked for.

"Thank you. I won't forget this. I'll prepare to go there right away." Lord Geoffrey was visibly relieved.

"Allow me to go with you. It will be easier to coordinate my resources from there." Kamenwati was developing a new strategy; this was a good excuse to be gone and looking for someone.

"And the Master? How will we present this to him?"

"I was just on my way to his quarters. I will handle the explanation. Meanwhile, get ready and we'll go as soon as I've had my meeting."

KAMENWATI ENTERED ABADDON'S quarters to find him in a true rage. It seemed to the Egyptian that the Master was more erratic and more volatile with each passing day. He was not sure what set off this latest episode, but he must work around it in order to move ahead with his own plan.

"There you are, Kamenwati. It's about time. Where have you been? What took you so long?" Abaddon simply rambled in his thinking process.

Kamenwati cleared his throat and spoke calmly. "My apologies, Master. I was in a meeting and came as soon as I received your summons." The indistinct response seemed to deflect Abaddon's anger and he focused on other issues.

"Do you know that our leadership in Russia is reluctant to follow my directives? It is an outrage! And they have slowed down Consortium payments to a trickle."

"No, Master, I did not know that."

"And I sense other areas, like the Far East, and even South America, are leaning that way." Kamenwati was aware of the growing mutiny, and in fact he was instrumental in fomenting much of the instability. What Abaddon did not know is that they were preparing to align with him and submit to his leadership.

"No, Master. I was unaware of these troubling developments. What will you do?"

"What I want to do is rain death on them all."

"Master, you are reacting from an emotional place. You are unused to any dissent, but you must know that during your recent absence much changed, both in the organization and in the world."

"I don't want to hear about change. The only change I want to see is the implementation of my plan. There are simply too many people in this world and they are all clamoring for more wealth, more position, more, more, more."

"But isn't that good, Master? More people competing for fewer resources will eventually result in wide-scale conflict, even wars."

"In a sense, you are correct, but the culling of humanity must be done in such a way that they loose theall connection to their technologyies is lost. It must all be stripped down to the most basic of conditions. Only then can I step onto the world stage and lead them, free from nationalistic loyalties and untethered from political control. I will emerge as the savior of mankind, my Brotherhood the new stabilizing force in the world. And they will respect Magick once again, and I will wield powers that will cause them to stand in awe and fall down in worship."

The Egyptian stood quietly before the Master, letting him ramble on, knowing the anger he'd built up over the coming defections would drain off.

"Master, there is a matter I must attend to. I am reluctant to bring it up at such a time, but you need to know what is happening."

Abaddon stopped, and looked sharply at the Egyptian. "Go on."

"Sir, it relates to Lord Geoffrey and his organization. It seems it has been penetrated by American intelligence and they are seeking to attack you directly."

For Abaddon it was another weight added to the load he was carrying. He sat heavily in his chair. "What is it you wish to do?"

"We have reports that spies are in Baden-Baden, presumably trying to find Krugerschloss. I propose to go there, locate them and neutralize the threat."

"They cannot locate this castle unless I permit it. The Word of Deflection keeps all casual detection away."

"Of course, but should the Americans, with their satellites, or their surrogates in the German government, seek us out in earnest with cameras and other detection devices, the Word will be of little use. We must deflect that threat before it is ever deployed."

Abaddon was now fully focused on the new topic and he calmed down.

"Master, we need you to be our spiritual leader and demonstrate your power sparingly. Don't worry over these matters. Let me do that." Abaddon was proving himself to be less in control than Kamenwati ever imagined, and he knew supplanting him in the leadership role would be easy.

"And what of Dekker? I have had no report on him."

"He is in hand and I am waiting for the proper ceremonial time to bring him before you for punishment." The explanation, though flimsy, seemed to satisfy Abaddon.

"You are proving to be a resourceful and reliable chief of staff. Carry on."

Kamenwati left with a smile on his face. *It's working out perfectly*, he thought as he went to find Lord Geoffrey. He was still unsure whether the Englishman would be an asset or a liability. It was time to find out.

ABADDON WAS IN full ecstasy, reciting the familiar vision. Yet, for all his pride there was something troubling, something he couldn't quite put his finger on. He'd sensed dissention but could not determine its source. He was increasingly troubled that the American, the cause of all his troubles, was still alive. He acknowledged Kamenwati's wisdom in holding off Dekker's sacrifice until a more propitious time, but the fact that he was still alive bothered him in a place deep inside, one he could not precisely define.

It was as if there were alternate forces working through Dekker, quietly pushing against the Abaddon spirit within him.

The man, Kambrian, had given himself long ago to the influence and control of the Abaddon spirit. The power and control promised was irresistible to the youthful sorcerer whose odd powers of control and influence were greatly increased once the Abaddon spirit was invited in.

At first the "possession" was under Kambrian's control. He could turn it on or off at need as he grew in riches and power. But somewhere along the line he'd lost the desire to turn off the outside influence, and he'd become the temporal manifestation of a very powerful force. There were now few times when the real Kambrian was at the forefront, but the dominion of mankind the Abaddon spirit promised seemed an acceptable trade.

It had been many years now and still the promised dominion had not taken place. He had control over many people around the world, but the collapse caused by Dekker eliminated some of the most important political and economic influences he held.

Abaddon/Kambrian was forced to rebuild his secret empire and he rationalized it was perhaps for the best. There were flaws in the old system that he was determined to correct. For example, he had relied too heavily on the Brotherhood, that remnant of an ancient order and belief system in place from before the age of Babylon and Sumer. Their superstitions served well to coerce Brotherhood members to follow his lead, but it was an allegiance based in fear of retribution. While fear made a good leash, Abaddon/Kambrian found he could not let people off that leash to act independently to pursue his interests. The recent case of Kara Triberg came to mind.

Kara was perhaps the most gifted and promising acolyte he had trained. He quickly elevated her to the ranks of the Adepts, her skills in Magick and the other arts being exceptional. And then she turned on him, defecting and leaving him to aid the American. That disaster cost Abaddon/Kambrian dearly and resulted in his entrapment in a stasis that was seemingly unbreakable. The Abaddon spirit guiding Kambrian had retreated within the stasis and offered no power or aid in his escape.

It was Kamenwati's efforts that finally released Abaddon/Kambrian from the stasis. At the time he was too exultant to look to closely at the Egyptian's motives and accepted his offered loyalty at face value. Now, after a time in his pyramid chamber, he looked more closely at Kamenwati, the talisman of the Succubus he carried, and the entire landscape of the Brotherhood.

The developments in the capture and return of the American seemed to be a pivotal point in a larger developing scheme. Abaddon had to ask himself, who was with him and who was against him? In his heart he knew no one was truly with him, so he began to focus on those he perceived as opposition.

In the past the Egyptian had resisted the full embrace of Abaddon's version of the ancient Brotherhood religion. Like a number of the elder mystics, he was suspicious of Abaddon's motivations. Abaddon's stated plan, to return mankind to a simpler life free from mechanization and technology, was very appealing to the vast number of Brotherhood members. But a few of the elder mystics, like Kamenwati, Salim, Galdur, and

Ulrig, resisted his control. A senior Adept had executed Ulrig the Scott, leaving Galdur the Icelander without a close ally.

Salim, he believed, was too immersed in the orthodoxy of the Order to become involved with the more secular objectives Abaddon espoused. His assessment of the potential areas of resistance satisfied his logic but left a hollow suspicion in his spirit. Why did Kamenwati release him from the stasis? What were his objectives? And why did he feel the need to hold the ashes of the Succubus over him? These questions gnawed at the back of his mind and had increasingly directed his inquiries within the Flows.

Abaddon sensed a growing conflict between Kamenwati and the Englishman. Abaddon had seen through the Flows that spies were coming and the Englishman was doing his best to keep this development hidden. What gain was there to Kamenwati in helping Lord Geoffrey find those spies? And then there was the troubling fact that Abaddon was unable to "see" the hated American, despite Kamenwati's assurance he was "in hand."

Something was afoot, and Abaddon was unsure whether it bode ill or well for him. This was an area where

Abaddon was not in control, and that was disturbing. Never before had he been in such a position and never had he felt so vulnerable. He knew he was thinking as his natural self, Kambrian, and it felt lonely. He needed the strength, assurance, and vision of the spirit that had controlled him for so many years.

Abaddon left his quarters and entered the Great Hall through the cleverly masked doorway in the back wall. He stood on the central platform made of one huge agate stone mined many years ago from the heart of the mountain. It glowed an eerie blue from the dim illumination within the hall. Oil lamps hung on the walls were kept lighted day and night, maintaining a mystical atmosphere within the Hall. Abaddon soaked in the dark atmosphere, tinted with shimmering blue light from the agate platform. This was the heart of his domain and the place he felt most powerful.

Basking in the feeling of his own presence, Abaddon sensed someone else enter the Hall. Annoyed by the interruption, he brought himself back to the here-and-now, expecting to find an Acolyte. Instead, he saw the Englishman approaching in a tentative hat-in-hand posture, clearly wanting to speak with his Master, but unwilling to disturb him.

"What is it you want?" The annoyance came through loud and clear.

"Master, I've discovered something you should know about. I suspect treachery, but I don't want to make unwarranted accusations."

Abaddon became immediately alert and suspicious, Lord Geoffrey feeding into the very thoughts and misgivings that plagued his mind.

"Speak."

"Sir, it concerns the Egyptian, Kamenwati. He has been, well, 'strange' and I wanted to bring it up to you."

"What do you mean strange? He has always been this way, and not surprising given he lives alone on an island in the middle of the Nile River."

"No, sir. It's not that. What I mean is about your directive concerning the American, Dekker."

Abaddon gave a slight nod of his head, the blue light from the agate below his feet highlighting his bright copper mask in eerie ways.

"I think Kamenwati is hiding Dekker from you for some purpose of his own."

Abaddon saw through the half-truths and suspected this interview had more to do with posturing for position and currying favor than revealing some supposed plot. He closed his eyes, allowing himself to be given over fully to the spirit that had been his refuge and his strength for all these years.

Lord Geoffrey observed Abaddon momentarily stiffen. "Are you all right, sir?"

Abaddon looked down on the man standing before him, his posture clearly communicating contempt. "There is nothing occurring that I do not know about, or I do not allow."

Lord Geoffrey dropped his head at the admonition. "Yes Lord. Forgive my impertinence."

"Get out—and solve your own petty jealousies."

Lord Geoffrey backed out, leaving Abaddon alone. Despite his declaration to the Englishman, Abaddon did not know all things and there were certainly events taking place outside his vision and influence. That shortcoming served only to inflame his anger and desire to strike out at someone or something. He spun around, facing the stepped-in pyramid that formed the back wall of the Great Hall. Lifting his fists he let out a loud shout of frustration. Had anyone been in the Hall, they would have seen fire streak from Abaddon's fists, striking the back wall with a scorching explosion. The outburst seemed to calm Abaddon's spirit somewhat and he left the platform, going back into his quarters behind the wall.

"No one will get in the way of my ascendency. No one!" His statement, hissed in the privacy of his chambers, only underscored his misgivings about how things were developing.

He took off the golden mask, flinging it angrily. "No one!"

CHAPTER THIRTY-EIGHT

THE INN WHERE DEKKER AND Galdur were to meet consisted of a small group of cabins arranged in an untidy arc fronted by a gravel parking lot. The forest surrounded the establishment, but somehow it lacked the warmth and "woodsy" appeal of other inns.

A large wooden structure was the anchor for the inn, serving as registration, restaurant, laundry, and various other guest services. People of mostly eastern European origin occupied most of the cabins. They kept to themselves, an artifact of a generation of oppression by totalitarian rule, and rarely made eye contact, even in the dining area.

After eluding the searchers and returning to their room, Dekker became more vigilant. He kept looking out the window to see if any new cars entered, or if new guests were checking in. It was his opinion they were in danger of discovery and he did not know how a confrontation would turn out. His danger alarm was sounding in his mind and the longer it continued, the more uncomfortable he became.

"We have to get out of here," said Dekker. "I think we're going to have more company very soon."

"But what about Galdur?" Dennis worried. "What if he shows up and you're not here?"

"If he shows up, and at this point it seems a very big if, he will have to follow. He'll know where I'm going."

Dennis had a puzzled look. "Where exactly is that?"

Dekker with a firmness and conviction that surprised Dennis, he said, "I'm going to cut off the head of the snake." And he explained the basic plan he had for getting to, and into, Krugerschloss.

LORD GEOFFREY'S TEAM was frustrated by the search for the spy and for Dekker, but their leader kept them moving, knowing persistence would pay off in the end. The others listened to what they considered platitudes from a leader who did not know what else to do. Nevertheless, they continued searching hotels, inns, and restaurants in Baden-Baden.

The search team began in town, figuring there were more places for their quarry to hide. Their inquiries left them tired and without clues, and were now working toward the outskirts of town. "We're definitely outside the trendy area of Waldenstrasse, boss," said one of the team. "If I were going to find a place to go to ground, this is where it would be."

The leader agreed, and with the help of false identity cards identifying the team as members of the Bundeskriminalamt, the BKA—a state police force—they were able to question proprietors and innkeepers without objection.

It was getting late and everyone was tired. "Can't we stop for the night? I'd like to get a good meal and a tall stein of beer," said one of the men.

"Yeah, me too," chimed in another.

The leader relented, pulling into a roadside inn, the small sign announcing its name: BKA Baden-Baden, the same inn visited earlier by Kamenwati's men.

Dekker knew almost immediately something was wrong. His danger alarm was making him more agitated and Dennis responded to his uneasiness. Dekker looked out the window once again, and when he saw a dark SUV pull up to the registration office, he knew it was the source of his discomfort.

"Dennis, take a look. There is a suspicious car out there."

Dennis peeked out the curtained window, and nodded. "This doesn't look good."

"They haven't found us yet, Dennis, but it seems they've gotten lucky. We need to know if they're on to us, or are just looking for a room for the night."

"It sounds dangerous to go out there and check," said Dennis.

Dekker said nothing while putting on an insulated vest he purchased, looking very much like a tourist who was there for hiking, and left the room.

Dennis watched from the window as Dekker walked to the main building and surreptitiously inspected the vehicle parked under the entrance portico.

Inside, Dekker saw four men standing before the clerk at the registration desk, with a fifth at the door, almost like a rear guard. Dekker casually walked in, stopping at a rack of flyers promoting various local attractions, tours, and activities. He picked up one flyer after another, seeming to read each. In fact, he was using them as a cover to watch the men.

Speaking German they questioned the clerk. "No officer, we've had no new arrivals today," said the clerk, handing back the man's identity card. "What interest does the BKA have here? This is a resort area, not a hotbed for anarchists or revolutionaries."

The man did not respond to the barb, but asked for rooms for the night.

"You'll have to double up, sir. We only have a small number of cabins."

"That is fine." He asked for keys, which the clerk handed over.

Dekker returned to his room, reporting the conversation to Dennis. "They identified themselves as BKA, but their bearing says otherwise. The German agents I have known are disciplined, and carry themselves like professional soldiers. These men did not have those qualities. They stood too loosely, too casual. And they left in an untidy group, not as a unit."

Dennis looked out the window again and turned to Dekker. "They're sure to find us."

"Yes, I'm afraid so, Dennis. The only saving detail is you did not rent a room, I did. Had that not been the case, they would know you are here."

Dennis looked afraid. "Can we get out of here? They're bound to find us."

"On the contrary, Dennis, we have the advantage. We know they're here, but they have no idea we're all just a few cabins down from them."

Dennis thought about that for a moment and seemed to calm down. "So, if we just sit here, they'll move on in the morning and we'll be okay?" Dennis stepped back across the room, sitting on the small couch.

"Yes, Dennis. We just sit tight, keep out of sight, and let the storm pass."

CHAPTER THIRTY-NINE

THE NEXT MORNING DEKKER AND Dennis awoke rested and ready to start the day. The cabins had small kitchenettes with propane gas stoves, a small refrigerator, and a set of dishes and pans. The two NCTC men could not go to the main building's café, since the false BKA agents were likely to be there.

"We can't risk exposure now, but I can get us a few things and bring them back," offered Dekker.

"That would be great," said Dennis. "Especially if you can bring back some coffee." He was rummaging around the kitchenette and proudly announced he had found a coffee press. "It's one of those fancy French things, but I guess it will work." Dekker congratulated the young man and left the room.

There was a small store on one side of the inn's registration desk, one for guests to buy simple packaged foods and snacks. Dekker found a box of donuts, a small package of ground coffee, and a plastic bottle of orange juice. While shopping Dekker saw the false BKA agents enter and sit in the café directly opposite his little market. The leader happened to be sitting in the chair directly facing the market and when he casually looked across, he saw Dekker looking at him. The leader leaned over to one of his men, speaking softly in his ear. The man looked at Dekker and shook his head. Dekker surmised the leader asked if the man across the lobby was the one they sought, but the other did not recognize him. The leader did not look satisfied and kept one eye on Dekker as he paid for his goods and left the lobby.

He is suspicious, thought Dekker. Instead of going straight to the cabin, Dekker stepped around the porch of another, waiting for the tail that was sure to come. It only took a minute for the lobby doors to open and the suspicious leader to step out, looking left and right. The man went to the left, inspecting each cabin as he walked along.

At that inopportune moment, Dennis stepped out, looking for Dekker. The false BKA agent spotted him and reached into his waistband for a pistol. "Halt!"

Dennis jumped back through the doorway. "Great job, Dennis," he said to himself. "Now I'm trapped in here. It'll take a miracle to get out."

Dekker watched the leader go into an alert stance, pull his gun, and shout. Something happened and Dekker had to do something; he had to neutralize the threat. He moved quietly behind the next cabin and crept along the side. Dekker peeked out to see the gunman cautiously approaching his cabin. Dekker had to admire the man; he was making the correct moves, even without backup, but that very caution gave Dekker his opening.

He moved swiftly around the corner of the cabin and leapt up to the porch of his cabin, directly behind the gunman. It was only at that moment the gunman sensed another presence and began to spin around to face it, but his move was too late. Sudden recognition of the man from the lobby immobilized him for the split-second Dekker needed. He deflected the gun hand and simultaneously delivered a gut-wrenching blow to the man's solar plexus. The result was all the breath in his lungs was expelled and the gun hand went limp, dropping the pistol to the porch. It all happened in the blink of an eye, but the noise of the pistol clattering on the wooden porch alerted Dennis, who opened the door an inch. When he saw the situation he flung the door open and rushed out to Dekker.

"Help me get this guy inside," Dekker said. "I hope we haven't attracted any attention."

They lifted the inert body and carried it into the cabin. "Is he dead?"

As an answer to Dennis' question, the man rolled his head and groaned. Dekker cut a curtain cord and tied the gunman's hands and feet, pulling his feet back to connect with the now bound hands behind his back.

Dennis was impressed. "A regular rodeo hog-tie. Well done."

Gathering their few things they went to Dennis' car. While Dennis got into the rental car, Dekker went to the hunters' SUV. A quick move under the hood released the latch, and in a flash Dekker disconnected the distributor, effectively disabling the car.

"That will slow them down," said Dekker climbing into the passenger seat of little sedan. "If they have any mechanical skills, they'll be on us fast, but if they don't, they'll have to wait for a mechanic to come from town."

As Dennis pulled out, the other fake BKA agents stepped out of the main building's front doors, looking for their missing leader. One of the men seemed to take charge, ordering the others to search around. Dekker looked out the rear window, watching the new drama unfold, but lost sight of the men as Dennis turned a corner and got onto the highway.

"Where to?" Dekker turned back around and instructed Dennis to head east toward Gaggeneau.

THE TEAM LOOKED around for their leader, finally finding him bound and gagged in one of the cabins. The man was embarrassed to have been caught and took it out on the others, screaming and waving his arms as he ordered them first do one thing, and then another. After some minutes of this behavior he realized they were getting nowhere and settled down.

Using his false credentials at the front desk, the leader questioned the desk clerk and discovered the room was rented to Adam Dekker—an American. "Isn't that the guy the boss has been griping about for days?" One of the team said as he looked over his leader's shoulder.

"Yes, it is. I told you it was no coincidence our man came here." Turning to the clerk, he asked in German, "Do you know if another man joined this Adam Dekker?"

The clerk looked up, as if the answer were written on the ceiling. "Why, yes, right after Mr. Dekker checked in."

"Did you see that other man leave?" It was too much to hope the dim clerk would have seen or remembered, but it was worth a try.

Again, the clerk consulted the ceiling, and then brightened up with an answer. "Umm, yes. Now that you mention it, he got into a car with Mr. Dekker and they drove off."

"I don't suppose you know which direction?"

"Yes, I do. They headed east on the road out of town."

The false BKA leader thanked the clerk, telling him his government would be proud of him, and he'd be sure to mention his name in a report. He never bothered to get the clerk's name.

The other team members were standing in a quandary, arguing about their black Mercedes SUV. When the leader walked up they launched into a string of excuses. The leader surmised the problem was the car would not start and ordered the men to be silent. He sat in the driver's seat, turned the ignition key, and heard only a *click* followed by silence. Confirming what the men said, the leader pulled the hood release lever and went to check it out. The problem was immediately apparent and he waved the loose distributor cables at this men.

"Here it is. A juvenile trick and easily fixed." The leader leaned into the engine compartment and began the repairs.

"One of you go inside and borrow a pair of pliers so I can re-insert these wires."

Forty minutes later the false BKA team was on the road, racing as fast as possible to the East. The clerk was very happy to see that crew leave, believing only trouble would follow where those men went.

CHAPTER FORTY

THE DRIVE THROUGH THE FORESTED hills was relaxing for Dekker, and Dennis seemed to settle down from the excitement at the inn. Once in Gaggeneau, they turned south toward the town of Schiltach, where they connected with Highway 33 and then on to L107. "Hey, I remember this road from before," Dennis said.

"You're right, but we're coming from the opposite direction," Dekker said. "We'll intersect L109 and turn south." He leaned over to the back seat, grabbed a ball cap, and pulled it down over his eyes. "Wake me when we get there."

After turning onto L109, Dennis leaned over to rouse Dekker. "Wake up—we're getting close." Dekker was glad to have taken a nap. His Ranger training taught him to eat whenever possible, since you never knew when you'd be eating again, and you take every opportunity to sleep because during an operation it was often a scarce luxury. He consulted his folding map and told Dennis to look for a turnoff.

"It's an unpaved road, like a fire road back home. It will be on your right." Dennis nodded.

"Do you think those guys back at the inn are still following us?"

"I'd bet on it. They seemed determined."

"How could they know where we're going?"

"The same way I would if I were in their shoes. I'd ask the desk clerk, even the staff at the inn, to see if they knew anything. With their BKA credentials they'd have no trouble with cooperation. And there's something else: Those BKA IDs suggest a deeper and more sophisticated organization than simple bodyguards for Lord Geoffrey."

"Do you think it's the Abaddon Consortium?"

"Yes, I do. And when they find out I rented the cabin we left that attacker in, they will know I'm coming to Krugerschloss."

Dennis had a worried look. "Damn."

"That's right," said Dekker. "We need to get in as fast as possible."

"But what about Galdur?"

"I haven't counted him out of the game yet, but we can't wait for him. I just hope I can connect with him."

"You mean through the Flows?"

"Yes, the Flows. But it has to be done carefully, in a way that hides the communication from Abaddon's detection."

Dennis thought about that for a moment, and then seemed to understand. "You mean, like masking an IP address, or running a computer message through servers all over the world to confuse an identity search?"

"Yeah, like that, and that's what I've got to figure out."

"I wish I could help you. If you were working with computers, I'd be your man."

"You certainly would, Dennis. Unfortunately, in the realm of the Flows I am on my own, and I'm a novice. Galdur would know how to manipulate things."

"Well, maybe he'll do that. I mean, maybe he'll contact you instead of the other way around." Dekker hoped Galdur would do that, as he had when he was still in the grip of scopolamine.

GALDUR SENSED IT was time to chance using the Flows to reach Dekker. He was days late for their meeting, and he knew his friend would be worried. He might even try to strike out on his own to reach Abaddon, and going alone would be a mistake.

Extracting Salim from Iraq proved more difficult than expected, certainly more costly in time. And during the intervening days Galdur had to consciously avoid the Flows, knowing any activity might give him away, alerting Abaddon to his plan. Unfortunately, silence meant Dekker was in the dark and no doubt worried. It couldn't be helped, but now it was time to reach out to his American friend.

Salim agreed to be Galdur's surrogate in the effort to reach Dekker. By joining with Salim and utilizing his deep knowledge of the Flows, Galdur could connect with Dekker without revealing his identity to outside observers and, for a little while, keep the plan from exposure. Sitting in the back of a truck on their way toward Baden-Baden, the mystics were ready to try. It only required that Dekker be listening. "We could be at this for a long time, Galdur." Salim shook his head, signaling his uncertainty of their ultimate success.

"It is the chance we must take. The closer we get to Abaddon, the greater the chance of failure, and I cannot let it go on."

The two men sat in silence, reaching the deep meditative state necessary to enter the Flows.

CHAPTER FORTY-ONE

LORD GEOFFREY WAS RELIEVED WHEN Kamenwati told him he would assist in his search for the spy. He went back to his guest quarters in Krugerschloss, pleased he could rely on the strange Egyptian to be part of the solution. He expected Kamenwati to be an enemy, if not overtly, at least a stumbling block to his own ambitions. But this surprise offer of assistance made him reconsider his original bias, and wondered if they could actually become partners in the coming New Order.

As a politician, Lord Geoffrey knew enemies quickly became friends when interests converged, but he was having a difficult time discerning Kamenwati's goals. Was he truly just an administrator, content to carry out the orders of his master? His position with Abaddon gave him great authority, but it was in the name of his master, not his own. That was Lord Geoffrey's dilemma.

He'd learned through years in politics to "smell" a rival and sense his vulnerability to a political attack. Sometimes rivals were simply stupid and overconfident, believing their position unassailable. Usually they were blind in a particular area, and thus, open to attack. Lord Geoffrey had that same sense about Abaddon, and he was still trying to assess how to exploit the blind spot. He watched many in the Brotherhood fall into misunderstanding, or worse, underestimating Abaddon and his power. Geoffrey would not fall into the same trap, and so moved carefully to assess and plan. He knew Abaddon would not be denied his lust for power and control, yet in that was his opportunity to strengthen and expand control over Consortium interests. Geoffrey had a plan to consolidate operations and control, but needed time to make it happen.

Thinking over the wide range of Consortium people, he knew they were respectful of power, but were resistant to bullying. He had to build confidence in his leadership, and then loyalty to himself. Lord Geoffrey's reflection was interrupted by a message delivered by an acolyte. At first Geoffrey didn't understand the message from the search team, then, rereading, it the implications dawned on him, and he smiled. "Aah, Kamenwati's interests become clear."

The message outlined the search team's efforts to capture the spy who tracked Lord Geoffrey to Germany. The man was a problem, but not a huge one, and Geoffrey simply wanted to put an end to unwarranted meddling. He wished he had Origen and his team here; he would have wrapped up the spy in no time. Lord Geoffrey sighed, resigned to using the assets at hand, and read on. "We found the spy at an inn outside Baden-Baden, but he was in the company of another person—Adam Dekker." The team leader knew of Dekker, but only slightly. He did not know the importance of what he had discovered.

Lord Geoffrey left Dekker with Kamenwati, who said he would deliver him to Abaddon. But something had obviously gone wrong, and Dekker was no longer under the Egyptian's control. "How very interesting. I am beginning to see the roots of Kamenwati's interest in assisting my efforts," Lord Geoffrey mused.

He scratched out a reply and gave it to the waiting acolyte, waving him out of his quarters. Geoffrey needed to think about this incident and calculate its impact on his plans. Whatever Kamenwati was up to, it was not in Lord Geoffrey's interests. No, this was a propitious revelation, one that he must play very carefully, for in that play was the promise of life—or death.

Geoffrey would tell the Master how Kamenwati stopped him in Strasbourg to "prepare" the prisoner for presentation. It was fortunate that the Master was himself distracted and wouldn't press the point, but Geoffrey knew it was only a matter of time before Abaddon realized how flimsy Kamenwati's excuse had been and would demand that Dekker be brought to Krugerschloss. Geoffrey knew he would be facing a moment of truth. As he walked down the long hall to the inner chambers he went through optional excuses, each one more preposterous and unconvincing than the last. In the end he knew the only way out of his dilemma was the truth, or some version of the truth. Anything else would be spotted in a moment and he would surely die. He wiped the sweat from his palms as he entered Abaddon's chamber.

The room was not especially large, although Geoffrey knew there was another much bigger room beyond this one, the suite of rooms where Abaddon spent most his time. He knew the front room was used as a receiving office, a place to conduct formal business, and the thought added to his fear and discomfort.

An acolyte stationed in the office jumped up when Geoffrey entered and slipped through a doorway into the chambers beyond, while Geoffrey waited in a posture of attention before the large wooden desk. Soon Abaddon entered in full formal regalia: The bright copper mask and a full hooded cape, decorated with intricately patterned silver and gold threading. Geoffrey had seen this many times, but it still had the power to intimidate. Abaddon walked to the large carved chair behind the desk, sitting down with a flourish of the cape. He did not invite Geoffrey to sit.

The tension grew as the silence continued and Geoffrey remained standing. He was unsure what to expect, but he was certain it would not be pleasant. He realized Abaddon was taking stock of him, using his extraordinary powers of perception to gauge Geoffrey's thoughts and feelings.

Abaddon began, slowly and quietly. "It occurred to me you have deceived me regarding Dekker." The golden mask looked directly at Geoffrey, causing his blood to run cold. "Why?" Without warning Abaddon slammed his fist on the desk, creating a great echoing boom. "Why?" Abaddon shouted again with another fist slam, causing Geoffrey to jump.

Geoffrey expected to burst into flames, or have his guts explode from his belly, or some equally gruesome punishment. But none of that happened. Instead, Abaddon stood and paced behind his desk, ranting about Dekker. Geoffrey remained silent, waiting for the fit to pass. As the intensity of Abaddon's tirade diminished, Geoffrey saw his opportunity. "Master," he said quietly, "I understand your frustration and I think I can offer an explanation."

Abaddon stopped and turned to Geoffrey. "Go on."

"All this has happened because of Kamenwati's scheming. I don't pretend to know what he is up to, but somehow it involves Dekker."

"And where is Kamenwati?" Abaddon asked.

"I don't know, Master. Would you like me to look for him?"

"Yes—and bring him here to me."

"Of course." Lord Geoffrey breathed a sigh of relief, knowing he had escaped another trap. As he left Abaddon's office, he said quietly to himself, "That Egyptian has maneuvered me into danger for the last time. I must move quickly and get my team the support they need."

THE SEARCH TEAM leader received Lord Geoffrey's reply and it puzzled him. "It seems our objective has changed," he said to the other team members in the car. "We are not looking for one man, but two. And when we catch up to them we are to keep the one named Dekker and 'dispose' of the other."

The men looked at one another, a little confused. One spoke up, asking the leader an obvious question. "Do you mean we've been chasing the wrong man all along?"

"No, but it seems his value dropped while we've been chasing around Germany. Dekker is the new objective and it sounds like he's very important to the boss."

"They can't be too far ahead, can they?"

"No, I don't think so, but there are many little turnoffs along this road, so keep a sharp eye for them."

"Can we get some help from the locals?"

"Funny you should ask," said the leader. "The boss has already ordered up air support. A helicopter should be joining the search soon." They pulled off the road in an open area and waited. It was not long before they heard the distant beat of blades, drawing closer by the moment. The leader looked into the clear, blue sky, a set look on his face.

"Now the net will tighten and we can all go home."

CHAPTER FORTY-TWO

DEKKER SURPRISED DENNIS WHEN HE asked him to pull off the road. A little confused, Dennis complied and pulled onto the shoulder of the road. "Is that good enough?"

"Yes, it's fine. I just need a few minutes to concentrate. I've just been called, and I think it may be Galdur."

He got out of the car and sat by a large tree, centering himself. Reaching out with his mind, he inserted himself into the Flows and waited. Soon there was a repeat of the call, but he perceived it was not Galdur. What he received was an image of Galdur sitting quietly, eyes closed in meditation. The image shifted to an older man, the person communicating with Dekker.

Who are you?

Salim, a friend of your friend. He is with me and wishes to speak with you.

Relief washed over Dekker. He couldn't handle losing the old Icelander, not after Kelly.

He remained in contact with Salim and Galdur for many minutes, sitting beneath the tree. Dennis took care not to disturb him.

When Dekker emerged from the trance-like state, his companion was full of questions. He did his best to recount a narrative from the inherently nonlinear experience of the Flows. "Galdur is safe and on his way here. He has someone with him, another mystic named Salim, who is an old friend and head of his order. Salim is also committed to stopping Abaddon before he can re-assert his power, and has joined Galdur. They were delayed by a Brotherhood pursuit and had to make a complicated escape across a desert, and then a sea voyage."

"It sounds long and tedious," said Dennis.

"Yes, it was, but it was the only way to escape undetected. Abaddon's people know Galdur is on the move, and that Salim has disappeared. If they capture them, they will be executed."

"That's a stiff penalty for opposing Abaddon," said Dennis.

"Abaddon tolerates no dissent, and theirs is an act of open mutiny. He has killed others for smaller infractions."

"What are we going to do?" wondered Dennis.

"We're going to turn around, go back to the inn, and wait for Galdur. I was foolish for doubting his arrival and leading us out here."

"If you hadn't, we'd have been at the mercy of those thugs chasing us."

"I suppose you're right, Dennis. Maybe this little road trip will throw them."

THE RETURN TRIP found both men wrapped in thought, and the light banter of before stifled. After a while on the road, Dennis called out in alarm, "Hey, isn't that the black SUV parked over there?" Dekker peered out the windshield and ordered Dennis to pull off the road to get them out of sight. "The bunch of them are just standing around, but one is looking up, like he's expecting something." At that moment a large military-style helicopter dropped from the sky, landing in the field next to the Mercedes.

"So, I guess we know what that something is. They've got air support to look for us," said Dennis.

"Don't worry, Dennis. The reversal of our path is timely. They think we're running away and will be looking ahead, not behind. Now I understand one thing Galdur and Salim told me, 'watch the skies'."

"Can I get up yet? This is a little uncomfortable," complained Dennis from the well in the front seat.

"Just a minute more. I want to make sure they can't see us."

Dekker looked between the rearview mirror and the side mirror, and when the helicopter took off with one of the men, the others left in the car with a cloud of gravel and dust. "You can get up now, Dennis."

A few miles on, they heard the beat of the helicopter's rotors and again pulled off the road, stopping below several tall trees. When the noise from the helicopter receded they felt confident enough to continue on, reaching the inn without further incident. They returned to Dekker's cabin and the waiting began.

IT WAS THE next day before Galdur and Salim arrived, and Dennis was surprised how relieved he was to see the old Icelander. Galdur greeted the NCTC computer expert with a smile and a pat on the back. "It's good to see you again, my young friend. And Dekker, too."

The group crowded into Dekker's room for a strategy conference. "This news of helicopters and chasing cars concerns me, Dekker," said Galdur. "We may want to change our strategy."

CHAPTER FORTY-THREE

ABADDON EMERGED FROM THE MEDITATION pyramid in his quarters. It was a miniature of the multi-step structure forming the focal point of Krugerschloss' Great Hall. He had been inside for several days, neither eating nor drinking, sustained only by the forces within the Flows.

His time inside had taken him far; he inspected many areas under Brotherhood control, and areas not yet under their sway. Abaddon was puffed up with pride, believing his latest incarnation is a sign that he is unstoppable and invulnerable; fear went before him and destruction followed behind.

THE FALSE BKA team leader discussed a search plan with the helicopter pilot, boastfully proclaiming they would have their men by the end of the day. The pilot, somewhat less confident, said nothing as he climbed into the helicopter. No one noticed the small sedan moving up the road.

"I'm going with you," Klaus, the leader, said to the pilot. "My men will continue on the ground. Do you have walkie-talkies?"

The pilot pulled two small radios from a bin on the floor and handed them to the leader. "Perfect," he said passing one to his men. Looking at his own radio, he instructed the ground team to keep theirs turned on. They nodded understanding and went to the car to continue searching, while helicopter blades began spinning up to speed.

The pilot attempted to engage his passenger in conversation as they flew, but the man was unresponsive. Any question about their target, or the supposed infraction, was met with a shrug. The pilot gave up and pulled back on the cyclic, giving them more altitude to avoid updrafts and other dangerous conditions over the mountains and forests the BKA man wished to inspect.

After four hours of searching the southern area, the pilot announced it was getting late and he needed to refuel. Klaus was unhappy; their search was futile with no trace of the car or the men he sought. He called his team on the roads below, instructing them to turn back and meet at the Karlsruhe Airport serving Baden-Baden.

When the helicopter landed, the pilot quizzed the false BKA man. "What are your intentions regarding this search?"

The leader's answer was immediate. "We continue tomorrow, of course."

"Well, you'll have to arrange a different aircraft and pilot. I'm booked for the balance of the week."

The leader became angry with the pilot. "You can't abandon us now!"

"Look, sir, I don't know how you arranged this excursion today, but I am fully booked and cannot give you any more time. You'll have to do it from the ground, or find another helicopter and pilot."

Klaus sputtered but knew he didn't have the authority to order the pilot to cancel other obligations and return for another day's search. He came to grips with the setback, thanked the pilot, and walked to the main building to see what sort of aircraft or helicopter might be available for charter. Inside, he discovered that services offered from that airfield were sparse, and the attendant at the information counter only smiled at the request for a charter helicopter.

"You may be able to find one in Mannheim, sir. Would you like a contact telephone?"

The team drove up, asking the leader what was next. The leader grabbed their radio and took it to the helicopter pilot who was supervising the last stages of refueling his aircraft. With the radios returned, the leader got into the big Mercedes sedan.

"Where to now?" asked the man driving.

"Find us a place to stay for the night."

"Do you want to go back to the inn where we found those men?"

"I don't care, just get us somewhere I can collect my thoughts and make a report."

CHAPTER FORTY-FOUR

A BROTHERHOOD CELL RE-FORMED in the town of Bad Peterstal after the Krugerschloss diaspora. At the time of "the order," as the Brothers called it, there was great sadness and fear. The Master himself had given the order that all were to scatter, no two going the same direction. It was discovered later the order was not given by Abaddon, but by an imposter wearing his cloak and mask, and so loyal brothers began to gather in small groups to support and encourage one another.

For many years the Brotherhood kept a low profile, an underground movement, but now it was very much hidden and quiet. During the time of displacement and migration all Brothers associated with Krugerschloss hid their identity and moved with great care. A number of their order found themselves in the small mountain town of Bad Peterstal, a place small enough to keep them from the notice of officials, yet large enough to absorb them and give them a new life.

There were about twenty members in the Bad Peterstal cell, and each was a true believer in the return-to-the-natural-order worldview that received a virtual deathblow with the Master's fall. Their tenacity in maintaining traditional ways and beliefs in the Old Truths came to Kamenwati's attention. He'd ingratiated himself with the small group, through the Flows, gaining their respect and loyalty. For them he was a new Teacher, a man of deep wisdom who would help them rebuild the Brotherhood into a world-changing force.

Kamenwati cultivated the relationship with the Bad Peterstal group, not for their purposes, but for his own objective to ascend to the position of absolute leader. Now the relationship was paying off. Bad Peterstal was roughly halfway between Krugerschloss and Baden-Baden, making mobilization of the believers ideal to stop this unfolding disaster. The Bad Peterstal group was only too happy to enlist in Kamenwati's search for the man who almost single-handedly destroyed their world.

LORD GEOFFREY LISTENED to the report with increasing frustration. "He was just here, and it was why we couldn't find them—they were hiding out in his cabin two doors down from us."

"And where is Dekker now?"

"Well, since he was with the spy, we sort of lost him, too." Lord Geoffrey's initial feeling of satisfaction gave way to anger.

"You fool! How could you be so careless?" He went on with more verbal barbs until he finally calmed down. "Now listen carefully. I need you to understand exactly what is going on. There is another Brotherhood group loyal to Kamenwati that is also looking for the American. We cannot let them find him. If they do, the Egyptian will march Dekker in to Abaddon just as casual as you please, as if nothing was wrong."

"But, sir, what does it matter who brings the American to the Master?"

Lord Geoffrey was surprised at the lack of understanding his man had for the intrigues of politics and power. "If Kamenwati brings the American in, it appears nothing happened, and he will solidify his position at the Master's right hand. However, if I bring Dekker in, I will be able to expose the Egyptian's failure to keep control of the asset and position myself next to the Master." The search team leader said he understood, but really did not. It all seemed like a lot of silly posturing to him.

"Listen carefully now. You and your team must find Dekker before Kamenwati's people. You must stop them at all costs. Do you understand?"

"Yes, sir, I understand. We'll begin again first thing in the morning."

"No, you will begin tonight. There's not a minute to loose."

CHAPTER FORTY-FIVE

GALDUR, HAVING ARRIVED AT THE inn, found Dekker safe and sound. He was also monitoring the Flows carefully, seeking any hint of pursuit. Those chasing them were surely Brotherhood, and as such, were expected to convey their success or failure through the Flows. Salim was moving in the Flows as well, but his focus was on those he left behind in ancient Babylon to carry on the work of the Order, and so had no insight to offer Galdur.

"Salim, could you not focus on our immediate problem?"

"My brother, there are many responsibilities that continue, whether I am in the Temple or not. Surely you can understand this."

Exasperated, Galdur could only nod his head in acknowledgement.

"But I can tell you, there was a strange movement in the Flows, and it seemed to relate to your friend, Dekker."

Galdur perked up. "How so, Salim?"

"It seems there was a strange order given to a Brotherhood remnant near here, in a place called Bad Peterstal. They received orders to gather and to seek out and capture an American." Salim paused before delivering the final piece of information. "The order came from the Egyptian, Kamenwati."

"That *is* news, Salim. Is there more?"

"No, but it seems the gathering will take place tonight, but I'm afraid I don't know where."

"Don't worry, Salim. We know they are out there and looking for Dekker. We must tell him and head him in a direction they are not looking."

DEKKER TOOK THE news with a wry smile. "So we have two groups hunting us. How nice. We know where one group is, in that town of Bad Men."

"Bad Peterstal," Salim corrected.

Dekker fell right into his military strategizing mode, and began formulating a plan. "I think we need to play one group off the other, let them fight over us, as it were."

"I like it," Dennis interjected. "Lure them both in."

"It's not as easy as that," said Dekker. "We are outnumbered, out-gunned, and we only know where to find one group."

"Oh, yeah. That is a problem," agreed Dennis.

Dekker looked at his friends, Dennis, Galdur, and Salim. They willingly left their own lives and concerns to help him stop, once and for all, the growing rot of Abaddon. He was grateful for their dedication, even if they did not fully understand the threat they faced, and a sadness gripped his heart. Looking at them huddled and debating strategies, he knew he could not lead them to their destruction. An assault on Abaddon, any assault, could only result in their deaths. Even Galdur, for all his ability in Magick, in the end would be sacrificed to the cause. There was only one person who should die, only one who had nothing to lose and therefore the greatest likelihood of success: Himself.

Dekker made a decision and knew the course of action he must take. He would not sacrifice his friends, but he could help them distract and divert the forces of Lord Geoffrey and Kamenwati. In his estimation, Kamenwati's threat was the greater, and he would keep that danger away from his friends. He stepped quietly away from the group, excusing himself to get some air. It was some time before anyone noticed his absence.

THE GROUP DECIDED they were hungry and agreed to adjourn to the café, and it was then they discovered Dekker had not returned from his walk. Dennis called out for his friend, becoming concerned. Galdur looked thoughtful, and after pondering for a moment, had an assessment. "Friends, I believe Adam has gone."

There were general cries of alarm and disbelief, but Galdur quieted them. "I sense a certain fatalism in Dekker. You know, of course, he was deeply affected by the death of his wife, a murder he is determined to avenge regardless of the personal cost. I think he decided it was much too dangerous for us to follow him, and so left."

"Doesn't he know this is about more than him?" asked Dennis. "Abaddon has the means to bring disaster on the world—that's what we are here for."

"Agreed," answered Galdur. "And I believe Dekker intends to spare us the struggle. He thinks if he can cut off the head of the snake the whole thing will die."

"And what if the snake is like the Hydra?" Dennis asked. "Cut off one head, and two more grow in its place?"

"That's a very good point, Dennis, and our friend is so overwhelmed with a sense of vengeance he cannot consider all aspects of the situation."

"What do we do?" Salim asked.

"We help him, of course. But we must leave him to the path he has chosen and pray we converge at the right time."

"That's leaving an awful lot to chance," said Dennis.

"It is my experience that there is little chance or coincidence in this world. We must trust that the tidal forces of the Flows will carry us to our assigned destinies."

"Wait a minute," Dennis said. "What do you mean, the Flows? I thought they were only for communication."

"So they are, but they are much more than that." Salim nodded his head in agreement with Galdur. "The Flows can influence action and emotion, Dennis. They move us gently in the direction they want, and this is the great danger in Abaddon, for his ability to control the Flows can shape mankind's destiny." Everyone was quiet with this thought, each weighing the implications of what Galdur said.

"Does Dekker know this?" Dennis asked.

"No, not specifically, but at some level I believe he does understand, and his deep desire to protect people from evil also influences his actions."

"So, in a funny way, he is moving with the Flows," Dennis observed.

"Yes. As are we all," said Galdur.

CHAPTER FORTY-SIX

DEKKER PICKED UP A TRAIL map of the western reaches of the Black Forest from a kiosk in the lobby. His objective was Krugerschloss, but the mountain castle was not listed on any map, and walking in the front door was the worst kind of dumb. No, he must gain entrance by stealth, and use the secret entrance Kara had shown them high above the mountain castle. From there, assuming it was still open, he could enter and move down to Abaddon's private quarters.

There was a discernible shift in the Flows, as if a logjam was broken and a flood of energy poured out. Dekker felt oddly renewed, full of new energy and purpose, as if a heaviness had been lifted from his soul.

Dekker looked around a dark and somewhat forbidding forest. It was the same as a minute ago, yet he felt as if he'd stepped onto a lighted path through the trackless wood. He was armed with only a Swiss Army multi-tool, but he was not concerned. He knew a showdown with Abaddon would not involve weapons, at least what he knew as weapons. He would have to rely on resolve, cunning, and surprise—his greatest assets in this assault.

KAMENWATI COULD NOT believe his luck. Dekker may not have revealed his presence in the Flows, but he did sense his presence in the forest. This was a place to start and the Egyptian dispatched his Bad Peterstal brethren accordingly. "No need to search the town of Baden-Baden, the American is attempting an approach through the forest."

Twenty Brothers set out to follow Dekker into the Black Forest.

LORD GEOFFREY SENSED much the same thing as Kamenwati, but took a different approach to locating the American. Through the Flows, he ordered his search team to join him at Krugerschloss. From there they would work outward and capture Dekker as he approached.

Lord Geoffrey had no appreciation for the skills possessed by the American, and his presumed "simple" capture would be anything but easy. He assumed because Dekker had been so quickly found and captured in Maryland that it would be the same here.

Lord Geoffrey was heading for a rude awakening, not to mention a running battle with Kamenwati and his team.

SALIM AND GALDUR felt the shift as well, and quietly conferred with one another as to its meaning. In the end, Galdur could say only they must move with all haste to divert the pursuit and support Dekker. Galdur watched from the window as the false BKA people once again left the inn in a hurry, headed for destinations unknown.

"Do you think they know where Dekker is?" asked Dennis.

"No, they don't. They have been summoned and leave with haste."

"That's good," said Dennis. "At least they'll be out of our hair."

"Don't be so sure. I sense we will encounter them again before this is over."

Dennis looked out the window, watching Lord Geoffrey's team rush off, tires spinning, throwing up dust and small stones.

"Will they bring back the helicopter?" Galdur thought about the question for a moment, and then shook his head. "No, they won't. The search is in the forest, and a helicopter is no help." Dennis was relieved, glad they would not have to worry about being shot from above.

"We'll leave at first light."

"Where are we going?" asked Dennis.

"We are going to find the back route into Krugerschloss, where you were going earlier today." The group retired to their cabin, each considering what would happen the next day.

CHAPTER FORTY-SEVEN

THE DAY DAWNED CRISP AND cool. A mist hung over the canopy of trees, creating a sense of the forest primeval where magical creatures lived untouched by the world of man.

Galdur took a deep breath of the morning air; he held it long before expelling an extended, slow breath. Salim stepped quietly to his side, taking in the vista. "Very different from your desert home, is it not, Salim?"

"Yes, it is. But I still long for my own soil and my own people."

"Can you see our future here? Can you see an outcome?"

Salim shook his head. "No, it is hidden. But I discern there are two groups hunting for our American friend, and that they are on a collision course."

"Perhaps that is good, Salim. They can distract one another while we steal into Krugerschloss."

"We will have to take care to avoid the crossfire that is sure to take place."

"And Dekker? I get no clear sense of his location, except out there," said Galdur with a sweep of his right arm.

"It's quite odd. If I didn't know better, I'd say he was a wizard himself, masking his presence with a cloud." At that moment Dennis walked out of the cabin and approached the two older men. Dropping three backpacks on the porch, he asked if everyone was ready to go. Galdur and Salim nodded and the small group headed for the car.

The drive back to the L109 was uneventful, now that they weren't being followed. They soon found the unpaved road Dekker had marked on his map, made the right-hand turn, and followed it for about a mile into the forest where it came to a dead end at a wooden barricade. "End of the road," said Dennis. "We go on foot from here."

Dennis shouldered his backpack and handed water bottles and expanding trekking poles to Salim and Galdur. They were grateful for the hiking aids and set off into the woods. The folding map gave Dennis some sense of where they were, and the circles and lines drawn by Dekker provided a good guide to their destination.

The hike through the evergreen forest was pleasant, and not too difficult. The mature pine forest was surprisingly free of ground cover, a result, Dennis recalled, of the acidic soil created by pine needles and the high canopy overhead that allowed little direct sun to reach the ground. They hiked steadily westward, coming upon occasional openings in the forest canopy that created pleasant little glens with grass and small white flowers, like primroses. They rested frequently, giving Galdur and Salim time to concentrate on the Flows, but at each break they had nothing new to report.

The day grew hotter and they encountered no streams or pools of water. Dennis made sure they had CamelBaks in their backpacks, and they sipped freely as they moved on.

When Salim raised a concern about the heat and dwindling water supply, Dennis was quick to respond. "We went through this before. Don't worry, there is a fresh water stream ahead. We just have to get through this evergreen section."

The ground rose steadily as they hiked and soon, true to Dennis' prediction, the pine forest gave way to stands of oak and maple. Everyone was relieved when they heard the sound of a stream ahead, and foot weary, gladly stopped on the grassy banks of the unnamed stream. Cooling their feet in the water, the group discussed their next steps.

"We're not far from the field named Desolation," said Galdur. "From there we will have an excellent view of the eastern wall of the Krugerschloss mountain."

"I remember it clearly," Dennis said. "That strange open field with nothing growing, and the creepy Stonehenge-like thing in the center."

"Yes, Dennis, and I intend to stop at the megalith and pay my respects to Kara." An hour more hiking brought the group to the edge of an open field.

"Desolation," announced Galdur.

The field was aptly named: It sat like an ugly brown scar in the middle of the lush forest. Long ago it served as a smelting and processing center for the copper mine in the heart of the mountain, and it was the source of the original tribe's wealth. The copper, refined and smelted into bricks, was ultimately combined with tin that was mined to the east of Krugerschloss to produce bronze for weapons and armor. The bronze armaments, swords, and shields were the basis for the tribe's power in the region. It is also the reason Abaddon wears a copper mask.

As Dennis promised, there was a symmetrical rock structure in the center of the field, but it hardly looked like a temple or Stonehenge. As they approached the stones, their size and weight were apparent.

"These are massive stones," said Salim. "Where in the world did they come from?"

"I'm afraid I don't know the ancient history of this place, so I can't tell you how or when this structure was erected. I will tell you that until five years ago those three huge stones stood leaning on one another, creating a peak above an altar stone." The group walked in silence to the jumbled stones.

"This is where we faced Abaddon. The struggle was great and took all our strength, but in the end, we prevailed." Galdur walked up to one stone thrown down on its length. He knelt, placing his hand on the stone. "Kara was the bait and drew Abaddon in. In his distraction and extreme anger, he did not notice Dekker or myself behind the other upright stones, each of us exercising a different Word of Power. Kara let the evil one enter the confines of the temple where she created a stasis cube. It was floating high overhead, a beautiful thing with soft, swirling colors. But when Abaddon entered, the cube changed dramatically. It became dark and ominous, potent, and full of power.

"He mocked Kara's rebellion, and when he noticed Dekker and myself, laughed at our puny efforts to stop him. But he didn't notice the stasis cube growing overhead, slowly descending to finally envelop him. His surprise was complete when he realized what happened, and his mocking derision turned to fear and cursing.

"With a final Word, the containment was complete, but not before there was a terrible cracking sound. A beam of light shot straight up through the peak of the stone triad, shattering the delicate balance holding them in place. The stones fell and Dekker and I were able to avoid injury, but Kara was so spent by her efforts she was unable to move and was crushed by this stone, completing the blood sacrifice necessary for confinement.

"I think she went in knowing she would die, but after all Abaddon had taken from her, it was an equitable trade. Little did she know the thousand-year confinement of Abaddon would last only five years." The others stood around Galdur in respectful silence, taking in the tragic story of the brave woman who died facing Abaddon. "I pray we do not make the same mistake."

They left the ancient temple, heading for the edge of the field and the forest beyond. Galdur indicated there was a trail to the top.

"Won't trails be guarded?" asked Dennis. "We can't just march up, knock on the front door, and ask for the master of the castle."

Galdur laughed lightly at the comment. "You're right, of course. I was thinking of taking a more ancient way—the one Dekker discovered in the face of that cliff," indicating the sheer wall. "You can almost see it from here." He pointed up to the stark granite face of the cliff above them, to the right, where there was a cleft.

"How in the world are we going to get to that?" asked Dennis.

"Not to worry. There is a small ledge just below the edge of the cliff. It's a little hard to see from here, but it is there—or so Dekker told me." The others seemed satisfied with Galdur's explanation and were ready to move on. "But let me warn you: Abaddon still controls this area and monitors activity through the Flows. Salim and I will do our best to exercise a Word of Denial, keeping his attention away from us. But if Abaddon suspects he's being deceived, he will penetrate our cloud in an instant. And I don't need to tell you that discovery will end our ability to help Dekker."

"Yeah, and probably end our lives, too," said Dennis.

CHAPTER FORTY-EIGHT

DEKKER WAS RELUCTANT TO STOP moving, knowing it would give his pursuers the chance to catch up. But fatigue was beginning to slow him and he knew he needed sleep. In an effort to foil any dogs that might be sent on the search, he fashioned a bower twenty feet up in an especially large fir tree. He was grateful there wasn't much sap running, since the sticky substance tended to be an annoyance. Once he located a suitable spot in the branches, he settled in as best he could, making a mental note not to roll over in his sleep—which came on almost immediately. For the first time in many weeks he did not dream of Abaddon or the brutal attack on Kelly.

Dekker awoke with the first rays of morning sunlight peeking through the thick pine canopy. The aroma of the forest was invigorating. The fresh scent caused nostalgic memories of camping in the woods, fishing in mountain streams, and cooking fresh-caught trout in cast iron pans over a campfire. He basked in the memories for a moment, allowing himself to awaken slowly. He was surprised his night in a tree had been as restful as it was. His next sensation was hunger.

I need to find something to eat.

He learned in survival training to live off the land, whether a desert or a jungle. He knew there were many options in a forest, and it was only a question of how much time foraging would take. Dekker continued to "go with the flow" as he thought of it, relying on his feeling for the direction to take. He was familiar with some of the area around Krugerschloss, but he was completely in the dark on the approach from the Northwest. He didn't worry about it, instead looked for mushrooms, berries, and nuts that would constitute a breakfast. He found them in small amounts as he hiked through the forest, and was grateful for them, but would have appreciated a cup of coffee.

He thought of the many tales of fairies, sprites, and similar creatures of myth and legend, and how they often took pity on a lost and lonely traveler in their forest, guiding and feeding him until reaching safety. Of course, there were an equal number of tales about more mischievous, even harmful spirits that abounded in the Black Forest, but Dekker chose to be thankful to the benevolent spirits for his food. He didn't specifically believe in woodland spirits, but in a place like the Black Forest, he wouldn't take a chance, either.

About midday he crossed a well-worn path in the forest and wondered if he should take the easier route. As he stood there wondering, his "danger sense" began to ping and he concentrated on deciphering the threat.

He'd always had this "sixth sense," a skill he'd discovered during his time in the Rangers and brought to full realization with his Native American friend Eagle Claw's careful mentoring and training. Eagle Claw was an elder and leader of a Native community high in the Jemez Mountains of New Mexico. Dekker was fond of Eagle Claw, and the old man seemed to return the feeling. In the absence of a father or strong male figure in his life, the native elder filled the void. Remembering Eagle Claw's lessons reminded Dekker of the principles of his talent.

It is a passive ability, something difficult for a man of action such as you to understand. Instead of moving, you stand still; instead of striking out, you pull back; instead of talking, you listen.

Dekker smiled at the memory of Eagle Claw's simple lessons regarding what he came to know as his danger sense, and how it saved him time and again throughout his career. Feeling it again now, he stopped and focused his attention.

He sensed the danger coming from the left, or west. As he concentrated, he also felt a distant threat coming from the east. *Not good*, he thought. *If they've located me and they're using a pincer tactic, it will be very hard to escape capture.* Looking up and down the trail, he came to a decision: He would not go left or right; instead, he would follow the tugging that led him all morning. Stepping across the trail, he continued to let himself follow the forces that had seemingly seized control of his destiny. He walked back into the forest, taking care to leave no telltale signs of his passing.

Sometime later he paused when he heard the sound of people passing on the trail in the distance behind him. Stopping to eliminate distractions, he concentrated on the pursuers. He was unable to determine the number in the party, and it was clear they were looking for him. Squatting on the ground, Dekker attempted to discern their plan, but there was too much confusion among the searchers. Then there was a sudden mental "shout" and everyone stopped. Dekker sensed another person, someone with great power. Could it be Abaddon? After several minutes of intense questioning, Dekker realized it was not Abaddon, but Kamenwati interrogating the search team.

The Egyptian mystic was not physically with the search team, but controlling its actions from a distance. Dekker remained silent and motionless, since his proximity to the Flows made him all the more vulnerable to detection—especially by someone as experienced as Kamenwati. So Dekker sat, maintaining a psychic profile the size of a flea, hoping for the best.

The search group was released from the Egyptian's interrogation, and Dekker could feel a collective sigh go up as Kamenwati withdrew. But Dekker himself was not out of danger. He felt the leader of the search team, who had some skills in the Flows, begin to reach out and probe, seeking any feeling or sign of Dekker.

Two searchers were left behind as a rear guard while the main group continued on the path through the forest. Each of the men took one side, searching the underbrush, turf, and dirt, for any sign of human passage. The uninteresting duty was assigned to junior people, a fact not lost on the two men, performing their job with grudging indifference.

One of the searchers, a younger man named Eric, wandered onto the spot along the trail where Dekker stopped earlier to listen, and discovered the packed-down grass and other signs someone stood in that spot, and not long ago.

"Hey, Vincent. Come look at this." The other man crossed over the trail to join Eric a few feet into the underbrush. Vincent was by far the more experienced tracker, a fact Eric took into account. "It looks like someone stood here," said Eric.

Vincent stooped down to inspect the bruised foliage and agreed with his companion. "You're right, Eric. He stood there turning, undecided. Then he left—that way." He pointed across the trail. "Let's see if we can follow him."

Vincent and Eric had to search harder for signs of Dekker's passing, but eventually found what they were looking for: A bent and slightly broken branch on a bush. The lie of the branch gave them direction, and Eric wanted to run off and chase down their fugitive.

"Hold on there Eric, not so fast." Vincent held his elbow and explained. "You heard what Master Kamenwati said: This guy is experienced and probably dangerous, armed or not."

Vincent pulled a small revolver from his waistband, opened the cylinder and spun it. Satisfied, he held the gun before him and walked carefully into the thicker woods. Eric, taking his cue from Vincent, pulled a slim semi-automatic from his pocket and followed behind. Vincent noticed the younger man's weapon, and the fact he was walking directly behind. "Move over to the side, you dummy. I don't want you accidentally shooting me."

Eric, not liking the admonishment, nevertheless took a few steps to his left as they moved quietly through the woods.

CHAPTER FORTY-NINE

DEKKER WAS RELIEVED WHEN THE brotherhood search group moved on, but decided to remain where he was and see what developed. He was glad for his decision, when he realized two men were left behind. Concentrating on the sense of their presence, Dekker soon had a fix on the pair and knew they were heading his way.

He understood they would have to be neutralized, but how best to do that? He went through a list of the many guerilla-style traps he knew, discarding several for being too impractical or time-consuming to construct. Dekker began by salting a trail—breaking small branches, disturbing moss mounds, and leaving footprints in strategic places. Since they were alert enough to find his track crossing the trail through the forest, they were probably sharp enough to find and follow his false route into the deep woods. He needed to make the trail obscure, but not difficult. He also had to make the trail wander in such a way that his pursuers concentrated on following his trail rather than paying attention to where they were going.

Dekker led the two men on until he felt they had gone far enough, with sufficient twists and turns to confuse almost anyone. He turned the trail into a deep copse of hemlock trees, which was difficult to pass through, and a good ambush site.

Doubling back along his trail, Dekker found his pursuers arguing over a track and what it meant. "This is clearly showing us he is moving that way," Eric said.

"You're wrong. It shows our man continuing on straight," Vincent countered.

"Do you think it's a little strange we haven't seen or heard him?"

"Nah, he's probably gotten wary, especially with you making all this noise."

"I hadn't thought of that, Vincent. I'll be quieter."

The two men finished their direction discussion in whispers, but Dekker heard enough to know his little trick of misdirection was working. They selected a path reasonably close to the one Dekker blazed, and moved on into the forest.

Dekker took a clue from the overheard discussion and decided to stage open "sightings" to keep the men focused on him, and not their surroundings. He began with a soft cough, the sort of sound that was distinctly human yet difficult to get a fix on in a forest. At the first cough, the men froze and looked around, as if their quarry might be standing directly in front of them, or behind them, or perhaps to one side or the other. After a moment's indecision, Vincent indicated they should separate and search. This worked into Dekker's plan, and he focused on the younger of the team.

As Eric moved to the right, Dekker made a small scuffling sound with his feet, something only Eric would hear. The sound seemed to electrify Eric, who hefted his small revolver, thinking it an advantage. Dekker did not want the young man to fire the pistol, knowing the acoustics of the forest could work against him—a shot would be heard for a very long way, perhaps even by the larger group moving along the main forest trail.

Dekker was impressed with Eric's skill moving through the forest, but then, for a member of the Brotherhood it was not too surprising. Their philosophy of "nature first" made them naturally inclined to step in the correct place and follow faint trails with relative ease. Dekker's own training in the Special Forces, and his long association with the Native peoples at home, gave him an advantage, which he now put to good use. He teased the young man on, giving a slight sign whenever he seemed to be wavering. He led Eric into the dead-end copse of hemlock trees and observed the young man looking around in confusion.

"Now, where did he go? There's no sign of his passing through here."

That's when Dekker sprang from behind, knocking Eric to the ground. A choke hold, with one arm and a thumb placed on the carotid artery in Eric's neck, resulted in rapid unconsciousness. Dekker sat Eric up against a tree and used some rope he carried to secure him. When his prisoner was properly trussed up, Dekker stood back to admire his handiwork. "That will keep you for a while. And to keep you quiet, let's give you this." He stuffed a piece of cloth into Eric's mouth and took a length of vine, tying it into place across his mouth and around his head.

Satisfied Eric was going nowhere, Dekker moved obliquely through the forest to intercept Vincent. He found the man moving slowly through the trees, searching constantly for signs. Dekker used the same techniques to lure Vincent to the hemlock dead-end.

Vincent spotted Eric as soon as he stepped into the copse. He was unconscious and tied to a tree. Vincent moved warily to his partner, stooping down to untie the gag. He could see the younger man was out cold, and began untying his bonds holding him to the tree. Without the support of the ropes, Eric's unconscious body leaned to one side and would have fallen over had Vincent not grabbed him. That was Dekker's opening and he again sprang quickly to subdue Vincent. The struggle was short, resulting in Vincent's restraint.

With both men now immobilized and tied together, Dekker was confident he could leave them. They would escape their bonds eventually, but not before he was far away. He relieved the men of their weapons, figuring guns might be handy should he run into trouble. He set off on his original heading that he now realized was taking him to the heights above Krugerschloss.

He thought for a moment about Galdur, Salim and Dennis, wondering where they were.

CHAPTER FIFTY

GALDUR AND THE OTHERS MOVED up the hillside leading to Krugerschloss but made it a point to stay off the main trail, preferring side routes whenever they presented themselves. It made the going a little slower, but Galdur believed it was safer.

Salim was especially quiet during their climb and it was difficult to interpret his mood. Finally, Dennis put the question to him. "Salim, is everything all right?"

"Whatever do you mean?" responded Salim.

Dennis pressed on with his questioning. "You've hardly spoken a word since we passed through Desolation Field, and nothing since beginning our hike up the mountainside."

Galdur stepped into the conversation. "Dennis, please leave Salim alone. He is concentrating on maintaining a Cloud around us so we're not discovered." Dennis apologized for being a distraction and walked on in silence. Not long after they found themselves standing on the edge of the cliff they had seen from the field below. *The drop down is much scarier from up here,* thought Dennis.

Galdur spotted a small ledge about six feet from the top. "There's our highway to happiness!"

"Or more likely, our Highway to Hell," said Dennis, referring to the old AC/DC song.

Galdur peeked over the edge, examining the ledge, noting the smooth rock where the brethren stepped before going down. "Many have gone before us, so be heartened. What they could do, we can do." Dennis remained skeptical.

"Shall we begin?"

CHAPTER FIFTY-ONE

LORD GEOFFREY DISPATCHED HIS PEOPLE to prowl the territory around Krugerschloss, knowing that was the American's goal, and therefore, the surest way to find and capture him.

He thought Kamenwati a fool, but he would not discourage his wide-ranging search. *Besides*, he thought with a certain glee, *it keeps him away from here, and more importantly, away from the Master.* Geoffrey resented the influence the Egyptian seemed to have with Abaddon, and he would now do anything to discredit Kamenwati.

Geoffrey knew better than most the inner workings of palace politics, having spent a lifetime navigating the turbulent and frequently deadly waters of the British Parliament and royal court. Most people don't realize how deep rivalries and grudges go in Great Britain, but such was home waters for Geoffrey and he was ready to use his considerable experience to achieve victory.

Lord Geoffrey's men were not familiar with Krugerschloss or how many ways led inside. He gave them a quick rundown on the castle, saying it was virtually impenetrable. "There are only three entrances into the mountain. The first, of course, is the main structure built right up to the face of the granite mountain. One of you should be positioned out there, patrolling out to the alder grove and back. The next is the large, fortified door used for refuse removal. Keep an eye on that entry, as it is an obvious alternative to the front door.

"Finally, there is the ancient tunnel entry on the face of the mountain. It is a cleft in the rock that was originally used by the ancient clan to gain access to the interior. It used to be an underground river, dropping a waterfall into the field below, but the water has long since been diverted for use within the castle complex. It is still passable, but infrequently used. The only way into the cleft is along a narrow ledge. Young acolytes make a game of it, challenging one another to test their bravery, but other than that, it is unused. It is possible the American knows of this entry, so keep a sharp eye on it."

The men split up duties, heading off to watch for the expected intruder. Lord Geoffrey was quite pleased with himself and confident his men would capture Dekker. Unfortunately, the Englishman was unaware of a secret upper entrance that would be his downfall in the coming hours.

KAMENWATI LEFT HIS base on the barge, now convinced Dekker was truly gone. He was frustrated by his inability to detect the American using the Flows, but was confident his people from Bad Peterstal would locate the runaway.

Meanwhile, he had been gone from Krugerschloss too long and was receiving messages from Abaddon questioning his extended absence. The Egyptian had long since abandoned any thought of an alliance with Lord Geoffrey, perceiving the Englishman as shallow of thought and short on vision. He simply must capture the American himself and get on with his plan.

On the trail through the Black Forest, Kamenwati's searchers stopped for a rest. The leader looked around, counting heads and coming up two short. "Where are the two rear scouts?" None of the group could give an answer, and the leader became concerned.

"They should be right behind us," the leader said, and then turned to two others of his group. "Go back and find them. It wouldn't do to have them lost in the woods." Two men jumped up and trotted back down the trail, occasionally calling out for the missing men. The main group moved on, headed for the alder grove and the first confrontation in the struggle to control Abaddon's empire.

DEKKER HEARD DISTANT shouting through the forest and smiled, understanding it to be Kamenwati's force looking for the missing men. They would be surprised when they found them tied to a tree, but when they did, he knew the hunt would be on. He stepped up his pace, now heading into higher elevations and leaving the fir forest behind.

Oak and maple became the dominant trees, and passage between them was easier. The wall of trees blocked his view of the mountaintop but it didn't matter to Dekker. He knew where he was headed and pressed forward with purpose. Dekker began considering what he would do once he reached Abaddon. What steps did he need to take to confront and defeat his enemy?

The sun was setting as he reached the heights above Krugerschloss and he paused for a moment to look down. The late afternoon sun bathed the landscape in amber, and the edges of leaves seemed to glow with an inner, magical, radiance. He saw the alder grove far below, an open glen in the forest with a large stone in the middle. He wondered how many bloody sacrifices Abaddon made on that stone, how many lives shattered, how many dreams dashed. *No more*, he thought. *This is where your reign of terror stops.*

He turned from the overlook and began searching for the hidden entrance to the cave system below.

VINCENT AND ERIC were escorted back to the searchers' forest camp. The two men were embarrassed by their capture and were reluctant to tell their leader about it. After some stern coaxing, the men related the sequence of events to the laughing criticism of the larger group.

"You would have been fooled, too!" Vincent shouted. His statement was met with more jeers and catcalls.

"Stop it, all of you," ordered the leader. "What's done is done and we can't change that. What is more important is our American friend knows now he is being hunted and he's clearly taken steps to stop us, but in the end we'll find him." A general murmur of agreement came from the group.

"The American is obviously heading toward Krugerschloss but staying off main trails."

"What are we going to do?" asked one of the group.

The leader thought about the question for a moment, considering his options. "We must inform lord Kamenwati of this development and await his orders." The leader stepped away from the group into a secluded spot, and went into a meditative trance. Fifteen minutes later, the leader returned.

"Lord Kamenwati has instructed us to make our way to Krugerschloss with all haste. There we are to set up a perimeter along the western reaches of the castle and wait for the American." The leader prayed Dekker had not yet reached the mountain castle or its grounds. Finding him there would take an army; there were just too many places to hide.

The Bad Peterstal brothers moved out, although the dark evening skies made moving through the forest more difficult, and their progress was not what the leader hoped for. With much coaxing the group made it through, arriving in the alder grove at midnight. The group was split into teams and assigned several posts; that created some discord since they had no rest or food.

"We'll rotate you into the main house for food and rest," offered the leader. "Meanwhile, everyone off to your posts."

THE DARK WAS no impediment to Lord Geoffrey's team, who discovered two strangers lurking on the cliff edge, apparently considering how to get down to the ledge leading to the cleft.

Geoffrey's team did not realize Dennis already descended and was proceeding along the ledge to reconnoiter, while Galdur and Salim waited above. The result was only two men were in evidence when the guard team arrived. The guards easily took the old men into custody, mocking their efforts to evade Lord Geoffrey.

The two captives were led back around to the front entrance of the cottage leading to the castle interior. Because of the size of the mountain rising above it, the cottage seemed quite small, but upon approach it was large, with a generous porch stretching the full length of the structure. A double door of heavy oak served as the main entrance, although farther down left and right there were smaller doors opening onto the porch.

The captives were directed to the right, into one of the smaller doors. Salim wondered why they were not going in the main doors and then dismissed the thought. Galdur knew why they were not being ushered into the front entrance.

Their captors did not want others to see them, or to whom they were being taken.

Galdur surmised it was not Abaddon they would see, and that gave him much food for thought. If not Abaddon, then who? And why would Abaddon be left out of the loop on their capture? There was more going on here than one might suspect.

CHAPTER FIFTY-TWO

RUSTY NOTIFIED TSA TO LOOK for the fugitive, Origen. He extended the notice to Ft. Lauderdale and even Palm Beach, knowing any of these airports served international destinations. He did not believe Origen would be so predictable in his escape plan, but it paid to be prepared on all fronts.

He suspected Origen's motivation for driving nine hundred mile was twofold: First, to get away from Washington, but second, to do it in a way that had a low probability of capture. Also, south Florida offered relatively easy access to unfriendly nations, like Cuba, that would receive and harbor him.

The first motivation, getting out of the hot zone of Washington, DC, was moot. He had gone and there was nothing Rusty could do about that. The good news for Rusty was his ability to fly and pick up more than a day on his fugitive. Now that he was in Miami, Rusty had to anticipate Origen's next move. Sitting in his rental car, Rusty thought deeply on his next action, knowing it would make or break his effort to prevent Origen from leaving the country.

Rusty considered the airlines, knowing his fugitive could take a flight to Jamaica and from there easily travel to Cuba, but he still considered that a long shot. Origen would know TSA had to be alerted, not only in the metro Washington area, but all up and down the eastern seaboard. It was possible for a single passenger to make it through, but it was more likely he would be detained and ultimately taken back to face justice in Washington. Rusty's money was on a short sea voyage. Regulations were much less stringent, if entirely non-existent, and a simple short-term charter would provide all the transportation Origen needed.

"It's going to be by sea," surmised Rusty. "I'm sure of it. The trick now is to figure out where, in all the marinas in south Florida, Origen will go." He needed information, and needed it quickly. He called in to the NCTC and asked for the

Forensic Investigation Unit. Instead of reaching Dennis, he spoke to an assistant in Dennis' department. Frustrated about Dennis' absence, he outlined his need for a listing of all marinas from West Palm Beach to Key West. The assistant was helpful, but Rusty was concerned Dennis was not there. "Where is Dennis Allende?" Rusty wanted to know.

"I'm sorry sir, but Dennis is not here. We're not exactly sure where he is, since he should have returned by now." The young assistant advised Rusty he would receive a full listing of marinas, harbormasters, and small boat rental operations within the hour.

TRUE TO HIS word, the NCTC assistant emailed Rusty the list he requested. He scrolled through pages of material with a growing sense of futility. "I had no idea there were so many places to rent a boat. How do I wade through all this material?"

He pulled into a nearby hotel where he printed out his document and went into the restaurant for a cup of coffee and a table to begin the work of guessing where his quarry would go. Several hours and many cups of coffee later, Rusty felt he had a workable list.

The largest commercial rental facilities were the first to be culled. "No way he's going to get into a computerized system like these will have. He's going to want a smaller operation." Next to go were the larger municipal marinas, like the West Palm marina, the Ft. Lauderdale marina, and several more in Miami. What he was left with were small operators who rented space at small, out of the way marinas, as well as those advertising on Craig's List for cheap charters.

Rusty looked over his list, getting into Origen's mindset. "What would I do? Would I go to one of these independent operators here in Miami, or would I go further south, like Key West, where I would be that much closer to Cuba?" He looked at the list of twenty possible locations, rolling the question around in his mind.

ORIGEN HAD PLENTY of thinking time as he drove south on US 95. He had several departure and escape plans, developed years ago with the knowledge that one day he would be discovered. At one end of the spectrum was simple deportation. At the other was a fiery shootout where he may or may not live. And then there was the Consortium. His entanglement with them was begun reluctantly but he had to admit, over the years they delivered on their promise. But if he feared the American authorities, he feared what the Consortium would do when it was discovered he was leaving the fold.

His various plans only considered the American officials and their anticipated actions—the Consortium left out of the equations. He was sorry for that now, as his schemes never included this present situation. He panicked, he could see the storm that was coming his way and he simply panicked, leaving as quickly as possible. Origen wasn't especially sorry about the men he left behind, and in retrospect he felt he had done them a service by disappearing.

Now he sat in a Jacksonville motel room, exhausted from the drive, but still unable to sleep. He needed to activate a plan, one that was only halfway developed. He needed to re-establish a relationship from long ago, and hoped the old man he befriended years ago would still consider him a friend. He came to a decision: He would buy a burner cell phone and he would call Key West Charters.

The decision allowed Origen to relax and he fell right to sleep. The next day he arose early, had a mediocre complementary breakfast, and found a kiosk in the lobby offering pre-paid cell phones. He purchased one with minimum minutes, knowing he would only use it for one call, and left the motel.

RUSTY BEGAN HIS search for Origen with charter boat services between Ft. Lauderdale and Miami. He didn't hold much faith these would be places Origen would go, but he had to be thorough. He visited each one, figuring a personal visit would get him much more than he could get from a phone call. The businesses were generally small, operating between one and five boats. He met each of the owners, all seemed legitimate, and none had any reservation for a man named Origen. His fugitive could be using an alias, but with the rough photo he had on his cell phone, he was sure Origen had not contacted these particular charter operators.

As he left the last company on his Miami list, heading south to Key West, Rusty needed more help from NCTC. His call found Dennis still away from the office, but the friendly assistant that helped him earlier was once again ready to help Rusty. "Great. Say, what was your name again?"

"It's Gill, sir. John Gill."

"Right. Ok John, I need you to access some files that Dennis recently compiled. It was specifically a name search, but I'd like you to take it a little deeper."

"Sure thing, Mr. Strickland."

"The file would probably be titled 'Origen'—that's with an E—and I'd like to know how he came to the United States and if he ever vacationed in Key West. I'm interested in anyone he spent time with who operates a fishing boat for hire." John Gill wrote down the instructions and promised to get back to Rusty as quickly as possible. "Thanks, John. You're a big help. I'm on my way to Key West now, so you've got a couple of hours."

It didn't take that much time. Gill called back within an hour and had some news for Rusty. "It seems your man entered the country in New York as an immigrant from Ukraine. His name was, or should I say is, Dmitry Kosygin. He listed his age as twenty-two and his occupation was a student. He apparently produced acceptance papers from a university in Binghamton, and was issued a visa. INS lost track of him, but fortunately our modern technology can reconstruct certain aspects of his life."

"John, please. Tell me if he ever went to Key West."

"Sorry. I get a little carried away. Yes, he did travel to Key West and it was all in those early years, while INS still knew where he was. There were two occasions when he went down there. The first was within the first year here. On that trip he stayed in a cheap place, and he chartered a fishing trip with someone called Reuben Pounder."

"That's great, John."

"Wait, there's more. Three years later Kosygin went back. He stayed at the same address but hired another charter company to take him out fishing. This time he didn't go out just for one day, he chartered an entire week of fishing."

"Who did he hire on this second trip?"

"A man named Dallas Cutts. Well, I assume it's a man. It could be a weird business name."

"Thanks, John. And have Dennis call me as soon as he shows up." Rusty was worried for the young computer wiz. *He should have been back from Iceland by this time,* he thought.

CHAPTER FIFTY-THREE

DENNIS MOVED AS QUICKLY AS he could along the cliff ledge, coming to the place where he discovered he had to hold onto the fold of rock and swing himself around into the tunnel entrance. There wasn't time to consider the danger; there was only the immediate moment demanding action. As he grabbed the well-worn handhold on the rock, he imagined Galdur and Salim attempting this stunt. Galdur, he knew, was surprisingly spry, perhaps from his mountain hiking in Iceland, and it was conceivable he could manage what Dennis was about to attempt, but Salim—that was another question.

He cleared his mind, making a conscious effort to ignore his fear and thrust himself outward, twisting in. He made it! It was surprising how easily he made it, landing in a crouch on a firm, flat floor. He was sure Galdur would be proud of him, and Dekker, too.

Dennis didn't want to be seen, so he immediately flattened himself against the wall. He listened carefully for his companions and heard voices above—they had been discovered! Dennis was sure whoever was above had not seen him jump down to the ledge, and he was far enough along to avoid detection. He realized he was on his own with only the slimmest idea where he was, but his friends had been captured and it was his duty to help them.

LORD GEOFFREY WAS surprised to see these two old men standing in his office. He expected his team to capture Dekker, but these others—that was unexpected. Galdur he knew from years ago, and Salim by reputation.

"Galdur, my old friend. It has been many years. I thought you were frozen in a glacier in Iceland. Why are you here? What are you trying to do?" With no response forthcoming, Geoffrey moved on.

"And Salim, the venerable Salim. What in the world brings you here? Are you following Galdur on some fool's errand? You should have known better and remained in your Babylonian temple."

Lord Geoffrey walked slowly around the men, his hands clasped behind his back.

"Nobody's talking? Well, it doesn't take a gift of clairvoyance to discern your purpose. You are here to attack the Master." He stopped to let the statement sink in, and to gauge their body language.

"It is futile, this plan of yours, if you even have a plan. Attempting to sneak into Krugerschloss is pointless. Galdur, you should know that."

Still no reaction from his captives, and Lord Geoffrey began losing patience.

"Very well. You can play tight lips all you like. But I will give you some time to think about your position, and to tell me where I may find Dekker." The mention of Dekker's name rocked Galdur back slightly, and Salim dropped his head.

"Oh, I see he is someone you know. Well, we'll give you some comfortable contemplation quarters and let you think about your situation." Lord Geoffrey turned to his guard team and issued an order to remove the prisoners. "Take them to the pit."

The pit is an ancient torture, literally a hole, that a prisoner is tossed in and left to die. The mental anguish in a deep, dark hole eventually makes any man go mad, and the physical deprivation of food, water, and even light, make it all the worse. The Krugerschloss pit was legend among acolytes and often used as a threat to motivate cooperation or concentration on lessons.

The pit was located deep in the mountain, in one of the very oldest tunnels, dug there by the earliest clan leaders and used to hold captive chieftains for ransom—or simply for torture. The pit had not been used in many years; in fact, Lord Geoffrey himself had not seen it since his youth when a fellow acolyte challenged his bravery and he was forced to go down the dark tunnel ending at the pit to prove he was unafraid. It had been a harrowing experience and he remembered wondering how anyone could last more than a day or two in that horrid place.

Lord Geoffrey did not accompany the prisoners to the pit, relying instead on his men to carry out the task. They enlisted the aid of some acolytes as they left Lord Geoffrey's office, stopping to collect up a rope ladder and some lanterns. They escorted the prisoners down a wide passage until reaching a crossroads with a narrower passage. They turned right and came to a stair leading down. The footing was easy and they descended the long stair until reaching a landing with three tunnels branching off. In the dark, and with only a couple of lanterns to light the way, it was difficult to see where the tunnels led.

This was an area of the castle that was not much used; in fact, it was hard to tell if anyone had passed this way in a decade. Dust covered the rough stone floor, undisturbed by footprints. The guards directed the prisoners to the right-hand tunnel, leaving evidence of their passage in the soft dust. The somber parade moved on in silence, the oppressive environment and the growing smell affecting all. They reached a place where one of the guards almost fell into the pit; it was so dark that discerning its presence was difficult.

Using the lanterns, the escort attached the rope ladder to pins sunk into the stone floor, flinging the ladder into the void. One of the guards leaned over, lighting the pit.

"Hey, there's someone down here!" The leader came over and inspected the find from above.

"So there is. Looks like he fell in there. See how his legs are broken? He'll make good company for our friends here."

"Your turn," said one of the guards to the prisoners. "Down you go."

Galdur and Salim had no choice but to obey. They descended the rope ladder into the pit, stepping carefully around the desiccated body. The ladder was pulled up and stored on the edge of the pit, and the escort team left without another word.

Galdur and Salim could do nothing. There were no handholds or seams in the smooth dressed-rock surface of the pit, and it was much too deep to have any hope of climbing out.

"What about Dennis?" Salim asked. "He's in here somewhere, right?"

"Yes, you're right," said Galdur. "Let us see if we can reach Dennis and guide him here."

CHAPTER FIFTY-FOUR

DENNIS SAT FOR A LONG time, unsure what to do. Should he go back to see what had become of his companions, or should he move forward to the tunnel leading into the heart of the mountain? He wanted to go back but knew that was futile. The others had been seen and captured, and were by now long gone.

Where would they be taken? Into Krugerschloss, of course, Dennis reasoned. *Therefore, I have to go into the mountain to find my friends.*

While Dennis did have some prior knowledge of the mountain castle's layout, the tunnel reaching into the inky black before him was unknown territory. He reached into the leg-pocket of his cargo pants and found the small Maglite he carried. He felt the pocket on the opposite leg to verify his multi-tool was there—it was, and he felt much better. He moved into the long passageway, twisting the small flashlight to the *on* position.

He walked in the middle of the tunnel, swinging his flashlight left and right. The walls, he noted, were rough-hewn and unfinished. He remembered the chambers and halls above as being finely finished, and quite lovely. These walls, by contrast, were unlovely and strictly functional. If this were truly the original tunnel of what was to become Krugerschloss, he could understand the lack of workmanship.

Dennis noted occasional crude etchings in the walls, and even handprints. Those, he reasoned, must be Neolithic, and probably worthy of some study, but not today, not now. He had to move on. The floor began to rise slowly and the walls became polished and finished. Even the floor gave way from the raw stone to inset pavers. *Coming to civilization,* he observed. Still unsure of his location, he could do nothing but move forward.

He came to an open area, a vestibule of sorts. The path led forward to stairs that seemed to go a long way up. Before moving on he looked around and noticed footprints in the dust on the floor. He swung his light behind him and discovered he had been leaving a similar trail all the way up the tunnel. Turning back to the vestibule he noticed the footprints went into one particular passage. He wished he had Dekker's knowledge of such things; he would know how many passed this way, and probably how long ago. But he didn't have those skills and was about to press on to the stairs when he had a strong feeling, almost a call, in his head.

He stopped to consider what it meant. Is it Dekker calling me on the Flows? As he considered the question it became clear it was not Dekker, but Galdur. He concentrated on the feeling he was receiving.

"Damn—it's a call for help." Dennis knew it was from Galdur—it just felt that way. The more he concentrated, the clearer the pictures in his mind became. He saw a hole in a stone floor and a rope ladder rolled up at its edge. It dawned on him what Galdur was saying: He was trapped in a pit and the only escape was the rope ladder. Dennis had to find Galdur and help. The question was, where to search. He looked once more at the confused footprints on the dusty floor and understanding dawned.

"Coming, Galdur!" His shout was unnecessary, but it gave him heart as he set off down the dark passage.

CHAPTER FIFTY-FIVE

DEKKER SEARCHED AS BEST HE could in the dark for an entrance to the caverns below, but was unsuccessful. He would have to wait until daybreak to inspect the area and find the trapdoor. He was tired after being chased through the forest, capturing the two pursuers, and continuing up the mountain. He sat down with his back to a tree and fell into a deep sleep.

A rustling sound awakened him. The sun was up and at first he could not determine what made the sound he heard in his sleep. He looked around carefully, not wanting to make any noise himself, in case it was a searcher looking for him. After a moment he saw the gray head and floppy ears of a rabbit peek from under a bush, followed by a few hopping steps out from under the bush hiding him. The rabbit saw Dekker and was trying to decide if he was a threat or not. Of course, to a rabbit, any large primate was a potential threat and therefore to be avoided. The rabbit turned and hopped away from Dekker.

"Good-bye, little fellow."

He eased into a sitting position, took in the surrounding area and decided it was safe to move around. The forest below was still in deep shadow, but the rising sun was bright on the hilltop. He realized it had been many days, or weeks, even months, since he'd appreciated such a sight. It brought back memories of Kelly, how the morning sun made her auburn hair glow, almost like a halo. An ache gripped his heart once again thinking of her and it focused him on the task at hand: Find the trapdoor.

He searched his memory for the time, five years ago, when he'd followed Kara up here. She knew where to look, of course, so he didn't pay close attention and now criticized himself for not watching. He recalled they'd followed a game trail up here, so the first order of business was to find that trail. After some wandering he stumbled on the trail, still used by goats and other animals of the forest. Walking along the trail, certain landmarks came back to him. He was looking for a large tree stump a little off the trail. He was just about to give up, figuring he'd followed the wrong game trail, when the movement of a bird caught his eye. It was a large raven, blue-black in color, that landed to his left. With a few steps in that direction, Dekker saw the raven's landing site—his tree stump.

Dekker's relief was palpable. Now he could navigate his way to the trapdoor entry to Krugerschloss. A few steps through the underbrush brought him to a place clear of bushes and looked like any one of the many open spaces found in the forest, especially atop this hill. But Dekker knew it to be special, and went to the large, flat stone set into the ground.

He looked around for the instruments he knew were at hand and soon found them: a six-foot pole, tapered at one end, and a shorter pole that he remembered was used as a prybar for the stone cover. He carried the tools back to the center of the open space and found a notch on one edge of the flat stone. Inserting the shorter stick, he lifted the edge of the stone and propped it open with a nearby rock. He stood and grabbed the edge of the large stone, hoisting it high, like a weightlifter. He balanced the rock with an extended left hand, he took the longer pole, placed the tapered end into a round hole bored on the underside of the stone, and pushing it up to its full height. Securing the pole in a base rock seat, he let go, the stone now fully supported by the prop.

He looked down the stone steps and decided they were not wet or particularly dangerous due, no doubt, to the seal of the roof-stone. He had no flashlight, but the sunlight provided ample illumination down the narrow shaft. He descended the steps and hoped to find a torch or lantern at the bottom. He found a lantern, and with a box of stick matches stored nearby, he ignited it. Before moving on he thought it best to close the roof stone. "Wouldn't do having guests arriving here, would it?" He lowered the large stone, making sure it was properly set. Moving from the base of the stairs into a broader tunnel, he could tell there had been no traffic through this entrance for some time, years perhaps.

Soon he heard a rush of water flowing through the wall on his right and knew it to be ground runoff from Triberg Falls, and the source of power and water for Krugerschloss. Pressing on, he came to a low wooden door blocking his path.

He sat on the floor concentrating his proximity sense. There seemed to be no one on the other side, so he opened the door.

No locks, he remarked to himself. *I forgot—these people don't lock doors.*

Dekker stooped to get through the doorway and stood on the other side. He remembered this room as well. It had two doors, one leading to the water distribution center for the mountain castle, the other led to a large residence hall, appropriately called, Triberg Hall.

He again concentrated on sensing any presence on the other side of the door and felt none—at least, none close by. As he slowly opened the heavy wooden door he prayed no one was looking up at the platform and doorway high up the wall.

He crabbed out from the door onto a landing. As far as he could sense or tell, no one noticed him and he breathed a sigh of relief. A waterfall shot from the wall to his right, plunging almost one hundred feet down to a pool and recreation area in the Hall.

He scanned across the cavern walls, marveling once again at the industry and workmanship represented by the three levels of dwellings hewn from the rock. Each dwelling had its own porch and unique décor; all connected by sturdy walkways. Ladders were positioned along the way, offering access to other levels.

The brightly colored trim defined the entrance to each home and was an expression of the resident's personality. The whole made a bright kaleidoscope of color and design that was quite pleasing.

Dekker noted there seemed many fewer residents than five years ago, not surprising given Galdur, who played a false Abaddon, ordered everyone to abandon the cave system. But as true believers slowly returned, they naturally gravitated to their original clan residence halls. He moved down the long stairway leading up to his platform and wondered why there was no guardrail. *I guess they'd be in trouble with OSHA.*

As he reached the landing for the top residence level a door opened. He froze, knowing he was totally exposed, and hoped the emerging acolyte or Adept would turn the other way. Fortunately, the door of the residence opened outward and offered some masking. He was thankful that the builders did not hold with the convention that a proper door open inward; he supposed it arose from the need to mount a door on a wooden frame set into stone, and opening inward required additional stonework. Whatever the reason, Dekker was happy because he could hide behind the open door.

The unsuspecting Brother emerging from the residence closed his door, which of course exposed Dekker. The gray-clad brother let out a startled exclamation, but Dekker moved quickly to incapacitate him. Looking around as he dragged the Brother back into his home, he was confident they had not been seen.

Inside the stone residence Dekker looked for additional robes, found several hanging in a richly carved wardrobe, and took one. The resident was still unconscious, but would not remain so for long. Pulling the robe over his head he decided to leave the man there and left, closing the door behind. Now costumed to fit in, Dekker moved quickly down the residence levels to reach the floor.

There were several freestanding open structures on the main floor of Triberg Hall, very much like pergolas, with trellised ceilings and sturdy, carved logs at the corners for support. Beneath the pergolas were tables and benches, complemented by several Adirondack-style chairs. A large central area was built for general gatherings and community meals, and as it happened, was empty. There was only one small pergola occupied, and it was at the far end of the expansive floor. People were talking in low tones and the body language suggested they were being careful not to be heard.

Moving through the hall toward the main entry tunnel, Dekker kept structures between himself and the people in the far pergola. As he began to approach the tunnel there was a loud shout. It was the Brother who was left unconscious, shouting in German.

"Stop! Hey, you, stop!"

The shout alerted the people huddled in the small pergola, and they immediately stood to see what the shouting was about.

"That man knocked me out and took a robe. Stop him!" It took only a moment for one of the onlookers to spot Dekker who was now disappearing into the tunnel.

"There he is, I see him!" Several others echoed his shout as they set out in pursuit of the intruder.

As he ran, Dekker remembered that the primary tunnels, or "highways," all ran down to the main building attached to the front of the cave system. He also knew there were side passages allowing free movement between residence halls.

Dekker took the first cross tunnel, hoping to throw off his pursuers. The tunnel ceiling was considerably lower than the main highway, but still passable. All along the walls were doors opening onto storerooms, each neatly labeled as to its contents. As with every other door in Krugerschloss, there were no locks and Dekker once again marveled at the civility and lack of crime evidenced in the castle.

Dekker stopped to listen for sounds of pursuit, which soon echoed off the tunnel walls. The question was whether they would run down the main highway, or investigate the side passages. It took only a moment to determine that some were dispatched down his side tunnel, while the main body of the group moved farther down the highway toward the administrative center.

He had to convince them this tunnel was not his escape route, but there was almost nowhere to hide—except in the storerooms. Stepping into a room, he discovered it filled with furniture: Large pieces like tables, beds, wardrobes, and chests, and smaller items like chairs, mirrors, and end tables.

This is where residence furniture is stored, he thought.

Dekker listened at the storeroom door, hoping the pair dispatched to check out the cross tunnel would pass by. His enhanced proximity sense told him there were only two people, and he knew he could easily surprise and defeat them, but then it would only alert more Brothers to his location. He waited to see if they would give up, having gone far enough toward the next hall, called Germania, to send them back to the main roadway/tunnel. But the searchers were not content to look for him out in the open. They recognized the potential for concealment each of the storerooms offered, and began inspecting each one.

As the brothers approached his storeroom, Dekker stepped behind a tall wardrobe and discarded the robe he had taken from the residence cell above. *Better for my mobility.* The searchers opened the door, waving lamps, and soon decided their quarry was not there. Dekker breathed a sigh of relief as they stepped back into the access tunnel to continue checking successive storerooms.

After many minutes Dekker heard the men move back up the hallway, grumbling about the "wild goose chase" they were on, hoping the others managed to corner the errant Brother.

Satisfied the hallway was empty, Dekker stepped out of his hiding place, heading back toward the main Triberg Hall passage. Approaching the intersection, he moved carefully, alert to any human presence. There was none, so he turned back up the highway and re-entered Triberg Hall.

Dekker knew each of the residence halls had a large kitchen and he headed down the interior wall toward two large double doors providing access to the kitchen area. When he entered he had a sense of déjà vu, as the layout was exactly as the one he recalled from Kruger Hall, the farthest residence area.

It was in Kruger Hall five years ago that a lone Brother, lagging behind the call to assembly, spotted them. Dekker chased the man through the rows of food preparation stations and finally down a trash chute, which gave him a harrowing ride into the huge utility cavern below. He had no wish to duplicate that wild ride, but knew his best bet to shake pursuit and get to Abaddon was this direct route.

In his previous experience Dekker had only noticed the trash chute and had not seen a smaller dumbwaiter carved out of the rock wall opposite the trash.

Perhaps that is my escape route, he thought.

CHAPTER FIFTY-SIX

ABADDON'S SPIRIT STIRRED DEEP IN the heart of Krugerschloss. There was something amiss and the spirit sensed it. The unease manifested as a troubled demeanor in Kambrian, the man carrying Abaddon's name and hosting his spirit. Kambrian/Abaddon was acting erratic, issuing orders and commands that were contradictory or vengeful. Word came that a team sent to find and kill Galdur lost him somewhere in the Syrian desert and had no idea what direction he might have taken.

"Fools!" he yelled at the acolyte delivering the message. "It is where he is going that is important, and that destination is right here."

"Yes, Master. Is there a message to send back?"

"There is indeed. I want every incompetent in that search party executed. And I want it done right away."

"As you wish, Master." The acolyte backed out humbly, hoping as the deliverer of bad news to escape the Master's wrath.

Kambrian/Abaddon suddenly wondered where his chief of staff, the Egyptian, was keeping himself. He sent out an angry call on the Flows and was quite surprised when Kamenwati responded in person.

"Where have you been?"

"I told you earlier, Master, I was looking into some troubling rumors."

"Well? What did you find? And where is the American?"

"Sir, I have been reluctant to tell you, but Dekker seems to have escaped." With that revelation Kambrian/Abaddon began to see the world tinged in red, and his already delicate mental state came unhinged. Kamenwati watched in silent satisfaction.

"There is something else, sir. We have found a seditious faction within our Brotherhood, right here in Krugerschloss. I have men searching out the traitors and plan to bring them before you for justice."

"And who is the ring-leader?"

"It is the Englishman, Lord Geoffrey."

Kambrian/Abaddon couldn't believe the Englishman would betray him. He had known him since he was a boy, had instructed him in the deeper things of Magick and the Old Truths, and now this betrayal. Why? Kamenwati supplied the answer to the unspoken question.

"Lord Geoffrey sees you as weakened and vulnerable. He wishes to displace you and take control of the Brotherhood."

"Find the traitor, my faithful Kamenwati, and bring him to me."

"As you wish." The Egyptian left Abaddon's presence with a smug satisfaction, knowing he had just sealed his rival's fate.

IN THE ALDER grove a standoff of sorts developed between Kamenwati's men coming in from the search for Dekker, and Lord Geoffrey's men guarding possible points of entry to the castle. It was a race of sorts; the team capturing and presenting the American to the Master would receive the prize of ascendency within the hierarchy of Krugerschloss.

Both Lord Geoffrey and Kamenwati hungered for the prize, along with the belief each could replace the man Kambrian as the undisputed leader of the Brotherhood and all its enterprises.

Lord Geoffrey's team discovered the Egyptian's men as they entered the alder grove. When questioned about their purpose, Kamenwati's team from Bad Peterstal became combative, claiming they were on an important mission for Lord Kamenwati. The invocation of the Egyptian's name in a manner suggesting he was the Master only served to anger Geoffrey's team. A struggle ensued with each group claiming authority to arrest and detain. Unfortunately for Lord Geoffrey's men, the Bad Peterstal group outnumbered theirs, and soon had them restrained. With Lord Geoffrey's men bound, and several unconscious, the leader of Kamenwati's team gathered his troops.

"Men, I believe our immediate objective has just changed. We must find any other 'guard' teams roaming around the castle, arrest them, and bring them to justice before Lord Kamenwati. When that is accomplished we will continue to track and capture the American."

Inside the castle's administrative center a strange undercurrent began. People were uneasy, and there was a sense of trouble, like an approaching storm. Lord Geoffrey felt the dissonance and searched for the source. Only when he crossed paths with the Egyptian in the administrative center did it became clear. No words were spoken, only false, polite nods exchanged, but Geoffrey knew that the truce between them was over and that he must be on his guard.

The encounter with the Egyptian was followed by a breathless report to Lord Geoffrey of the clash between the groups in the alder grove. Geoffrey stiffened with a bolt of fear, understanding his rival made the first move, and then relaxed remembering his trump cards—Galdur and Salim. He would neutralize Kamenwati's move in one bold stroke, and since the Egyptian did not have the American, he could present no adequate parry to Lord Geoffrey's move.

CHAPTER FIFTY-SEVEN

DENNIS MADE HIS WAY DOWN the ancient tunnel. He would have fallen into the pit himself if the piled-up rope ladder had not stood out like a boulder in the light of his small flashlight. Peering down the deep hole, he could not believe men were held in such a terrible place.

"Galdur? Are you down there?" Galdur's relief hearing Dennis' voice was palpable.

"Roll the ladder down, my boy. We'll stand back."

Dennis wasted no time complying with Galdur's request and kicked the rope bundle over the side of the pit. He pointed the flashlight into the dark hole but could make nothing out. He saw the ladder stiffen and swing slightly, indicating someone was on the way up. Dennis saw the top of a head climbing up the ladder; the man looked up and Dennis recognized Salim's face.

"You're almost here. Keep climbing."

Salim pulled himself over the edge and Dennis called down to Galdur, telling him to begin his climb. In a matter of minutes Galdur, too, sat on the edge of the pit, catching his breath along side Salim.

"Thank you, Dennis," said Galdur. "You saved our lives." Dennis was a little embarrassed, claiming he did nothing, but still enjoyed the accolade.

"What a nasty place, Galdur. I had no idea Krugerschloss had this Medieval torture chamber."

"It has not been used in many years, Dennis. It is a relic from a time of constant conflict among the clans of the area."

"And someone decided you needed to reopen those old customs?"

"I'm afraid Lord Geoffrey was none too pleased to find us prowling around the grounds."

Dennis looked around with his flashlight wondered out loud, "So what's our next move? I can guide us back out the way I came in, but from there, I don't know."

"We go forward. Dekker will need us soon, and if we can remain hidden from Abaddon's view, we can help."

Dennis led Galdur and Salim up the tunnel and back to the chamber where the main tunnel continued up wide stairs. Galdur stepped forward. "Let me take the lead, Dennis. I remember this part from our march down here, and I think we need to be especially careful not to be seen or heard by any residents."

Dennis gladly gave up his lead position as they ascended the stairs. When they reached the top Galdur called a halt. They sat gratefully on a landing under the arched entry to a large chamber beyond. While his companions rested Galdur went forward to reconnoiter, and returned after several minutes.

"The chamber is an intersection of six tunnels. I went a short way up each to get a sense of where they go. Our tunnel continues on straight across, and without stairs, you'll be happy to know. The others lead up to the residence areas, Triberg Hall, Germania Hall, and Kruger Hall," Galdur said, shaking the dust from his clothes.

"We go straight across. This tunnel leads to the Great Assembly Hall and to Abaddon's private office and chambers."

"Is it guarded?" asked Dennis.

"The closer we get to Abaddon, the more likely we are to encounter guards. I sense turmoil and conflict, which serves to have everyone on alert—as we must be."

"All right then, let's go," said Galdur. Stepping into the chamber beyond he stopped short, giving a closed-fist signal to stop. He listened for a moment and turned to the others. "Quick, back down the tunnel. Someone is coming—and coming fast."

Dennis and Salim moved back down the stairs a short distance, following Galdur's instruction to stay low and hug the wall. Soon they heard the sound of people running down one of the stairs leading from the residence halls above. Galdur turned, raising his forefinger to his lips.

A group of six men and two women, some in white acolyte robes, some in the gray worn by Adepts, spilled into the chamber, stopping to catch their breath.

"Quiet, everyone," announced the leader, a gray-clad Adept. "Listen and reach out in the Flows to get a sense of our fugitive."

The three men heard their intention to use the flows and Dennis began to panic, realizing they would be found in an instant. But Galdur placed a calming hand on his arm and looked to Salim. The old man understood what needed to be done and set out to create a masking cloud to hide their presence.

The pursuing group fell silent as they concentrated their energies in the Flows, but two more men, those who searched the side passages, interrupted entering the chamber. A little annoyed, the Adept questioned the men. "Anything to report?"

"No, sir. We checked the storerooms between Triberg and Germania and found nothing."

"Good. That means he went forward." Another commotion on the stairs brought an acolyte messenger to the search group.

"There is a great conflict developing between Brothers loyal to Lord Geoffrey and those loyal to Kamenwati, and Master Abaddon commands all brethren in residence come to the Great Hall at once." A collective gasp from the searchers indicated the severity of this order.

The Adept leader looked around the chamber, knowing his search was far from complete, but he could not ignore the order. "Off we go, everyone—to the Great Hall."

Galdur breathed a sigh of relief and waited for the search party to leave the landing. When it became quiet Galdur stood, looking at the granite walls as if he could see through them. "They are gone," he said softly. "Salim, you may drop the cloud."

The three moved quickly across the open chamber to the tunnel opposite, continuing on. As they moved through the tunnel, Dennis had questions for Galdur.

"If Abaddon is calling everyone to the Great Hall, how are we going to interfere?"

"Don't worry, Dennis. If we are not too late, our very presence will be the distraction needed to allow Dekker to make his move."

"Dekker? Is he here?"

Galdur got that faraway look again, and said, "Oh, yes. He is here."

Dennis stopped, forcing the others to stop. "We've got to find him and help him."

"No, Dennis, we cannot. What Dekker has to do, he must do alone. Our job is to create an environment that will allow him to face and defeat Abaddon." He turned and looked down the tunnel. "The back door to Abaddon's quarters are down there, and that is where we must go."

CHAPTER FIFTY-EIGHT

ORIGEN CALLED KEY WEST DIRECTORY assistance, asking for the number to Dallas Cutts Fishing Charters. After a few moments he heard ringing on the other end, but it took a long time before the line was answered.

A gruff, older voice announced the charter business name, followed by, "How can I help you?" Origen knew Cutts would remember only his original name, Dmitry Kosygin. "Cutts, this is Dmitry, Dmitry Kosygin, do you remember me?" There was a long silence and then a dawning remembrance.

"My old friend. It has been years. I thought maybe you'd forgotten about your friend Cutts."

"Never, Dallas. But these intervening years have been very busy and I just couldn't get away like before."

"But now? Are you coming here for more fishing and talking?"

"Yes, I am. As a matter of fact I am only a few hours from you." Origin set a meeting time and made sure no one else would be around. Hanging up, he smiled to himself, believing this impromptu plan was going to work.

RUSTY WAS PLEASED that Dennis' department could sift through the details of Origen's existence and set him on the right path. He still had a nagging feeling that Dennis was in trouble, and because he was not a field agent, his peril would be that much more grave and likely to end badly for him.

He knew there was nothing to be done until this Origen episode was done. He only hoped Dennis would be back when he returned to the NCTC. "But now, my focus and energy needs to be directed to Origen." Rusty left his concerns for Dennis behind, heading for the A1A highway where the last stop was Key West. He only hoped the day wasted investigating marinas and charter operators had not put him behind Origen, that he could still beat the fugitive to the fishing charter operator he used those many years ago. He pressed down on the accelerator in an unconscious reaction to his fear of being too late.

ORIGEN LEFT JACKSONVILLE after talking with Cutts. He was not out of the woods yet, but he was confident his old friend still held with his patriot/survivalist beliefs, a system of thought that claimed taxes were illegal and the government must be opposed at every turn. Cutts beliefs were what Origen would play on, would use to convince the old man that the government was "after" him and only Cutts could help.

He passed through Miami about the time Rusty was first calling the NCTC and discovering Dennis' unexplained absence. The time between the call and the follow-up meant that Origen had about ninety minutes head start on Rusty. Neither knew it, but a race was on.

Two hours of driving found Origen just outside Key West. He remembered the sleepy town as a last outpost of individualism and self-expression. Key West always felt itself a place apart, and its history included the establishment of the Conch Republic in 1982, a not so tongue-in-cheek move to secede from the United States to create a sovereign nation. While the Conch Republic was short-lived, the underlying sense of freedom from laws and regulations remain.

Dallas Cutts still held to the principles of individual freedoms—free from federal government prying, spying, taxing, and regulating. He wasn't an outlaw; he simply believed he had the right to live without laws.

Origen found the turnoff from Florida A1A onto Suncrest Road and looked with nostalgia at the small trailer he rented all those years ago. "A long way from the manor house," he said. He continued on to Shrimp Road to the end, where pavement gave way to hard packed earth and sand. The area was littered with boats of all sizes, lying at odd angles and lining the end of the tiny isthmus. There was little change during the thirty years since his last visit. The beached boats were still in varying states of disrepair and most looked like they had been abandoned years before.

This was not a pretty area. It was a place where the poor underbelly of Key West found refuge, and Dallas Cutts was no exception. Origen drove around the curve that ended at one of the few boats in the water. A small, hand-written sign planted in the hard earth announced, "Cutts Fishing Charters." Origen parked his car along the road and walked back to the boat.

"Ahoy! Anyone aboard?" called Origen. Inside he heard the scrape of a chair and the sound of a small refrigerator being opened and closed. Soon an older version of the man he knew from three decades before emerged. He was still a big man, but Cutts had aged and let himself go. He easily weighed two hundred fifty pounds, and his puffy, round face was red—Origen wasn't sure if it was the sun or excessive alcohol—his hair had turned from the bright red he knew to white; it was still long, and tied off in a ponytail.

Cutts grinned at his old friend and held his hands up, like an Olympic athlete celebrating a victory, displaying two bottles of beer he just pulled from the refrigerator. "Kosygin! You haven't aged a day. Here, join me for a cold one." He offered one of the bottles of beer to Origen.

"And you look great yourself, Cutts. May I come aboard?"

With a great laugh, Cutts invited Origen up. "We don't stand on ceremony here, Dmitry. Just get the hell up here and tell me what you've been doing for the last three decades." Origen gladly accepted the offered beer and invitation to board. He took a long swallow from the bottle and pronounced the beer "perfect." He gave Cutts a serious look and whispered, "Let's go into the cabin. There is much to tell." Cutts looked around suspiciously, a reaction developed over many years avoiding the law.

They sat in a banquette on one side of the small salon. Across from the table was a galley with the natural gas refrigerator Origen heard earlier. Cutts quickly downed his beer and opened the refrigerator door revealing shelves packed with beer. Only beer.

"Looks like you're well stocked, Cutts."

"Yeah, I'm ready for an invasion. Now, what's brought you to our little republic?" Cutts sat down next to Origin with a fresh beer. "I take it this is not a call for a pleasure cruise."

Origen went into a rapid summary of his life in Washington, DC. He emphasized his anti-government activities and told how he compromised many high level officials. "But now they have turned on me. They discovered I never paid taxes, and now the IRS is pursuing me. I had to leave my home quickly, without even a suitcase of clothes. As I ran, I thought, who would sympathize with this illegal act of a taxing agency created to oppress the masses? Dallas Cutts, I said. That's where I must go."

"IRS, you say? I hate those guys. They do nothing but take what little we've got, and do nothing for it. Tell me, what do you need?" Origen was pleased he hit all Cutts' hot buttons and pressed on.

"I need to get away. From here—the United States."

"Where is it you want to go?"

"To Cuba. It's the closest and best bet for me."

Cutts took a long drink. Setting it down on the table he laid out some of the problems with Origen's plan. "Cuba's close, no doubt of that. But we would have to time it in such a way that we're not seen by Coast Guard boats."

"You're right. But if I remember correctly, you keep tabs on those patrols. You probably know the best route to take." Cutts scratched his head and took another drink of beer.

"Yeah. I do know how the Coast Guard operates in these waters. I'll take you, but first we need to draw up a charter agreement so if we are stopped, I can claim we're just out fishing."

"Perfect. When can we leave?"

"Now is as good a time as any, and I can see you are anxious to get under way."

RUSTY, GUIDED BY GPS coordinates sent to his cell phone, rolled up to the location of Cutts Fishing Charters only to find an empty slip. A telephone call back to Dennis' team in McLean confirmed the coordinates. "There's only an empty slip here. Any ideas?"

"Look around, maybe he moved since we gathered that information."

"It's more likely Origen beat me here and Cutts has taken him somewhere. I'll get back to you."

Rusty drove around the dilapidated buildings looking for another charter operator. He finally found one housed in a small shed-like structure with a weathered front door and one small window set into the wall next to it. A weathered sign affixed to the door announced the operator's business name: Thompson Charters. Hoping this man had a fast boat Rusty went inside.

A man, perhaps in his mid-forties, sat at an old desk with feet propped up, watching an old television mounted on the wall. "Afternoon. What can I do for you?"

"Do you have a boat for hire, a fast one?"

"Well, fast is relative, and we generally don't do things fast in Key West," said Mickey Thompson as he took first one foot then another from the desk.

"Do you know another operator around here named Dallas Cutts?"

"Sure do. He's just down the road, right after the curve."

"Is your boat faster than his?" Rusty was desperate. "Cutts is gone, and I need to catch up with him."

"You gonna arrest Cutts?"

"No, I'm not interested in him. Just his passenger."

"You a government man?" asked Thompson. By way of an answer, Rusty produced his NCTC badge. Thompson looked it over carefully. "What the heck is this NCTC? Never heard of it."

"Most people haven't, but we're part of Homeland Security. Can you help me?"

"You got cash? I only work for cash." Rusty pulled out his wallet, looked a little forlorn and asked if there was an ATM somewhere nearby. "Sure, up to Rudy's store, back up Shrimp Road."

"I'll be back."

THE DAY WAS perfect for sailing. A slight breeze blowing offshore, no swells to speak of, and plenty of beer. Cutts was into Origen's adventure by this time, regaling him with stories of his own daring escapades in the Florida waters.

"Drug runners don't use this route much anymore, but back in the day, I had to weave and bob like the dickens just to stay out of their way. And then there were the refugee boats. Small skiffs, really. Jam-packed with people and piloted by jackasses who had no idea where they were going. I kept my distance from them, too, so's they wouldn't jump on my boat and swamp me."

"Sounds exciting. How much longer until we're in Cuban waters?"

"That's the thing. I can't just go straight there; we have to sort of ease around Uncle Fidel's patrols and radar. I don't want to have my boat confiscated—oh no, I don't want that."

"Nor do I, Dallas. I'm just wondering how long it will be until we are beyond the reach of the Coast Guard."

"I'm headed for a deserted stretch of beach that the human smugglers sometimes use. About four hours from here. It's in some heavily shark infested waters, so you're gonna want to keep your hands inside." The thought of sharks had a peculiar, visceral effect on Origen.

"I couldn't imagine being eaten by a shark." They travelled on in silence, Origen contemplating how many sharks might be around the beach, and Cutts consuming a steady flow of beer from the refrigerator.

RUSTY RETURNED FIFTEEN minutes later with Mickey Thompson's fee. He was certain the amount was inflated, but there was no alternative: He had to catch Origen and bring him to justice.

"My boat's not as large as Cutts, but it is faster," said Mickey, who was now into the excitement of a chase. "Do you know how much lead he's got on us?"

"Not exactly," said Rusty. "Maybe an hour or so."

"And where is he headed?"

"My best guess is Cuba. That's where I'd go if I were him."

"You'd better hope we catch up to Cutts. Once he reaches Cuban waters, your man is as good as gone."

"Then there's not a minute to loose," said Rusty.

Mickey's boat was tied up to a short dock. It was a Crestliner 1850 Fish Hawk, an eighteen-foot open boat with a Bimini canvas top for the sun and a one hundred fifty horsepower engine mounted on the rear transom. "This is nicer than I expected, Mickey."

"Yeah, it's fairly new. She'll do almost fifty miles per hour in these waters." They stepped aboard and made a stop to top off the thirty-two gallon fuel tank, and to fill spare fuel cans, before heading out. Once out of the fueling station Mickey opened her up and soon reached her cruising speed of fifty miles per hour.

Mickey did not have the same aversion to being spotted as Cutts, and was able to take a more or less direct route south. The chase was on, and Rusty could only hope they would reach Cutts' boat before entering Cuban territorial waters.

ORIGEN MOVED FROM the co-pilot seat to the rear transom. He couldn't listen to any more of Cutts' fishing stories, or the endless complaining about government oppression. He just needed to get safely away and plan his next move.

He considered his options with the Romani that wandered throughout Europe. His closest ties were with a family group travelling between France and Germany. He remembered fondly the half dozen fifth-wheel trailers his people called home, and how they moved from one place to another completely free. That freedom was an intoxicating thought.

"Hey, my friend," called out Cutts. "We are right in the middle of the Gulf Stream, and if you look overboard you can see schools of fish migrating north." Origen obliged his friend and looked over the gunwale. He was surprised to see they were moving through a huge school of fish. "What kind of fish are these?"

"They're Bonitas. Good game fish, and good eating. I'm sorry we aren't fishing today." Origen made no reply.

After another hour of travel Origen happened to look around the vast, open ocean, grateful Cutts had modern navigation equipment to tell him where he was going. He had never been this far out, and the loss of the sight of land caused a slight panic. He trusted his skipper, though, and let it fall to his hands. As he swept his gaze across the open ocean he noticed a tiny speck. He wasn't sure what it was; it could be anything, a reflection or something else.

"Hey, Cutts, what is that behind us?" Cutts slowed the boat and brought it to a full stop. He grabbed a pair of binoculars and peered to the stern for a long moment.

"I can't tell exactly, but I think it's a boat. And if I'm not mistaken, it's following us."

"Get us the hell out of here," said Origen in a low tone.

"Yeah, you've got it," said Cutts.

Origen stood in the rear, watching with Cutts binoculars. "They're gaining on us, Cutts. Can't you go any faster?"

"She's going flat out now," said Cutts.

Another half hour passed and Origen could plainly see the small boat carrying two men. He wondered just who they were.

THE CRESTLINER GAINED steadily on the larger, bulkier boat ahead. Mickey had identified the boat as Cutts', to Rusty's great relief. He knew they were after the right boat and their smaller craft was definitely faster.

They continued on for another half hour, gaining steadily. Rusty now stood in the cockpit, his binoculars trained on the boat ahead. He could make out the man standing in the rear transom—it was Origen.

"How far to Cuban waters?" asked Rusty.

"Maybe a couple more hours," replied Mickey. "By the way, what is your plan when we catch up?"

"We'll show him this." Rusty pulled a large caliber pistol from his coat, showing it to Mickey. "And we have to hope the skipper makes the right decision."

More time passed and Rusty watched Origen moving frantically around the boat. "He knows they can't outrun us," Rusty observed coolly. "When you reach them, pull along on my side." Mickey nodded his understanding of the order.

ORIGEN, NORMALLY SO cool and in control, was frantic. There was nowhere to escape from this boat in the middle of the ocean, and screaming at Cutts seemed to have no effect. He watched with horror as the other boat closed the gap, coming closer with each minute that passed. He didn't know where to turn first, and simply moved back and forth from the captain's control console to the rear transom.

He watched the pursuers with the binoculars, suddenly realizing the shock of red hair could only belong to the NCTC agent who questioned him in his foyer. *When was that? A thousand years ago?* He cursed the agent.

"I'm going to have to stop, my friend. It seems the game is up," said Cutts. Origen looked at the man in horror.

"No! You have to keep going. We can make it to Cuban waters, I know it."

"I have to slow and let them approach, but I have a plan. Just go back there and watch them." Origen followed Cutts' command and stood in the transom, binoculars now fixed on the rapidly approaching boat.

Cutts began to throttle back, letting the other boat know they would let them approach. But Cutts had spent the last hour thinking about his own skin. How had he gotten himself into this situation, especially with a man he hadn't seen in thirty years? Cutts weighed the options and calculated the odds he could escape this without harm to himself or his boat. He knew his only option was to dump his passenger and bug out.

Cutts looked back and saw his passenger standing close to the gunwale in the transom. "This will be perfect," he said to himself. He continued to slow the boat until they were traveling at a no-wake speed. The other boat moved to the starboard side and he saw a determined looking man with red hair and a very large gun, pointing it in the general direction of his head. He got the message and lifted one hand off the wheel in a sign of surrender.

Origen dropped the binoculars and saw Cutts' sign of surrender. He was in an awkward position, feet twisted around and his balance unstable. At that moment Cutts shoved the throttle forward causing the rear of his boat to dig deeply into the water. The other boat, thirty feet off the starboard side, was caught by surprise, but none was more surprised than Origen. He was thrown off balance, and fell overboard. He was in the middle of a school of fish, which also meant sharks. He cried out for Cutts to stop, but the man either did not hear, or did not care, as he sped away. Origen was adrift in the open ocean.

RUSTY WAS CONGRATULATING himself on a successful capture. His gun produced the desired effect on the captain, who throttled back to a no-wake speed.

To his shock, Cutts dropped his lifted hand and pushed the throttle forward. The effect was immediate and caught Mickey by surprise. As the boat dug in to its full power he watched his fugitive, Origen, lose his balance and fall overboard. Rusty heard Origen calling over the roar of the rapidly retreating boat, but there was no response. "I think that guy has dumped his baggage overboard," said Rusty.

He looked to Mickey, who didn't know what to do—chase the boat, or bring the other man aboard. Before Rusty could give him an order there was a great commotion in the water around Origen.

"Look," said Mickey. "There's a school of fish all around, and sharks feeding on them!"

"Oh, my God," said Rusty. "It's a feeding frenzy."

Origen stopped shouting after the boat, instead screaming at the sharks now surrounding him. "My God, no!"

It only took a moment for Origen to be pulled under in a wash of blood, one hand lifted up in supplication, as if asking for someone to grab him. But Rusty could only watch the gruesome sight of Origen's death.

"Justice indeed," he said. "Let's go home, Mickey." The Crestliner turned around, heading for safer waters.

Rusty's pursuit was over and justice had been served.

CHAPTER FIFTY-NINE

THE GREAT HALL WAS FILLING with acolytes and Adepts, the noise of anxious questioning filling the hall. The last of the torches set into the walls were lighted, bathing the entire space in eerie, flickering light. The agate platform glowed with blue light, while the multi-planed pyramid structure behind the platform glistened with faint lines of silver and red. The entire setting was meant to impress and overwhelm the senses, creating awe and reverence.

Those inside Krugerschloss could not see the phenomenon developing outside the mountain castle. The skies darkened and clouds rolled in, covering just the area over the castle. It was the manifestation of a great anger building within.

Abaddon sat in stony silence inside his private quarters behind the Great Hall. He was livid such treason as displayed by Lord Geoffrey should even exist under his rule. He knew of the scuffle in the alder grove, and of the subsequent conflicts between men loyal to Kamenwati and those belonging to Lord Geoffrey. The very thought sent Abaddon into another wave of anger.

"These are all my people. Where do they get the idea to follow another?" His shouting reverberated off the walls and those assembled in the Hall heard something like distant thunder. Many concerned looks between brothers created a tense, expectant atmosphere in the room.

Galdur and the others in the back passage also heard the booming, and it brought them to a halt. "What was that?" Dennis asked. "I didn't think we could hear a thunderstorm inside the mountain."

"We can't," Galdur said. "That was the sound of an evil spirit's rage."

"Evil spirit? What spirit is that?" Dennis asked.

"Why, Abaddon, of course. Do you not know that the man Kambrian has long been the vessel for the ancient spirit we call Abaddon? And I perceive that spirit is most unhappy with things in his realm." Dennis looked around as if expecting a nightmarish demon to pounce on him.

"This door leads to a side alcove, adjacent to the altar in the Great Hall. There is also an entry to the private quarters behind."

"Yes, I remember, Galdur," Dennis said. "That's where we stopped Abaddon's doomsday machinery and you impersonated him with a mask and cloak, ordering the Brotherhood to disband." Galdur nodded, disappointed in his naïve belief that his actions could end the threat of Abaddon.

The group stood around the door, each wondering what was next.

IN THE ADMINISTRATIVE center Dekker stepped from a storage closet dressed once again in the gray robe of an Adept. His escape down the dumbwaiter was a quick ride to the castle's administrative offices and a much better experience than last time. He was afraid he would have to take the chute down to the trash room as he did five years ago, but this route was much more pleasant. He made something of a racket when he came to a stop at the bottom of the shaft, and was prepared for guards to pounce on him when he opened the doors of the lift. But there was no detail awaiting him, and he breathed a sigh of relief.

He crawled out to discover he was in a large storage room. Looking around, he saw piles of folded white and gray robes and took a gray one. *Better to have people follow my orders than expecting me to follow theirs*, he thought.

He grabbed a rope sash from a group hanging on the wall, cinched it around his waist and pulled up the cowl hood, deciding he looked like a proper Brother. He eased out the storeroom door into the now-deserted administrative office area and wondered where everyone might be. He decided to walk through the space with bold assurance, like he belonged there. When he was about halfway across, a white-clad acolyte burst into the room. Seeing Dekker he stopped and gave him a quizzical look. "What are you still doing here, Brother? We are ordered to the Great Hall."

Dekker could only shrug his shoulders and the acolyte shook his head. "It's your ass, my Brother. I hear the Master is in a terrible rage." With that pronouncement the acolyte took off running and disappeared through a door leading toward the Great Hall. Dekker followed, but with more circumspection. He didn't want to alarm or alert anyone.

Before Dekker could reach the door, another one opened with a *bang*. He stopped, letting himself into an adjacent office. A man marched out of the other office, clearly angry, followed by a group of acolytes.

It must be his entourage, thought Dekker.

In the few seconds he had to observe the man, Dekker realized who he was: Lord Geoffrey Stapleton.

Dekker looked around the office he was hiding in, recognizing it as belonging to someone senior. He rifled through some documents left lying on the top of a large wooden desk and realized this was Kamenwati's office. Intrigued, he began to look around more closely.

There was nothing of particular interest until he opened the bottom left-hand drawer. There he found a very old wooden box. He lifted the box carefully and opened the lid to see what it held. His initial reaction was disappointment, discovering the relic was empty. It was only a receptacle for dust or ashes. "An ashtray," Dekker mumbled.

Dekker was a little murky on the details, but he recalled Galdur's explanation five years ago of Abaddon's origin and ascendency to power. Kambrian, who was the host for the Abaddon spirit, was born of the unholy union of Baroness Kruger and a demonic Succubus. He looked at the empty box realizing it must have held the ashes of that very Succubus, but those ashes were now missing. He could only surmise Kamenwati was keeping the artifact close at hand, perhaps even on his person. And he knew there was only one reason Kamenwati would have such an artifact—to gain leverage over Abaddon.

Lord Geoffrey and his retinue were exiting the door leading to the Great Hall. Dekker decided it was good cover for him, so he jumped into the end of the line and went inside unnoticed—just another one of the group.

As they entered the Great Hall, Dekker lagged behind, finally finding himself well separated from the others. He stepped out of the central aisle and took a place at the end of a row and watched Lord Geoffrey and his escort move up to the glowing blue platform. A man stepped out of the dark shadow on the right side of the stage, moving to a position slightly off center, but placing him in a clearly superior standing to Lord Geoffrey.

"Ah, Lord Geoffrey. There you are. I thought you might miss the Master's assembly."

Lord Geoffrey simply glared up at Kamenwati and moved around to the stairs, allowing him to mount the platform. Reaching the top, Geoffrey faced Kamenwati, his entourage stepping up behind him. He noticed the Egyptian was unsettled, even nervous. He was handling a small pouch tied around his waist, as if coaxing tranquility from the gesture.

Before Geoffrey could speak there was boom like a clap of thunder. Kamenwati and Geoffrey looked up and around, and when no obvious source of the startling noise was found, turned back to one another. Except now Abaddon was standing between them. Both men immediately dropped to one knee in a show of submission to the Master. Turning his bright, copper-masked face to the left, he addressed Geoffrey.

"Lord Geoffrey, it has come to my attention you have assembled something of an army to oppose me." A sweeping gesture toward the escort group behind Geoffrey resulted in the instant death of all six men. Lord Geoffrey swallowed hard and stammered out an explanation.

"Master, these men were not opposed to you. They were devoted to you and were guarding me to assure Kamenwati's schemes would not touch me."

Kamenwati took up the challenge coolly and with assurance. "My Lord, the only schemes were his own, and this is hardly all his followers."

No one noticed Galdur, Dennis, and Salim slip through the side doors and hide in the shadows of the wing. Dennis witnessed the execution of the Geoffrey's guard detail and truly understood what kind of power they were attacking. He had no idea how Abaddon killed the men without a weapon, but his belief in conventional weapons as an invincible shield against evil now seemed foolish.

"We shouldn't be here," he whispered to the others.

Galdur looked at him, understanding his lack of training in the ways of Magick was a handicap. Dennis encountered the powers of the Brotherhood and Abaddon before, but he now relied on Galdur to guide them through the next few minutes.

Galdur raised a hand and said, "Wait."

DEKKER STOOD WITH the Brotherhood audience, awed like everyone else with Abaddon's demonstration of power. He knew this was the method used to kill his wife and so many others, and he could not bear to think this man could do such a thing and suffer no consequence. *Your day of reckoning has come, you monster*, he thought.

On the platform Lord Geoffrey stood dumfounded. He went from a feeling of security to totally vulnerable, and he saw Kamenwati smiling at him, all the while caressing the leather bag at his waist. Geoffrey had the urge to run, to escape the terrible tableau of which he was a part, but found he could not move. Invisible bonds clamped around his body, keeping him immobile. He began to shout and cry, and make excuses, blaming his failures on his inadequate people, on Kamenwati, and on the American. "Master, I have two captives in the pit, evidence that I am loyal to you!" Abaddon was unimpressed behind the gleaming copper mask.

"You are a disgrace to me and to the Brotherhood. Your desire for my power has driven you to this point, and now it is time to pay the price." With that pronouncement Lord Geoffrey let out a long wail that echoed through the Hall.

"Kamenwati, move him into position."

Kamenwati stepped forward shoving Lord Geoffrey backward toward the pyramid carving on the back wall. Geoffrey struggled, but the invisible binding prevented anything more than a small movement. The Egyptian lifted each arm up to clamps set into the stone, and when he finished he whispered, "Farewell, my brother. You played your hand badly."

Kamenwati stepped aside to await the Master's judgment—his final judgment if all went according to plan. He stepped off, close to the position of the three intruders huddling in the deep shadow off-stage. Not thinking, Dennis reacted instinctively, and with his pocketknife neatly sliced the bag from the belt on the unsuspecting Kamenwati's waist. The Egyptian was far too distracted by the struggle to secure Geoffrey to notice the theft. Dennis did not know what the bag contained, only that it was precious to Kamenwati, and therefore important to himself and the others.

Galdur saw what Dennis did and nodded in approval.

Salim and Galdur knew a bloody sacrifice was about to take place, and while they were powerless to prevent the sacrificial death, they could begin to create a diversion for Dekker. They slipped into a trancelike state with each exercising a Word of Power. Salim, being the keeper of the Great Nexus, had the ability to control and even stop the Flows, which would be critical in the coming moments.

Abaddon turned to the bound man on the back wall and lifted his arms. "No one defies Abaddon, the power of the ages!" As he spoke a discoloration appeared in the air above the platform, to some in the audience it looked like a cloud.

"Who dares challenge me?" asked Abaddon rhetorically of Geoffrey. "Surely not you!"

At that moment Lord Geoffrey seemed to fold in on himself, crushed into the wall by some great weight. There wasn't even time for him to scream as he died with a surprised look on his face. The distorted body inside the pyramid sculpture continued to flatten until blood ran onto the floor of the platform, collecting in channels cut into the agate stone. The rivulets of blood moved slowly through a network of channels, glistening crimson against the cool blue of the agate, creating a complex web surrounding Abaddon.

The cloud above formed into an identifiable mass: dark, billowing, and tinged with lights, as if lightning were shooting through it. Abaddon, in the ecstasy of the kill was consumed with proclaiming his power.

Dekker stepped out from his place in the crowd and moved down the central aisle toward the platform. He seemed in a trance himself, or at least driven by a force outside himself. As he approached the platform Abaddon looked down and noticed the object of his recent obsession. "Aah, Kamenwati has brought my prize."

Dekker kept walking up to the platform.

"Take down the traitor so I may replace him with this heathen," Abaddon ordered Kamenwati.

"No!" Dekker's voice boomed with authority. "You may not continue. You do not have power over me, foul spirit, and I will am not be subject to your cruelties."

The storm cloud, now boiling with angry life, suddenly erupted with thunder and lightning. One bolt struck the agate platform near Abaddon's feet, causing a large crack in the stone.

"You cannot defy me, little man. I am Abaddon, alive before this world began!" Abaddon began lifting one arm upward toward Dekker, the hand gripping like a claw, when Galdur and Salim stepped out. Taken by surprise, Abaddon could only bluster.

"Fools! You haven't the ability to stop me!" But the two deep practitioners were unmoved as Salim suspended the Flows and Abaddon effectively lost his power.

Dekker reached the platform during Abaddon's distraction and smiled, seeing his two allies. Kamenwati slunk back on the platform to await the outcome of this confrontation. Abaddon swung his attention wildly between Dekker and the two mystics, uncertain of the direction to expect a threat.

Dekker's voice boomed again, this time punctuated with thunder from the angry cloud above. Dennis stepped behind the distracted Abaddon, holding Kamenwati's bag in his hand.

"You have no power, no authority, no rule on this earth. Come out of the man and face your doom," commanded Dekker.

Abaddon squirmed and shook like he was being electrocuted, and when Dekker said, "doom," he dropped to his knees. A shocked gasp came from those observing, and Kamenwati snuck off the platform, frightened and confused.

"You are finished, spirit of Abaddon. Come out!" Dekker's command was punctuated by a cloud of Succubus ashes flung by Dennis, falling like snow over Abaddon.

The scream from Abaddon was truly terrible. The host body of Kambrian was flung up into the air and came crashing down on the platform. Everybody in the stunned audience winced at the sound of breaking bones. The dark, swirling cloud overhead filled the Hall, roiling with harsh colors and sharp lightning. The congregation fell to the floor in panic and fear. Dekker held his ground as Kambrian's body was flung up and down two more times, finally adding to the flow of blood in the channels, but now all the red fluid ran back to the fracture in the stone, collecting in a pool deep in the heart of the platform.

"Be gone, Abaddon," Dekker ordered. "You have no place in this world. Go to the place prepared for you long ago and do not bother mankind any more."

A disembodied scream echoed throughout the Hall and then seemed to disappear into the now frantically swirling cloud above. A light erupted from the center of the cloud, a bright, blinding light, like a nuclear explosion, a light far too bright to look at. In a moment the light was gone, sucked back in on itself to a singular point, which then flicked out of existence.

The cloud dissipated, leaving the room in absolute silence. Kambrian's body, broken and almost unrecognizable as human, lay in the center of the platform. The copper mask had come off, now battered and twisted, a perfect representation of Abaddon's ruin; next to the mask lay the empty bag of ashes from the Succubus.

Galdur and Salim came down from the platform and took up positions on either side of Dekker. Dennis, in awe of what he just experienced, followed the two mystics to Dekker's side. Dekker was coming out of his daze. He knew what happened, but it was as if he watched a movie of the action. He couldn't believe they had defeated Abaddon. He'd accomplished what he'd set out to do, but he wasn't altogether sure what he had done.

"Is he gone? Is he dead?"

Galdur put a hand on Dekker's shoulder. "He is gone, for good I hope, thanks to you—and Dennis' quick thinking. But he is a spirit and cannot die as we know it."

Salim stepped forward, saying, "The man Kambrian is dead, of course, but he was only a vessel used all these years by the spirit of Abaddon. Unfortunately, that spirit will search for another willing person to possess. I can only hope it will be licking its wounds for a long time."

Galdur looked at Dekker. "You have had a trying experience, Adam. Let's get away from this place and its evil memories." The others agreed with that suggestion and walked to the back door of the Hall, the one leading to the front building.

Dennis stopped to pick up the twisted mask of Abaddon and the empty leather bag.

At the door Dekker stopped, turned around and looked through the remaining brethren in the room. "Where is Kamenwati?" No one seemed to know, but he was not in the Great Hall.

"He has escaped," Dennis said. "Should we search for him?"

"No, we've had enough searching and running. Let him go," said Galdur.

"Won't he be a problem?"

The question was left unanswered.

CHAPTER SIXTY

KAMENWATI COWERED IN THE BACK of Abaddon's chambers, still stunned by what he experienced. An unschooled and inexperienced novice in their ancient practices successfully appropriated and used the ashes of the Succubus to destroy Kambrian, the host. And Dekker somehow accessed the spiritual powers necessary to cast out the spirit of the mighty Abaddon. Unbelievable, yet somehow Dekker hooked into the Truths and used them for his purposes.

Was it luck, or instinct? The Egyptian did not know. But whatever the source of his power, Kamenwati would have to take care not to cross Dekker, at least until he was ready.

In that moment of reflection Kamenwati felt a presence come over him, envelope him, and comfort him. His state of fear was instantly turned to one of steel-hard determination. He felt a strength flow in and through him, a strength not his own. And the Egyptian realized what it was—the spirit of Abaddon.

"My Master," Kamenwati said aloud. "I am here. What do you wish?"

An inaudible laugh resonated through his head and Kamenwati knew what he must do. He spoke someone else's thoughts, and in a strangely familiar voice. "That weak fool was not the man to carry out my plans. But now this new vessel, with considerably more subtlety and cunning, will take those plans forward."

Kamenwati stood up, walked to a wardrobe, took out a beautifully crafted robe, and swung it around his shoulders. He next opened a velvet-lined drawer where a new mask waited. He picked it up, looked through the eyeholes, and put it over his face. Turning to a mirror he was pleased with what he saw. It was the personification of Abaddon and he could feel power rushing into his body.

"There will be no stopping me this time."

Author's Notes: The names of several characters and certain terms have significance that may not be immediately apparent to the reader. To illuminate more of the nature of these characters, the author offers these translation/definitions.

Magick—A concept used to describe a mode of rationality or way of thinking that looks to invisible forces to influence events, effect change in material conditions, or present the illusion of change. Within the Western tradition, this way of thinking is distinct from religious or scientific modes; however, such distinctions, even the definition of magic, are subject to wide debate.

Galdur: Means "sorcerer" in ancient Icelandic

Kamenwati: Means "dark rebel" in ancient Egyptian

Cambion (Kambrian)—A cambion is most often depicted as the offspring of a Succubus and a human woman. At birth, the infant has no pulse and no breath. This continues until the child is about seven years old, whem it becomes increasingly difficult to differentiate from a human. A cambion is devilishly cunning and angelically beautiful, able to persuade even the most strong-hearted individual to do his or her bidding. According to the *Malleus Maleficarum*, demons—including the Succubus—are incapable of reproduction. Moreover, to beget a child is the act of a living body, and devils cannot bestow life upon the bodies they assume. Because life formally proceeds only from the soul, and the act of generation is the process of physical organs that have bodily life. Therefore bodies, which are assumed in this way, can neither beget nor bear.

Due to this inability to create or nurture life, the method of creating a cambion is necessarily protracted. An Incubus will have sex with a human male to acquire a sperm sample. This she passes on to a Succubus. The Succubus will, in his turn, transfer the sperm to a human female, impregnating her.

It is said these devils assume a body not to bestow life, but to preserve human semen and pass it on to another body.

Source: Wikipedia

Origen: The Greek name *Ōrigénēs* probably means "child of Horus." His nickname, or cognomen, *Adamantius* derives from Greek meaning "man of adamant." He acquired this name because of his severe ascetical practices. Origen was a prolific writer in multiple branches of theology, including textual criticism, biblical exegesis and hermeneutics, philosophical theology, preaching, and spirituality.

Some of his teachings quickly became controversial. Notably, he frequently referred to his hypothesis of the pre-existence of souls. As in the beginning, all intelligent beings were united to God. Origen held out the possibility, though he did not assert so definitively, that in the end, all beings—perhaps even the arch-fiend Satan—would be reconciled to God in what is called the *apokatastis*—the restitution.

Origen's views on the Trinity, in which he saw the Son of God as subordinate to God the Father, became controversial during the Arian controversy of the fourth century, though a subordinationist view was common among the anti-Nicene Fathers. A group who came to be known as *Origenists*, and who firmly believed in the preexistence of souls and the *apokatastasis*, were declared anathema in the sixth century. This condemnation is attributed to the Second Ecumenical Council of Constantinople, though it does not appear in the council's official minutes.

Source: Wikipedia

About the Author

Lawrence Miller is a long-time television and media producer, well versed in creating entertainment. As an international media consultant, he journeyed deep into the jungles of South America and across the Caribbean Sea, where pirates still roam. On seemingly idyllic tropical islands he found black magic and dark intentions living just below the surface of polite society.

He is a native of Los Angeles, California, and now lives in New Mexico.

Connect with Mr. Miller online:

Twitter: http://twitter.com/@lmillerabq

Facebook:

http://www.facebook.com/pages/Abaddon-Rising/174295432630205

Email: author@lawrencemillerbooks.com

www.ingramcontent.com/pod-product-compliance
Lightning Source LLC
Chambersburg PA
CBHW071111290626
47170CB00018B/51